SANDRA CHASTAIN

—

THE RUNAWAY BRIDE

BANTAM BOOKS

New York   London   Toronto   Sydney   Auckland

THE RUNAWAY BRIDE

A Bantam Fanfare Book/July 1999
FANFARE and the portrayal of a boxed "ff" are trademarks
of Bantam Books, a division of Random House, Inc.

ISBN 0-553-57584-8

Published simultaneously in the United States and Canada

*Bantam Books are published by Bantam Books, a division of Random
House, Inc. Its trademark, consisting of thewords "Bantam Books"
and the portrayal of a rooster, is Registered in U.S. Patent and
Trademark Office and in other countries. MarcaRegistrada. Bantam
Books, 1540 Broadway, New York, New York 10036.*

PRINTED IN THE UNITED STATES OF AMERICA

OPM   10   9   8   7   6   5   4   3   2   1

THIS BOOK IS DEDICATED

WITH LOVE AND APPRECIATION

TO MY FRIEND NICOLE JORDAN

MY EDITOR KARA CESARE

AND NITA TAUBLIB, WHO HAS

ALWAYS BEEN THERE FOR ME.

THE RUNAWAY BRIDE

1

New York City—December 1868

"Let me see if I understand you correctly." Annalise glared at her father. "You want *me* to *marry* one of your Wall Street associates to protect you from financial ruin?"

"It isn't just what I *want*, daughter," Roylston Sinclair said solemnly. "It's what I need. Without your help, the bank and its investments will perish. The famous Sinclair Banking Company will no longer exist."

Although Annalise had always known her father was a risk taker, she never thought he could lose everything at once. "How could this happen?"

"I'd hoped not to have to tell you this, but I invested most of the bank's funds in the building of the Union Pacific Railroad, and the bank doesn't have a leg to stand on if the railroad does not get built. In another six months, if they are finished, we'll be rich, but in the meantime, I need a way to provide security for my depositors. Marriage to the right man would make my associates less anxious about doing business with the Sinclair Banking Company since we will have another family's power and money to depend on. If you insist on practicing medicine, I don't know what they'll do," Sinclair said nervously wringing his hands.

"They'll keep right on trusting you with their money. It's what *you* do that matters, not me, and they know it's only your money you risk."

"You matter, Annie. It just isn't proper, what you want to do. I mean, a woman—treating—men?"

He was finally getting to his objections. Her father always got himself out of financial trouble—if he really was ever in it. But, he never seemed to accept her need to be a doctor.

"Now, Father," Annalise said in wry amusement at his fatherly outrage, "what do you think female doctors do, ogle naked men?"

He gasped. "Annalise, I'm shocked."

"No, you're not. You're an old fraud. You just think you ought to be. Why did you let me go away to school if you never expected me to make use of my education?"

His eyes grew moist and distant. "Annie, you were inconsolable after the deaths of your mother and your brother. I couldn't refuse you anything at the time."

"And then Teddy Miller bet you I wouldn't finish the first year. You could never refuse a bet, either."

Roylston finally gave way to a grin. "You know me too well. And you showed him, didn't you?"

"And you were so happy about winning ten thousand dollars that you let me stay another year to study surgery under Dr. Lindsey. Oh, Father, there probably aren't fifteen women in the state of New York who've done what I have. I thought you'd be proud of me."

"I am, but you're a woman and a woman needs a husband. I understand, I really do and I'm proud of you. But no matter what you think, a woman cannot practice medicine."

"Father," she said softly, "you never truly understood Mama's struggle to live. She hid it from you. But I watched her die and she died because she didn't have proper medical care. Then Steven died because he had none at all. I need to do what I can to prevent this from ever happening again."

Roylston clenched his fist. "Steven died because he was a soldier. He died an honorable death. And your mother's illness could not be cured."

"No," she argued quietly, "he died because there was no one to care for him and although Mother could not be cured, her pain could have been lessened."

"Perhaps." Her father looked at her for a long silent moment. "Annalise, the truth is, no self-respecting man will marry a woman who fancies herself a doctor."

Fancies herself? Annalise blanched. She'd gotten that from her teachers, the nurses in the infirmary, and even some of her patients and she still couldn't help but be hurt by it. But she'd thought her father at least tried to understand. "Sweet Papa," she said, reverting to her childhood name for her father, "I made a vow to heal the sick. I'm sorry, but I won't give it up."

Roylston Sinclair planted a sad look on his face. She knew what he was doing, for she'd seen him do it before. "I'm sorry, too, Annie. But no one will accept you."

She could defend her case forever, but after having the doors to every top medical office in New York slammed in her face for the last three days, she knew her father was right about a woman not being accepted as a doctor. She also understood that Wall Street marriages were arranged. Because of her father's wealth, or the perception of it, they'd forgive almost anything except her decision to heal the sick. If he truly needed her help, maybe she was in a position to give it and to bargain for what she wanted at the same time, if only for a short period, or at least until she had another plan.

"If you'll give me a chance to practice medicine," she finally said, "I'll start looking. I'll accept any man as a suitor who will accept me as a doctor."

Her father gazed at her thoughtfully, then nodded. "Suppose you fail? Suppose you are never accepted?"

"I'll know soon enough, won't I."

"All right," he said slowly. "I'll agree to that. You'll begin your search by attending Teddy Miller's New Year's Eve ball. It's a welcome home party for his son, Daniel."

"Daniel?" she questioned, trying to put a face with the name. She knew his father, for not only was he a close friend of her father's, but Mr. Miller was also affectionately known as the rogue of Wall Street.

"During the war, Daniel was appointed to a diplomatic post in France. Always thought Teddy had something to do with that. Anyway, Daniel's been studying over there ever since."

"I don't remember him. Because of Mother's health, I never did much socializing."

Roylston sighed. "I know. But the New Year's Eve ball is a good place to see and be seen. Go out and buy yourself a fancy gown and one of those French masques."

"French masque?" she repeated. "Why?"

"Teddy always has to show off with grand parties, sporting the latest trends. He says this ball is his wife's idea. I doubt that. The only thing Laura ever wanted was a house full of children and grandchildren. Don't understand it myself, but these balls are the latest thing—one of those parties where nobody knows who anybody is until midnight. Still, it ought to please you. With the masque, you can look at the eligible bachelors without anyone knowing who you are and Daniel happens to be one to consider."

Daniel's eligibility was a not so subtle suggestion that Annalise ignored. "I'll go on one condition. Promise me that you won't tell anyone there who I am. If I'm going to look at prospective husbands, I want to do it anonymously."

"All right. I agree." Roylston rounded the table and came to stand beside her, placing his knuckles beneath her chin and tilting it up. "Ah, Annie, I'm not trying to be difficult. It isn't really about the money. It is about your life. I know how much you have to offer a man, if you'd give yourself the opportunity. No matter what you may think, I just want your future to be secure and for you to be happy. I promised your mother."

"I know you did," she said, remembering the gentle, loving woman who thought a woman's life should be dedicated to pleasing her husband. Now, it all made sense— her father calling her in to discuss business trouble, when he really just wanted to convince her to take a husband. In Annalise's heart, she knew her father wanted only the best for her and was only trying to do what he thought her mother would have wanted. And she owed it to her mother to please her father if she could. "I'll try."

Exhausted and a bit disheartened, Annalise bade her father good night, left the dining table, and went up the stairs to her bedroom. She hadn't expected her return to New York to be an occasion for celebration by the medical community but she also hadn't expected to be turned down without having had the slightest chance to prove herself.

And now she had promised her father that if she were not successful soon, she'd choose a husband. Not only that, but in the meantime she had to consider the bachelors available. The only consolation lay in the fact that at least, for now, she only had to look.

Three blocks south of Fifth Avenue, Daniel Miller sat across from his father's desk, too stunned to move. "You called me back from France to do *what*?"

"To choose a bride, son."

Teddy Miller had always been a shoot-from-the-hip sort of financial maverick, but until now, he'd usually made some kind of sense. "To choose a bride?" Dan repeated. He'd heard his father's words, but he couldn't quite believe them.

Teddy cleared his throat. "It's like this, son. I've run into a bit of business trouble, only temporary, mind you, but a difficulty I can't seem to overcome."

Daniel studied his father. He looked troubled, almost old. Daniel had never thought of his father as old before. More important, he had never heard his father ask for help.

"Fine," Daniel said quietly. "My expertise may be in government, but I've learned a thing or two about business in Europe. I'm ready to use what I know. Tell me what the trouble is, and maybe I can find a solution."

Teddy Miller rose and walked over to the window. He stared out for a very long time before speaking. "It's business, yes, but it's personal, too. It's your mother, Daniel. She's sick."

Daniel didn't have to be told; he'd known it the minute he'd seen her this morning. "What's wrong?"

"It's her heart. I've had her to one doctor after another. They don't seem to know what to do, except tell her to rest."

"You should have told me. I would have come home sooner."

"She wouldn't let me."

"So what made you send for me now?"

"I know she wanted to see you. Ah, Daniel, I don't want to force you into marriage when you're not ready, but so long as she has this house she can still believe that she'll live to see her grandchildren." He hesitated, then went on. "What it's come down to is this: Your marriage could keep us from losing our home."

Daniel frowned. "I don't understand. Why are you going to lose your home?"

Teddy Miller sat back down. "I foolishly put the house up as collateral for a private loan. The man I borrowed from is demanding payment, else he'll take the house and I don't have the money."

Daniel recalled the circles beneath his mother's eyes

and the birdlike frailty of her tiny body when he hugged her, and knew that this was serious. "Just out of curiosity, what did you do with the loan?"

"I made investments. Mostly in the Union Pacific Railroad."

"And how long before you expect to see any profit from that?"

Teddy let out a deep breath. "If that fool Durant hadn't kept changing the route, we'd have made a profit long ago, and wouldn't be in the financial trouble we're in now."

"Who's Durant?"

"If you ask *him*, he was personally appointed by President Lincoln to get the Union Pacific up and going. The truth is, he was just a small-time operator when the South threatened to secede from the Union and take California with it. Congress couldn't let that happen. When all the railroaders heard the government was handing out land grants and charters, they smelled money. In all the wheeling and dealing Dr. Thomas Durant, the worst of the bunch, ended up in charge. He's making a fortune, and in the meantime, those of us who bought stock are going broke waiting for a profit that he hasn't delivered."

"Never known you not to have an ace in the hole before, Father," Daniel said.

"I thought I did. We bought a prime stretch of land in Wyoming along the route where the rails were to be laid. We were ready to sell it to the railroad, when Durant demanded a consultation fee for his services. My associates said it was a bribe and refused to pay. He found someone else who would pay without questioning his motives, and he moved the line farther south."

"And you don't own land farther south?"

"No, and temporarily, there is no money to buy it. I could have held out, but suddenly I can't get an extension on my loan, and I could lose the house. That's why I sent for you."

"Father, I have very little money. I spent most of what I earned traveling and studying. But you're welcome to what I have left."

"Thank you, but it's not enough. Daniel," he hesitated. "Daniel, I wouldn't have proposed this solution if it hadn't been for your mother."

Daniel frowned. "Mother? You never used to discuss business with her."

"I still don't. You know she's been waiting for you to choose a bride and give her grandchildren. Your marriage would not only solve this problem, but also raise your mother's spirits and give her some happiness again."

Daniel couldn't mask his consternation. "Do you want me to marry into a wealthy family so that you can pay off the mortgage on this house or do you want to make mother happy?"

At least Teddy had the grace to be embarrassed. "Come on, Daniel, you make it sound so cold. That's the way things are done. I mean, you're going to marry eventually. Your wife will most likely be someone from our circle of friends. Your marriage would make your mother happy if she could think about grandchildren and it could give me—us—a little breathing room. But, of course, your mother's happiness is my first priority."

Though it went against the grain, Daniel also knew that his father was right about the way marriages were arranged. And he knew how much his marriage would mean to his mother. "Why can't you sell your Wyoming land?"

"There's a tribe of Sioux camped on it. The Army would have moved them to build the railroad from Laramie through to Cold Springs, but now that the main line's route has been changed, nobody else will go up against the Indians. You're my last hope, Daniel."

Troubled, Daniel shook his head. "Marrying a wealthy woman would be taking the easy way out. I won't do that again."

"What do you mean, you won't do that again?"

"Father, I studied law and government because of you. When I graduated from the university and war broke out, I was flattered that President Lincoln asked me to join the diplomatic corps in France. But it was a decision I regret. I should have stayed here and enlisted like everyone else."

Genuine surprise flashed in Teddy's eyes. "Daniel, you went to France because President Lincoln knew you could convince those idiots not to buy cotton from the South or supply them with weapons."

Daniel sighed.

"You served your country, son. Without you, the war could have lasted years longer, and more people would have been killed."

Daniel shook his head. He'd heard whispers that his appointment had been bought but, at the time, he was sure he could help the President and he knew how proud his mother was. And his father was right. He had done a good job. "I'm not a businessman, father, but let me look into your problem," he finally said, "and I'll decide."

"Never mind, Daniel. I shouldn't have burdened you with this. I'll find another way. I'm glad to have you home. *Theodore Miller and Son.* I've waited a long time for that."

Theodore Miller and Son. Those words kept echoing in Daniel's mind. His father was right about one thing; it would be Miller and *Son.* But Daniel couldn't run his life as his father did. When it came to business, Teddy was a gambler. He'd worked hard and he'd always been generous with his money. He'd done well and he liked living lavishly, but he was as rash as he was generous with his money.

He did love his family though, and Daniel adored his father for that. Every ragtag relative who came to America got a stake from Teddy, along with anybody else who asked. As imprudent as Teddy sometimes was, Daniel loved his father's big heart.

The door to the study opened and his father's look of concern vanished instantly when Laura Miller came in.

"Daniel?"

"Mother." Daniel came to his feet. "You should be resting for the party tonight."

"I will. I just wanted to see you for a few minutes before I get ready." She slid her arm around his waist. "I'm so glad you're home. You've been away so long."

He hugged her, realizing again how fragile she'd become. "Too long, Mother. But I'm home now."

"Teddy, don't make him listen to you go on and on about that railroad. He's just gotten here. He needs to get out and visit with his friends, meet some new ones. Find a girl," she said with a chuckle.

There it was, his mother's wish, obvious even in her casual statement.

He gave her a kiss on her forehead. "The only woman I'm interested in is you, Mother. You don't want to share me, do you?"

"Of course I do. I'd love a daughter and grandchildren. Besides, it's time you got out and found yourself a wife."

"You really want me to marry?"

"Is there something wrong with my hoping that you'll find someone you care about and be happy?"

"No, of course not. And I promise I'll look around."

She smiled. "Good. I believe I'll go up now. I'm so glad you're finally home."

"So am I, Mother."

"And don't let your father worry you." She whispered in his ear, "he'll figure out a way to handle the trouble he's trying to keep from me. He always does."

Daniel nodded slightly and decided that no matter what it took, he wouldn't allow his mother to lose her home.

And later, he would think about fulfilling her wish for grandchildren.

2

—❦—

Annalise heard the sound of choking. She strained her ears to listen. It came again—violent retching. She took two more steps into her bedroom and caught sight of Ginny, the friend and personal maid she'd left behind when she went away to school, bent double over the porcelain washbasin.

Annalise flew across the room to Ginny's side, noting the paleness of her skin and the look of anxiety on her face. "Ginny, what's wrong?"

"Nothing," Ginny said, trying to swallow and attempting to stand. "Just a little digestive upset. I'll be all right. Let me help you into your nightclothes."

Ginny swayed, reaching for the bedpost, but missed and collapsed in a heap at her mistress's feet.

Annalise gasped and knelt beside Ginny, cradling her head in her lap. "Ginny?" There was no response. Annalise instantly relied on her training, checking Ginny's eyes—glassy; her pulse—faint; her breathing—steady.

Ginny began to stir, then froze. She twisted her face

away, a tear sliding down her cheek. "I'm so ashamed, Miss Annalise."

"Stop calling me Miss Annalise. We've been Ginny and Annie too long for that. Now, what's wrong?"

Ginny sniffed. "I've disgraced you and my father."

"You've never disgraced us, Ginny. Tell me why you're so upset. You don't have to hide anything from me. You know I'll help you."

"The only thing that could help me is a wedding. I'm going to have a baby, Miss Annalise."

Annalise took a long look at Ginny, noticing for the first time the bulge of her stomach pushing against the starched white of her apron.

"Oh, dear. When?"

"I'm over six months gone."

Annalise didn't know what to say. She'd been so involved in her own problems she hadn't noticed.

"The father? Who is he?"

"His name is Robert, and . . . oh, Miss Annalise, he's gone, too. He was working down on the docks, but he lost his job. A man came along and offered good wages building that railroad. Everybody's going west. They told him a man can get rich out there, be anything he wants to be, so he up and left."

Annalise bit back an impatient sigh. The building of the transcontinental railroad was apparently the most world-altering event since the War Between the States ended three years ago. Even her normally wise father had gotten caught up in the railroad's promise of wealth and new prosperity.

"When did Robert leave?" Annalise asked.

"It's been five months. I'm so scared. What am I going to do? I can't go home."

"You'll do nothing for now."

"But what happens when the . . . baby comes? My papa will kill me."

Annalise looked down at the woman who'd been not

only her maid but her friend for more than ten years. She could understand a father's disapproval. She'd fought it ever since she'd announced her desire to attend medical school. At least Roylston Sinclair was a bit of a gambler. Ginny's father was a minister in a little town along the coast, where the Sinclairs had a summer cottage. He'd bitterly opposed Ginny's coming to the city as a lady's maid, but her father had promised the elderly man that Ginny would be safe. Roylston would feel responsible for Ginny's disgrace.

"Ginny, do you know where Robert was going?"

"Not exactly, ma'am. Just that he was going west to lay rails."

Annalise sighed. "Do you think that Robert was serious? Would he marry you if he knew about the child?"

Ginny hesitated for a moment, then answered, almost too enthusiastically. "Oh, yes. I know he would."

But Annalise could tell that Ginny was unsure. The irony of the situation was that Ginny, the one who needed a husband, didn't have one and she, an heiress who didn't need one, would have more prospects than she wanted to imagine. Nothing was fair. A man who couldn't find work in New York City could find it in the West. A woman . . .

Wait a minute. She was beginning to see a solution to both their problems. "If you want Robert, we'll just have to find him."

"How?"

"Simple, we'll go out west. That way we'll both get what we want."

"Go out west?" Ginny echoed. "Us?"

"Yes." Then Annalise remembered her promise to her father. "But first I have to go to a masquerade ball."

"Why?"

She closed her eyes and gave voice to the promise she now knew she'd never be able to keep. "To look over prospective husbands."

In keeping with a reluctantly given promise, Annalise's father waited in the carriage and allowed her to enter the Miller mansion alone. At least she was wearing a masque. And she had a good excuse not to speak. If she didn't talk, she wouldn't have to give her name.

Inside the entranceway, a butler took her cape and ushered her into the ballroom. She couldn't have felt more unprotected if she'd been entering a cage of angry lions. In fact, the first man who caught sight of her could have been a lion, a sad, old, red-faced lion.

Overweight. Wispy blond hair. How could she make it through the evening? Then it came to her. Look at the men as patients, not as suitors, and she might survive for at least a little while. Mentally, she undressed him, diagnosing his palpations as exertion and too much alcohol. His attempt at conversation was met with silence on her part and, short of breath, he gave Annalise up to her second partner.

Chicken lips. Ears about to slide off his face. Not medical, but an accurate description. Probably not too bright.

Pale skin. Weak mandible. As she described the third, she wondered what other weaknesses lay beneath the velvet jacket that hung from his skinny frame, then decided she didn't want to know.

Her fourth partner stuttered. Physically, he seemed fine, though he limped a bit. His hair was full and dark, both on his head and in his nose. She didn't want to imagine him without clothes. He probably looked like an ape. And on it went. She'd dissected better specimens than these in medical school. If these men had really been patients, she wouldn't have been so unkind. But as husband material, she reasoned, they were fair game.

After a half an hour of being stepped on, breathed on, and fawned over, she escaped and found herself a place to hide in an arbor of greenery. Smothering a laugh, she decided she was doing exactly what her father had suspected;

she was ogling prospective husbands. They weren't really naked men; she only mentally undressed them. After all, it was only a game.

Spinsterhood was becoming more and more appealing.

Daniel Miller skirted the balcony overlooking New York City's most elaborate ballroom. The house was filled with party-goers celebrating the arrival of 1869. In France, he'd celebrated the birth of too many new years away from his family. He'd enjoyed a life that now seemed far-away and unreal, a life he'd been ready to leave even before his father had sent for him.

But to choose a bride? He knew his mother wanted grandchildren, and someday he'd give them to her. He could even believe that he'd been called home because his father was in financial trouble. But one thing Teddy had never done was use his wife in one of his schemes. She'd married him against her parents' wishes because she loved him, and he'd treated her like a queen for thirty-five years.

Daniel didn't have to be told that his mother wasn't well. Her breathing was much too shallow and her movements painstakingly slow. But the thing that made her condition most evident was the elevator his father had contracted for with a Mr. Otis, so that she wouldn't have to use the stairs. If there was anything Daniel could do to prevent her losing her home, he'd do it—without a marriage of convenience.

Now Daniel looked out at the crowd and frowned. For most of the afternoon, he'd visited his father's accountants and advisers. Miller Investments and Manufacturing was bordering on bankruptcy, and without selling the Wyoming land his father was in serious trouble.

From what he'd been able to find out, there were plenty of Wyoming cattle ranchers who would have bene-fited from the Union Pacific passing through Teddy's land

at Cold Springs. Since the war, Eastern cities were booming, and western beef was in great demand. But the main
line had been moved south, through Laramie. It was too
bad Teddy wasn't interested in railroad building; he could
build his own spur from Cold Springs down to Laramie to
transport cattle to the Chicago meat-packing plants. Such
a project could be very feasible and profitable—were it
not for the Indians.

Daniel stood on a balcony overlooking the ballroom,
listening to the music, watching the blur of indistinguish-
able faces dancing down below. He didn't see his father,
but he knew he had to be somewhere in the crowd,
searching for his son.

How many of the guests really wanted to be here? Or
had they come to curry favors from the top financiers on
Wall Street? Daniel hadn't expected so much excess. Only
three years past a war that depleted the country of both its
men and wealth, he'd assumed they practiced more restraint. He'd been wrong. There was too much of everything; too many guests, too many musicians, and too many
servants serving too much punch, whiskey, and fine wine.

There were no costumes at this ball, only elaborate
masques worn by both men and women. He'd seen such
disguises before, in Paris at the Arts balls, where the person's face and head were completely covered by creations
of satin and jewels. The masques were designed so the
participants could do whatever they wished and remain
anonymous. Daniel had decided not to wear one.

According to his father, the newest vogue was silence.
Until they were unmasked, the party-goers were not supposed to speak. He smiled wryly. As much as his country
wanted to be independent, it still adopted the latest Euro-
pean trends and fashions. Apparently the evening and the
refreshments were too far advanced to honor the custom
of silence, for the sound of laughter and conversation rose
and fell with the music.

After he'd greeted his mother, Daniel had dutifully performed the role to which he'd been assigned—dance with every woman there. One partner blended into the next, as did their names. Like butterflies, they fluttered brightly over the ballroom floor, their reflections blurs of color in the mirrors overhead. The men might have resented Daniel's failure to fight for their cause, but the women didn't care.

Finally, he managed to relinquish his last partner, bowing gallantly and explaining his need to check on his mother. But when he went in search of her he learned that she'd excused herself for a brief rest. Now he stood on the balcony alone, overlooking the ballroom where he could watch without being seen.

So far, even if he had been looking for a wife, he hadn't met anyone that caught his fancy. The woman he married, if he ever did, would have to be a woman of ideas and goals. All his dance partners were united in one purpose—marriage—but not a single intelligent statement had come out of the mouth of a single one of them. There were too many jewels, too much satin and lace. Everything to excess.

His father was as guilty as the women. In one corner, a platform had been constructed and covered with Christmas holly and imported fragile flowers. In the dining hall beyond, tables laden with turkey, whole roasts of beef, and blocks of ice filled with seafood were constantly being depleted and replenished.

How much had this cost his father? Probably nothing. Daniel would bet it wasn't paid for yet.

And then he caught sight of *her*. She was directly across the ballroom, concealed behind a bank of silvery ferns where she, too, was secretly observing.

Bathed in the glow of a gaslit wall lamp, the jewels on her white feathered masque twinkled through the leaves like a million candles on snow. Her gown was the same dark green color as the bank of ferns. She was so still that she blended into the arbor. Guests strolled by her without even noticing. For several minutes Daniel stood in a trance, caught by her stillness.

She didn't see him at first. Then, as if he'd reached out and touched her cheek, she lifted her head and looked up, a jolt of awareness arcing between them. Suddenly, everything and everyone around them disappeared, and for that one moment, they were connected.

Who was she, this ethereal creature?

Daniel felt as if all the air were being sucked out of his lungs, and a tremor raced from the back of his neck down his spine. He'd heard about "moments in time," but he'd never experienced one.

Then his father and another man walked by, blocking Daniel's view. Impatiently, he swore and stepped forward to catch another glimpse of her, but by the time they'd moved away, she was gone.

Daniel headed down the stairs, plowing through the guests to the spot where he'd last seen her. But she'd vanished. Frantically he searched the crowd. Then he found her again, circling the wall to reach the same stairs he'd just come down. Daniel angled his path, cutting through the dancers and intercepting her just as she reached the urns of silver flowers flanking the riser.

"Wait. Please," he said.

She lifted her chin and looked at him, her dark eyes frantic, like some wild animal caught in a trap. Then she shook her head. She didn't speak but he could feel her confusion. It matched his own.

He caught her hand and felt her tremble. "Don't go," he whispered with an urgency he didn't understand.

She pulled away and lowered her head.

"Please, dance with me."

Then she stopped struggling. From behind spiky lashes that covered her eyes with a fringe of black, his mystery woman studied him. A whisper of her fragrance teased him, not flowers or musk, but the clean, crisp smell of the wind in a winter forest. Petite and elegant in a green brocade dress, she looked like some kind of exotic creature from a fairy tale, plumed to remain hidden in a forest of evergreens frosted white with snow.

For a long tense moment she simply stood. Slowly, she nodded. He slid his arm around her waist and pulled her onto the ballroom floor.

Her disguise was different from the others. Except for her eyes and mouth, her head and face were concealed by a skintight white satin covering on which hundreds of white feathers, tiny pearls, and diamonds were sewn. The masque fastened beneath her chin, disappearing over her bare shoulders and trailing down her back like a feathered plume. A stylized beak made of blue feathers curled over the raised portion of the mask that covered her nose.

Only vaguely conscious that the orchestra was playing a waltz, he drew her into the mass of dancers. Gliding with the music of the night like lacy butterflies, they swept around the floor. Her white masque enhanced the illusion that she was some elegant winged creature, whose shadow had merged with his, their eyes hypnotically fastened on each other.

"Do I know you?" he asked.

She shook her head once more, then closed her eyes as if she were caught up in the music. In truth, Annalise was dazed by the strange feelings that swept over her when he touched her. She'd never had such a reaction before. She felt weak from the heat of his touch.

She had never been so conscious of a man. Everything about him was perfectly matched. The stranger had a powerful body that moved as gracefully as the wild animal she could see him to be in her mind, a sleek, black creature that lived in the night.

To know him was a dangerous risk. She knew it instinctively, as she felt herself go soft and limbless in his arms.

To her astonishment, something inside her began to sing. She tried to summon her practical knowledge in an attempt to understand. But the doctor who depended on her mind had vanished, leaving a woman who could only feel.

"Are you a friend of the Millers?" he asked in a whispered voice.

She nodded.

"Why won't you speak?"

She remained silent.

At the close of the first dance, he pretended not to hear the music end, forcing her to remain on the floor. For the next two dances he waved off other partners who attempted to claim her during the intricate moves of the quadrille and the Virginia reel.

"Let me go," she said finally. "I've taken far too much of your time. There are other women—"

"You're the only woman here," he said, "and I don't even know your name."

"Nor I yours," she said in a voice so low that he scarcely heard her.

"I'm Daniel Miller, and this," he gave a glance around, "all this is my father's idea of welcoming the new year."

"How would you have preferred to welcome it?" she asked, before she could stop herself.

"Alone, with you. In a carriage in Central Park. With a soft blanket covering us while the snow falls in big lacy flakes, creating a wall to close out the rest of the world."

"You have a way with words."

"I should," Daniel said. "That's what I was trained for." He glanced at the face of the grandfather clock as they moved by. "Almost midnight, my lady of the night," he said. "When the clock strikes twelve, all masques are removed and you are required to identify yourself."

Panic fluttered her lids. *Dear God, what had ever made her think she could do this?*

His dark eyes focused on her as he let go of her waist and grasped her satin-gloved left hand which was resting on his shoulder. He teased her fingertips with his, then said, "You are not married."

His words were a statement, not a question. She didn't answer. She'd already said far too much. Every word she uttered seemed to tie her to him in an indescribable way.

At that moment the clock began to chime.

"The bewitching hour," Daniel whispered, as the dancers began to count along with the deep bongs of the clock.

"Eight."

"Nine."

"Ten."

"Eleven."

As the clock struck twelve, the gaslights went out and a burst of fireworks ignited the sky outside the large French doors of the ballroom. Annalise let out a soft gasp of wonder. She felt as if she'd been caught up in a dream, the kind of dream she'd never had, never even wished for, but never wanted to end.

Daniel stood behind her, his arms around her waist. "I believe," he whispered in her ear, "that it's customary for a man to claim a kiss to begin the new year. Let me remove this lovely creation. I have to know who you are."

"No!" she tried to scream, frantic now to escape but unable to pull away.

That's when he kissed her.

She thought it might be a little like dying. Her body felt as if it were being washed in some hot liquid that left her skin so exquisitely afire that she moaned with pleasure. That same fire she'd already experienced raced through her body madly, bouncing off her ribs and lungs and skittering off in every direction of her body. His lips ravished hers, and she felt her own open and move against his in ways she had never known before. She didn't know how long she could bear his touch.

The grand finale of lights, colors, and explosions filled the sky, finally jerking Annalise back to reality. This time she did pull away. Before he could stop her, she ducked under the arm of a man standing in front of them and disappeared into the crowd, leaving only the tip of a silver feather caught in the buttons of Daniel's vest.

One minute she'd been in his arms and the next she was gone, a mystery, an illusion that lingered. Daniel tore through the guests, and ran up the stairs and out on the balcony where he could study the people removing their masques and bringing in the new year with kisses and laughter.

But there was no sign of her.

Then he saw it, a bead of silver glistening like ice against the dark rug on the floor.

Daniel picked up the bauble. He tucked it into his pocket along with the feather and started down the stairs to the corridor below.

The appearance of the woman in green had changed everything about the evening, including Daniel. He was still too caught up in the fantasy to understand what had happened or to explain the terrible loss he felt.

Even to himself.

3

—✿—

As Annalise left the Miller house, she felt her heart pound and her breathing grow shallow. The physical reaction she was experiencing was more stunning than the fireworks she'd seen in the night sky.

She ripped off her masque, drawing in the cold night air. Where had the sensible, controlled Dr. Sinclair gone? She'd known that it was a mistake to go to the ball, but she hadn't realized that it could be life-altering.

She'd expected her silence to discourage prospective suitors. Instead, her reticence had only intrigued them. Once she'd managed to escape and find a spot behind the ferns where she was hidden from view. She could easily claim she'd followed her father's directions to look over the eligible bachelors. Look was all she'd needed do to know that she would never marry any of them. She'd been just about to slide out the veranda doors and walk home, when she saw Daniel Miller and their eyes met and locked.

In the flickering gaslight at the top of the stairs, he'd looked like some kind of Dark Angel. For a dozen heart-beats, time stood still and she felt as if she'd been struck by some paralyzing drug that immobilized her. She'd known at that moment that if she stayed there, her life would change forever and she couldn't let that happen. She'd done the only thing she could: run. But the man without a masque had intercepted her and put his arms around her, forcing her to dance. Their feet had moved; she knew that because they didn't stay in the same place. But beyond that she felt as if she'd been swept into some kind of fairy-tale land.

What had happened to her?

She'd always had a vision of her future, a destiny that she'd vowed to fulfill. She thought she'd brought herself too far for anything to knock her off course. Then a stranger had touched her, and Dr. Annalise Sinclair had become the one thing she'd never expected—a woman.

What made the event even more catastrophic was that the man who'd cast this spell over her was Daniel Miller, the son of one of her father's associates—one of the men her father hoped she'd consider as a husband. A man she now considered more of a powerful threat to her life than her father.

Now snowflakes melted in her eyelashes, dripping onto her frozen cheeks. She ran silently across the untraveled white carpet of snow as if she were a cat moving on the soft pads of her feet. Leaving her cape behind, she'd thought the cold air and the removal of her masque would break the spell. But she suddenly felt exposed, vulnerable, and for the first time, fearful.

What on earth was she going to do? If this evening had proved nothing else, it had made it clear that she was right about her resolution not to marry. She knew her de-cision would be a disappointment to her father, but to-morrow morning she'd start making arrangements to leave. To stay would compromise everything she'd worked for. When she told her father that she'd made a vow, he thought it was to herself. It wasn't; it was to her mother and her brother. He would understand. She knew, in his heart, the only thing that mattered to her father was her happiness.

Annalise slowed down her pace and forced herself to take long deep breaths.

She made it down Fifth Avenue.

Past Delmonico's, brushing quickly by exiting patrons, in hopes that she would not be recognized.

Thank God for the masque she'd worn to the ball. She'd never again have to see the man who'd awakened some secret yearning inside her, for he hadn't learned who she was. Tonight, for a short while, she'd been an ostrich disguised as a beautiful swan. But the ostrich was back.

Daniel looked everywhere, but she was gone. A quick survey of the guests revealed that they were as much in the dark as he was about the identity of his snowbird.

Now, he stood in his father's study staring out into the cold December night. No, it was no longer December 1868. It was January 1869. The gaslights along New York City's Fifth Avenue flickered brightly, casting an icy glow on the snow that was still falling.

He forced himself to concentrate on the facts, his method of dealing with problems that seemed overwhelming, while he was working out his solution. So his mystery woman remained a mystery. Somewhere there had to be a guest list. She couldn't have appeared out of nowhere. Her gown and masque were too expensive for her not to have had an invitation. She was no mirage, and what they'd just experienced was no fantasy. She had a name. She existed.

But she was gone, and his father and his associates would arrive any second. The real world was something he had to deal with before he could look for his mystery woman. Though nothing about his return had felt real, except his reunion with his mother. Somehow, he'd lost any genuine attachment to place. He didn't know where he belonged.

Six years ago, Daniel hadn't wanted to leave New York. But once he'd arrived in France, he'd understood that Lincoln needed him there. The foreign businessmen he dealt with quickly learned how honest Daniel was in his negotiations and that, because of his father, he was in a position to influence their business dealings with the United States in the future. And Daniel knew that if he left France, they would resume trade with the South, prolonging the war and costing more lives. So he stayed and learned how to handle people.

Daniel had hoped he could use his negotiating skills to find an answer to his father's troubles. But that was before he learned the severity of the problem and was forced to face the truth. His father's situation required more than negotiation. His expertise would not help. This situation might be beyond anyone's expertise. Yet, his mother had asked him to help, so he had to figure out something.

Sheer frustration coupled with anger drove him to the meeting. Why had his father brought them to this state? Daniel suspected the associates were all cut from the same mold as his father: free-spending risk-takers. The sound of conversation in the hallway told him he was soon to find out.

The door opened, and Teddy followed the group in and locked the door behind them. "Daniel, these are my associates, Albert Bolt, Roylston Sinclair, Robert Townsend, and Louis Riddenhouse. Gentlemen, my son, Daniel. I've asked him to join us while we discuss our mutual financial troubles."

The round-faced, balding man, identified as Roylston Sinclair, gave a forced laugh. "Now, Teddy, what makes you think we're *all* in trouble? Your son is home from Europe. My daughter, Annalise, is home from . . . finishing school, and I, for one—"

"Don't lie, Roylston," Teddy said. "When the Union Pacific's main line was relocated to bypass Cold Springs, our boat started to sink. Everything we have is invested either in railroad stock or land that we can't sell."

"Yes," Albert Bolt jumped in, "and they keep asking for more money to repair and rebuild what they've already built. What the hell are we going to do?"

"Why not sell your stock?" Daniel asked.

All five men laughed. Bolt gave them a warning look and answered, "We couldn't get half of what we paid for it, Daniel. If the line had gone through our property, or somebody else wanted to build a spur into Cold Springs, we might have had a chance."

Daniel had been right about the investors. They were gamblers, just like his father. His inclination was to let them stew in their own juices, but he remembered his mother's plea for his help. "I know about Durant's moving the line, but what would stop another smart railroader from building a spur line into Cold Springs?"

His father opened an engraved metal box and offered cigars to the men. "Two things. Snow and Indians. Casement and the government troops stationed at Fort Laramie could have handled both, but nobody else wants to take on old Black Hawk and his Sioux."

Daniel knew about construction problems, but the elements and wild Indians were an unknown factor. "I have some friends in Washington. Maybe they could be persuaded to change the route back between now and spring."

Riddenhouse swore. "Not enough time. Normally the construction is shut down by Christmas, but Durant is so afraid that the Central Pacific's Chinese workers are going to outdistance the Union Pacific's crews that he's got his men working straight through the winter. It's crazy. It's obvious that they'll have to do it all over when the snow melts."

Their construction practices might be crazy, but the

idea of a railroad from New York to California had caught Daniel's fancy long before he returned to New York. He liked the thought of going places not already spoiled by cities and big money, places where a man could make a new name for himself based on what he accomplished, not what he was able to buy.

Teddy Miller let the men talk for a moment, then reined in the conversation. "It seems we're all in agreement about our situation. None of the investors have any control or real knowledge of what is happening and this, my friends, is what we have to change."

Bolt turned to face Miller. "How is that going to help? If I invest any deeper, I'll lose my house, which my wife won't like, or my business, which will make me unhappy."

Daniel had remained quiet. Now he walked forward. "Maybe there's a way. What if the spur were built? Would it generate enough traffic to ensure a fair return on your investment?"

"Well, yes," his father agreed. "At least it would be a temporary fix. There are immigrants and farmers ready to use a new spur, and ranchers already driving their cattle east to the stockyards in Chicago. If we could line up a few shipping contracts, then we could pull this thing out."

"Doesn't matter," Roylston said. "If we can't sell the land, what makes you think we can find anyone willing to put up the money to build a spur from Laramie to Cold Springs? Investors have already bought into too many pie-in-the-sky ideas. They are more interested in the Union Pacific. At least it's backed by the government, for whatever good that's worth."

The men discussed the options for a moment before Riddenhouse finally offered his opinion. "We're beating a dead horse, boys. The spur isn't going to be built. Nobody's willing to take the risk."

But Daniel had the answer. As illogical as it seemed, it could work. He took a deep breath and said, "What if *we* build the spur?"

"Us?" The men responded in unison. "How?"

"Yes, son? How?"

"You already own the land. I'll build it."

This time the response was unanimous laughter. "You?"

"Yes, me. I spent the war learning how to negotiate. Maybe my connections in Washington could get us some help with the Indians. As for building the railroad, I stayed in Europe long enough to learn about manufacturing and construction. One of the factories I visited was a locomotive manufacturer. Any other knowledge I need, I'll find. You could hire someone else to do it, but if I build the spur, you'll have some control over how your money is spent."

There was no laughter now. Instead, the men began to consider Daniel's proposition. One by one they looked at each other.

Daniel stood and walked toward the French doors, as much to give himself time to reconsider what he'd just volunteered to do as to give the men time to discuss it. Would it be enough to put off Teddy's creditors and save his mother's house? Would they have the confidence in him to let him try?

Immediately, the investors broke into a debate. "Is it possible? Where will we get the money for supplies? How long will it take? Suppose . . ."

Those might have been serious questions for other groups where the decision would take a lot of time to make, but Teddy's friends needed only a few moments. Although it would be a long shot, they were willing to risk it. By the time Daniel turned back around to face them, Teddy was already setting out glasses and opening a bottle of bourbon.

"I think we're agreed, aren't we?" Teddy asked. "We've always taken chances. Why stop now?" He filled a glass for each man and lifted his own. "To my son, the man who is going to build us the Cold Springs Spur."

Daniel's gaze circled the room, returning briefly to his

father. Here it was, his chance to claim a future for himself, separate from his father's. He was about to walk a path he'd never taken. He didn't know where it would lead or what he'd find at the end of it. But he'd taken the first step, and he'd see it through to the last one.

One by one, the men lifted their glasses, their mouths formed into wide smiles. There was one glass left on the table. "To the future," Teddy said, and handed Daniel the glass.

"Do you believe in fate, gentlemen?" Daniel asked.

"Hell, no," Teddy answered. "A man makes his own fate. He wants something bad enough, he'll figure a way to get it."

"I hope so," Daniel said and sipped the whiskey, feeling it refuel the fire still smoldering within him. It looked as if he'd found a way to help his father without marrying. That was what he wanted. Then, why didn't that make him feel better?

As Annalise made her way down a crowded Fifth Avenue, she saw people walking home from other neighborhood parties, laughing and celebrating the arrival of the new year. The new year—she thought, the year she'd expected to come home and begin her new life.

At the corner, hired carriages were loading. The departing guests called out final cheery greetings to their hosts and stole final forbidden kisses as they wished each other "Happy New Year."

A window swung open overhead, accompanied by a harsh call. "Stop that noise. People are trying to sleep here." A clanging sound of something metal hitting the cobblestone sidewalk immediately followed, and Annalise broke her gait.

It was a chamber pot, bouncing into the haunch of one of the coach horses. The horse reared and backed up, thrusting the coach into a young man standing close behind.

Annalise heard the snap of bone and the scream of the victim. "God's eyeballs!" someone yelled. "The bloody carriage broke his leg!"

Annalise tore through the gang of onlookers, pushing them aside until she reached the man beneath the lamppost. His trousers had been ripped and she could see the unnatural bend of his lower leg. She knelt beside him, hearing the rip of her gown as she leaned forward to examine the moaning man.

"Don't move," she said, and was surprised when he complied. Tenderly she ran her fingertips beneath the fabric and felt for breaks in the skin. "Good," she said, unaware of the quiet that had descended on the crowd.

"Good?" He grimaced, sucking in a quick breath. "Madam, if you're interested in my body, your timing is atrocious."

"Please. I live just down the avenue." She looked up at the crowd. "If someone will bring him to my house, I'll see what I can do for him."

Laughter broke out behind her.

"I'll just bet you will, sweet thing."

"She can examine me anytime she wants," another male voice offered. "I know she can cure my problem."

Someone pushed her aside. "Sorry, darling, looks like you're going to have to find yourself another way to make some money tonight. Somebody give me a hand. We'll take Willie to the hospital."

"Yeah, and he'll die in that hellhole," one of his friends observed. "Better to go with the woman. He might still die, but at least he'd be happy."

"He doesn't have to die!" Annalise said calmly as she stood. "I'm a doctor, and I can set the leg."

"Yeah, and I'm the mayor," the roughest of the onlookers said, pushing her away. "Go home, girl. The only women doctors I know of take care of foolish little girls who get themselves in trouble and old ladies drawing their last breaths. Willie still has all his male parts, even if he don't quite know what to do with them."

Willie's screams as they put him in the carriage brought another barrage from the window overhead. Nothing Annalise did convinced the makeshift ambulance crew that she could help their friend.

Soon they were all gone. The snow picked up its intensity and covered their footprints so completely that it was as if they'd never been there at all.

With a weary heart, Dr. Annalise Sinclair made her way to the end of the block and up the steps to the brownstone mansion. She stopped, hugged her stomach with her hands and leaned forward as she sucked in a deep breath. Her father would be disappointed that she'd left the ball early. But that wasn't the worst of her troubles.

Daniel Miller was. Daniel Miller had become the greatest obstacle to attaining her dream. More than ever, she knew her only salvation was in going west to find Ginny a husband. The search would make certain that Annalise Sinclair wouldn't find one.

She didn't know how she'd explain this to her father. Nor did she know what kind of catastrophe would befall him if she left New York, but she knew that she had to go, and go quickly.

When she went inside, Ginny was waiting up for her. "What happened to your masque and cape?" she asked as they climbed the stairs.

"I—I took them off. I couldn't breathe."

"You breathed all right before you left here."

"Well, it was—very warm, dancing." That was the understatement of the year. From the moment Daniel Miller touched her she'd felt as if it was the middle of summer on Long Island Sound. Running through the snow hadn't changed that.

Inside Annalise's bedroom, Ginny studied her carefully. "Are you sure you're all right? You look a little odd."

"I'm fine, Ginny. I've just made up my mind."

"Made up your mind to do what?"

"We *are* going out west. It's the only logical thing."

"Annie, I can't let you do that for me."

"I'm not doing it just for you. I'm doing it for me, too. Now, unbutton this dress. I need some air. My chest aches on the outside and inside."

"Why would your chest be bruised on the inside?"

"Because my silly heart—never mind. You wouldn't understand. I don't think I do."

Ginny looked at her with a narrow gaze. "Your lips do look a little odd, too. And your dress is torn. Did something happen tonight?"

"No, I mean yes. I tore my dress while examining a man's broken leg. He refused to let me treat it. He'd rather suffer than accept a woman's help. That's the way it's always going to be, Ginny. I'll never be allowed to be a doctor here. And if I stay, I don't know how to be a proper wife even if there was a man . . . Maybe out west I'll have a chance. So we're leaving before something can stop us."

"You don't mean that, Annie. This is your home. What about your father? He'll never let you go."

"He won't know until after I'm gone."

"He'll come after you."

"Not right away. I'm going to tell him that we're going to the summer house. That . . . I . . . need to think about the men I met at the ball and consider the potential candidates for my hand in marriage."

Ginny's eyes widened. "Go on. How can you choose a husband from a bunch of masked men that you don't even know?"

"I'm not. Besides, there was one who wasn't masked," Annalise blurted out before she could stop herself.

Ginny had started to slide the gown over Annalise's

shoulders. She stopped. "And this one man whose face was bare? Was he handsome?"

"No . . . I mean, yes. I guess he was."

"So who was he?"

"It doesn't matter," Annalise said quickly, shimmying herself out of her dress and forcing Ginny to pull it over her head.

"Oh, I think it does, Annalise Sinclair. I think something happened to you that sent you scurrying home before the ball ended. Tell me."

Annalise took the dress from Ginny. "Unfasten this corset. I don't know why I let you talk me into wearing it. Medically, a corset is responsible for a good many of women's health problems. It keeps you from eating and breathing and moving around."

Ginny smiled and moved to Annalise's back where she unfastened the hooks. "But Annie, it gives you an hourglass figure that other women would die for. You look just like a China doll."

The corset was gone, and Annalise walked over to the dressing table and peered into the mirror. Ginny was right; she did look different, strong and sturdy, hardly the delicate female men wanted. "I don't know what a China doll looks like," she said crossly, "but I'm sure that description doesn't fit me. Go to bed, Ginny. Tomorrow we'll sell my mother's jewels and start getting ready. No, it's already tomorrow, isn't it? We'll begin today. If your Robert is working on building the Union Pacific, we'll find him."

"Annie, I don't think this is a good idea. Even if we go, I don't think we'd ever find him."

Annalise sat down and began to brush her hair. "Maybe not, Ginny, but there are other reasons we have to leave. Go to bed now. I have to formulate our plan."

Later, after Ginny had built up the fire and returned to her own room, Annalise started making lists of the chemicals and supplies she would need. Next she surveyed her possessions. The jewels her father had bought for her mother were impressive. She'd sell them, keeping only her mother's locket and her grandmother's watch. She ought to have enough—if she could keep her father in the dark about what she was planning. In a few weeks, with any luck, she would be on her way out west to start her new life, one where she could practice medicine.

Pressing her fingertips hard against her temple, she closed her eyes. Her mind was spinning in a hundred directions. But at the center was Daniel Miller. She could still see his black eyes, still feel the heat of his touch. For just a moment she wished she could see him again. Knowing that such a thing would only bring disappointment, she shut him out of her mind and began to pack.

4

—❦—

Once Daniel had the go-ahead, he began assembling the steel rails and pins. Next, he contracted with the agent of a lumber dealer to pick up timber on the other side of the Mississippi. Lastly, he sent out the word that he was hiring workers. Those interested in a job were to meet him at a pub near the docks on the fourth Wednesday in January.

By that day he'd used most of his funds, but he refused to ask for more. He'd said he could do the job with the limited amount given him and he would. In order to avoid the impossible task of laying the track himself, he came up with an idea.

The crowd of prospective workers overflowed into the street. Daniel was stunned that so many men were looking for jobs. He circulated among them, asking questions.

"Do you have a wife and children?"

Those who were responsible for supporting a family were eliminated. It would take a special kind of man to go for his proposal, a man willing to take a gamble on his future. Could he sell enough of them on his plan? Would his diplomatic skills help him now?

"I need men of vision," he stated frankly, "men willing to work for keep and a share of the profits, men who are willing to commit themselves to a project that will be risky but financially rewarding."

"You mean we get no pay?" a worker shouted as others began to drift away.

"That's right. No wages right now. What you get is a share of the railroad. When it's done, you own part of it." Daniel figured that if the other stockholders refused to honor the promise he was making these men, his father would have to make it good from his portion of the profits.

"Ah, go on, you're just bilking us. What man works for nothing?" one man asked.

"Me. And any of you who are interested in building a future for himself."

Finally he was left with eight men. Desperate men or men wise enough to see the potential, he couldn't be certain. Only eight, when he needed a hundred. But he figured that once he got underway, he'd be able to convince other men to join him. He winced. He never thought he'd become a gambler like his father, but he was doing just that.

He advanced the workers money to eat and outfit themselves while he bought supplies and made arrangements for them to be delivered to the station in Brooklyn, where he could book cheap train fare for the long journey. Daniel filled his days organizing the details of his project. But in the evenings, he attended every social function to which he was invited, looking for his masked mystery woman. He knew what he was doing wasn't smart. There was no place in his future for a wife, but still he searched every ballroom and dining hall, asking casual questions about the petite dark-eyed woman who'd run away from the ball. If she was one of the wealthy New Yorkers who belonged to his father's Wall Street circles, nobody seemed to know her. One by one he identified and rejected every single woman suggested as a possibility. His snowbird seemed likely to remain a mystery.

Finally, Daniel decided that fate had intervened. He was forced to give up his search and concentrate on his mission—building the transcontinental railroad's Cold Springs Spur.

At the end of January, Daniel joined his father's friends for one last report.

"Are you ready, Daniel?" Teddy Miller asked.

Daniel looked hard at the men standing in his father's study before answering. "I have purchased all of the necessary supplies, but I'm afraid that took most of our funds. I had to promise the crew a share in the line in lieu of salary."

Teddy stared at Daniel in shock. "You had to do what?"

"I had to promise them a share of the line. It doesn't have to be much, and there are only eight men. It's the best I could do, unless you come up with more money."

"Well, Miller, guess their shares will have to come out of your portion," one of the investors said. "It was your son who made the arrangement without our consent."

Teddy squirmed. He either had to reveal that Daniel had overstepped his place or swallow the loss. Saving face was more important. "Of course. It will come from my portion if need be."

Roylston Sinclair was still eyeing Teddy. "I hope we don't intend to waste money, cut corners, or pay bribes."

"Gentlemen," Daniel said, "I assure you, your money was spent wisely. And there is none left to squander."

"And when do you intend to start?" Riddenhouse asked.

"In the next week."

Roylston Sinclair patted Dan on the shoulder. "We're depending on you. I've put a private car at your disposal."

"No, I'll be traveling with my crew, like any other worker."

"Really, Daniel, that won't be necessary," Teddy argued. "There's no reason for you to be uncomfortable."

To Daniel, there was every reason. Even his father wouldn't have recognized the burly roustabout with the railroad cap on his head and the canvas knapsack over his shoulder, walking shoulder to shoulder with his crew in only a week's time.

Daniel didn't tell his father, that he had no intention of trading on Teddy Miller's name. Not only didn't he want to give Dr. Durant a chance to do his father any more harm, but also he thought that building this spur was his chance to prove himself. He'd do it as Dan Miller, construction boss, working on the line like the other men, not as Teddy Miller's son.

He was determined to forget his father's last comment, "By the way, son, I'm thinking that, in spite of any temporary money problems, we'll get through this. A banker's daughter would be a good choice for a bride."

"And which banker did you have in mind?" Daniel asked.

"Roylston Sinclair."

Tiny snow crystals, captured by the swirling January air, were flung with reckless abandon against the travelers. They caught in Annalise's eyelashes and stung Ginny's cheeks until they turned her sallow complexion to a mottled red.

The ground crunched beneath the wheels of their cart as the horse moved slowly down the rutted mud street toward the Brooklyn train station. At the wooden platform outside the ticket sales window, they came to a halt. Annalise climbed out. "Help . . . Mrs. Wilson down," she told the driver. "Then unload our cases. Ginny, don't forget our carryalls and our blankets."

Annalise left Ginny in charge while she dodged the mass of human travelers hurrying toward the shelter of the roof overhanging the platform.

The smell of wool wet from melting snow, unwashed bodies, and unfamiliar food odors overtook Annalise's senses, as a cornucopia of dialects assaulted her ears. There was no mistaking the tingling of excitement among the passengers.

Looking around the Brooklyn station, Annalise decided that she'd chosen wisely. There was little likelihood of being spotted in the large crowd of workers, immigrants, and farmers, all looking for a new life. Many of them were pulling small carts filled with their possessions. Her own driver had pulled up to the platform and was unloading their cases of medical supplies.

Before she left, Annalise had written her father a letter of explanation, which she'd mail once they were away from New York State. She hated deceiving him, but she felt she had no other choice. When he learned what she'd done, he'd likely send someone after her. But he wouldn't know where she'd gone, and it probably wouldn't occur to him to begin his search in Brooklyn.

For the trip, Annalise had worn her oldest gray traveling dress and covered it with a sensible black wool cape with a hood and shawl. Ginny, on the other hand, masked her fear and uncertainty in a sassy blue travel dress that would have made her stand out, even if her pale skin and reddish brown hair hadn't. At least the cape she wore concealed her condition.

Annalise didn't have the heart to tell her that the dress would probably be ruined by smoke and cinders. Ginny felt as if she were going on an adventure, rather than a dangerous journey.

"Where to, miss?" the station agent asked when she reached his window.

"Two tickets to . . ." She faltered. She'd planned everything but an answer to this question. "Well, I'm not sure. How far west does this train go?"

"This train goes from Brooklyn to Chicago. From there, if you want to go west by the most direct route, you take the Rock Island or the Northwestern. Of course there's the Chicago Burlington and Quincy. It's not the best way to go, because it takes longer, but it's cheaper. Once you get across the Mississippi you head for Omaha. Then you'll be traveling on the new Union Pacific which, as of this morning, is just past Laramie, Wyoming, ma'am."

"Fine. I'll take a sleeping compartment for two ladies from here to Chicago and the Burlington and Quincy."

The agent laughed. "Sorry, ma'am. Only got regular seats. No sleeping compartments. You want seats that make into beds, you need to take one of the other lines."

"But Ginny—I mean Mrs. Wilson is—with child," she blurted out.

"At least she'll be inside, and not in a covered wagon," he commented. "That'll be thirteen dollars and sixty-five cents each. Only got six seats left. Make up your mind. 'Course, you could always travel in one of the freight cars with the farm animals and the people who can't afford regular fare."

"I'll take them," Annalise said. She opened the purse hanging from her wrist and handed the agent the money. He held out the ticket envelope and her change as she was thrust aside by the next anxious traveler.

As she pushed her way through the crowd a commotion broke out behind her. Suddenly there was a high-pitched scream and Annalise felt something strike her in the knees. While stumbling forward she felt a sharp tug on her wrist. Unable to stop herself, she fell over the edge of the platform. The last thing she remembered was her own startled yell, the hard jolt of the ground, and a shattering pain to her forehead.

Daniel Miller leaned against the railcar looking over

his supply list, checking items off as his men loaded them on the train. He glanced up just in time to see a dirty boy being cuffed by a man who then shoved him, sending him crashing into a woman from the rear. As she fell forward the same man stumbled into her. He looked for a moment as if he were going to catch her, then took her wrist and sent her over the edge of the platform. A classic pick-pocket move. Dan ran forward, lunging for and missing the wily boy as he tried to escape.

"Somebody stop him," Dan called out and made his way to the edge. The woman was sprawled across a rocky expanse at the bottom of an incline, her face turned away from him.

And she wasn't moving.

Dan swore under his breath. Behind him, a woman was screaming. "Help. Somebody please help us!"

A woman was hurt and nobody was going forward to help her. He couldn't walk away and leave her there. He sighed and jumped over the edge, sliding down the same slick surface she'd traveled.

Seconds later he was kneeling beside her, turning her face toward him. Her face startled him. For just a moment he had an unexpected urge to tenderly run his fingers down her cheek. It must have been leftover desire from his mystery woman, he told himself as he examined her. Bloody scratches covered her cheek, but the ticket envelope was still clasped tightly in her hand.

He took the envelope and stuck it in his pocket and lifted her, marveling at the exciting familiarity her touch elicited. As he made his way back up the bank the crowd began to thin, leaving only the anxious woman in the elegant travel dress who was apparently her mistress, or maybe traveling companion.

"Is she hurt bad?" she asked, her voice tight with worry.

"I don't know yet," Dan said, moving toward the back

of an empty wagon. Dan laid his charge down, pulled his handkerchief from inside his jacket, and began to brush away the dirt that had stuck to her face.

She moaned softly. At least she wasn't dead. Then she opened her eyes, her dark, jeweled gaze darting frantically back and forth.

"Are you all right?" he asked.

"What did you do to me?" she whispered.

"Me?" He gave her a smile. "It wasn't I who sent you flying off the platform. I'm the guardian angel who rescued you. Just be still for a minute."

Annalise couldn't have moved if she'd wanted to. She couldn't even breathe. This was a hallucination. This couldn't be real. She closed her eyes, then opened them slowly, waiting for him to disappear. He didn't. The man leaning over her was the man who'd sent her fleeing into the night, the man she'd thought she was leaving behind her—Daniel Miller.

"Annie, are you hurt?" Ginny's frantic voice cut in, bringing her back to reality. "I don't think so," she whispered.

"Your eyes," he was saying. "You have very unusual eyes."

Annalise jerked her face away and groaned as pain sliced into her. Suppose he recognized her? But that was impossible. He didn't know her name, and her entire face and hair had been hidden by the masque. There was no way he could know who she was.

"There's something familiar about you," he murmured. "Have we met? My name is Dan Miller."

"Please, let me go." She struggled to sit up. "We have to get on the train."

"I don't think you ought to move," he said, still holding her. "I think you may have injured yourself."

"No, I—I'll be all right." Emotion, confusion, pain, all swirled around inside her head. The intensity of the moment caused her to close her eyes again, losing touch with everything for a moment. Finally, she opened her eyes again and focused them on Daniel. Suppose Ginny panicked and called her father? "Help me to the train. He mustn't stop us."

"Who mustn't stop you?" Dan asked, concerned now for more than the injuries from her fall. "Your husband?"

"I'm not married. It's Ginny—Mrs. Wilson who is married. We're heading out west to meet her husband. Now, I need to . . ."

The train whistle blew. "Better get aboard," the conductor called out.

Daniel frowned. That statement didn't answer his question but if the maid and her mistress didn't get on the train they'd be left behind. Missing the train might be the best thing. Two women traveling alone invited only disaster. But he'd seen panic in her eyes and she'd asked for help. Dan couldn't refuse.

He lifted her, carried her across the platform, and climbed the steps to the railcar. "Get aboard, ma'am," he called out to Ginny. "Unless you've changed your mind about leaving." Ginny gave a vigorous shake of her head.

Dan softly placed his charge in a seat close to the potbellied stove at the front of the car. He had motioned to the occupant, a burly red-haired worker, that he should move. The man had complied, pulling his knapsack from beneath the seat and stepping into the aisle. Dan stood over the maid, waiting for her mistress to tend to her wounds.

But the lady seemed frozen, unable to move. "Annie," she was saying as she wrung her hands, "this is all my fault. Please, don't die."

Annalise's eyes were closed again now, but her breathing seemed to be steady and color was returning to her cheeks. It was Dan who finally opened her carryall and found a tin of paste marked *Wounds*. "Could someone get me a wet cloth?"

Moments later, the red-haired man handed him a wet handkerchief.

"This is going to hurt," Dan said as he wiped away the blood and grit from Annie's face. Next he blotted the paste, then rubbed it into the scratches. "You're allowed to yell," he said softly.

She was surprised at the gentleness of his touch and the way she reacted to it. A breath of warm air seemed to be settling over her, prickling her skin as if she were sensing the presence of an intruder. "I am not a yeller," Annalise managed to say in a gravelly voice.

Even in her dazed state she was aware of the danger she was in. The night of the New Year's celebration she'd learned two basic truths: No matter what a woman prepared herself to be, she was first, last, and always a woman, and women, whether they wanted to or not, responded physically to certain men. Especially men like Daniel Miller. What was he doing here in Brooklyn pretending to be a railroad man?

Annalise clenched her teeth, trying desperately to control the icy shivers that were building just beneath the surface of her skin. Shock! She'd learned about shock to the body's nervous system. It was a natural response to her fall. It had to be that. Daniel Miller's presence had nothing to do with her reaction.

"I think you'll be all right," he said, "but I'm no doctor."

"That's all right," Ginny began, "Annie—"

"Annie is fine," she said, and forced herself to sit up. No matter what happened, she had to be strong, for Ginny. Somehow she'd have to get through this and look after Ginny. *Doctor, heal thyself.* Except this time she might need a little help. Annalise clenched her teeth once more and forced herself to sit straighter.

Then her head began to spin.

She leaned forward, took in a few deep breaths, then waited as the earth seemed to tilt one way, then the other. Finally, when all movement stopped, she sat up. "Thank you, but I'll be fine. You go on and take care of your . . . yourself."

Dan nodded. Putting some space between them was definitely a good idea. He recapped the paste and stuck it back into the carryall. Looking around, he took the blanket Ginny was carrying and draped it over Annie, tucking it beneath her chin.

As his knuckles grazed her chin, Annie caught her breath. In spite of the cold, she felt a bead of perspiration form across her upper lip.

"Rest now," he whispered, and for a moment she thought he was about to kiss her. She held her breath. Daniel's kisses had already caused her hours of sleepless nights.

As he stepped away, he reached inside his pocket and retrieved the tickets, which he handed to Ginny. "Guess the thieves were after these. Better put them in a safe place. I don't know how she managed to hang onto them."

"Thieves?" Ginny said.

"A child hit her from the rear," he explained, "and his accomplice came at her from the side. They were obviously working together. But she held on."

Ginny gasped. "He shoved her over the edge."

"Your maid is pretty tough. She rolled over like a prize-fighter taking a dive."

Ginny stuffed the tickets into her carryall. "Thank you."

Dan looked up. "Did anybody catch the boy?"

"Nope," one of his men answered. "He disappeared like smoke. We looked around, but he was gone."

"Did you get our supplies loaded?"

"Yes, sir."

"What about the women's things?"

"Put them in the same car as ours. Boss, you need to know, the cook didn't show up."

"Damn!" Dan swore. Food was important to a work crew. "We'll, we'll just have to find a replacement."

"Where we gonna find a cook out west?" one disgruntled worker asked.

"I'm a fair cook," the Irishman volunteered from down

the aisle. "Wouldn't mind signing on, lads, if the wages are good and you like me stew. I'm good with a hammer, too."

"No wages," Dan explained. "The men are working for shares. Are you still interested?"

There was a moment of silence. "I'm interested."

"Okay, what's your name?"

He grinned. "Folks call me Red."

"Folks call me Dan. I'm going out west to build a rail line. Have you ever been out west?"

"Nope."

"Neither have I," Daniel said. "Come on to the back of the car and I'll introduce you to the rest of the crew. Then I want to check on our goods." They moved down the aisle.

"Ginny," Annalise said as soon as they'd gone, "are you all right?"

"Yes, Annie, but I was scared. Thank goodness for that Dan. I think he likes you," Ginny said with a smile, then added, "are you sure we ought to do this?"

"I'm sure," Annalise said with more confidence than she felt. She tested her arms and legs. They all appeared to work. She wasn't so sure about her lungs. They seemed to be permanently drained of air. Annalise took a few more deep breaths. "Where are our carryalls?"

Ginny looked confused. "I have this one, but I don't know what happened to the one with our clothes. It was right there beside me, but I had to hold the blankets and then you screamed. Now . . . I don't know."

Annalise swore silently.

"I'm sorry, Annie. I'll go and look." Ginny stood and wobbled into the aisle so quickly that she walked into the Irishman heading for the exit.

"Oh!" Ginny exclaimed, as she grabbed the back of the seat. The Irishman grabbed her.

Annalise, still dizzy from her fall, was incapable of helping either.

"Sorry, ma'am. I never meant to knock you off your feet. Are you trying to get off the train?"

"I seem to have lost one of the carryalls. I was going back to find it."

"Sit down, Ginny—Mrs. Wilson," Annalise said. "I don't want anything to happen to you."

"I'll go and look for it," Red said and helped Ginny back into her seat.

Ginny's "You will?" didn't sound quite so fretful. Annalise couldn't help but see that Ginny's attention had quickly transferred from the missing bag to the Irishman.

The Irishman was staring at Ginny, and behind him, Daniel Miller was staring at Annalise.

5

—❧—

"Give me a hand, Red," Dan said, pushing past his new cook without speaking to Annie or Ginny. "I want to make certain everything is loaded properly before the train pulls out."

Red nodded, and gave Ginny a reassuring smile and an "I'll look," under his breath as he followed Dan outside. "She's a tough lady," Red said.

"For a maid, she's a bossy wench," Dan snapped.

Red grinned. "I wasn't talking about Annie."

"Ginny's a married woman, Red."

"I know," he said, "the best ones always are."

Dan gave a sigh. Somehow he'd become saddled with a pregnant woman and her feisty maid. Why had he ever intervened? All he'd had to do was get himself and his men on board. But when Annie had opened her eyes, something had stirred within him. For just a second, he'd felt a strange awareness between them. He shook his head. This odd obsession had to stop.

Red stopped on the platform. "The ladies lost one of their carryalls."

Dan glanced around. There was no sign of a carryall. "It probably disappeared with the thief."

The livestock carrier was the last car. It was filled with wooden crates containing chickens and pigs, several horses, and a cow. The next car held his own equipment and supplies. He and Red climbed inside and checked the list once more, satisfied that everything was there. Then Dan paused, his brows knitted together. "Where are the women's things stored?"

"Sorry, that happened before I became a partner in building a railroad," Red said. "I don't know. But we can look."

Dan climbed down and moved to the next car, packed with immigrants and their goods. "I don't know why I'm so concerned, but if we don't check, Annie will probably try to do it herself and she is in no condition to get out of that seat."

Red nodded and followed, tipping his head to the people inside as they searched. Finally, in the back corner, he spotted a stack of crates with the name Wilson printed on them. "Here they are."

Dan studied them curiously. "For two women who travel light, these are pretty heavy crates."

"That they are," Red agreed. "And they really did a good job of sealing them."

"Makes you wonder what's inside," Dan said.

"Maybe they're bank robbers and this is their gold," Red jested as they left the car.

"Good, we could use a couple of wealthy ladies."

Wealthy ladies, just what his father had told Dan to look for. He smiled. Wouldn't it be something if he found one out here? He thought about the girl in the masque, then about Annie. No, what he'd found was trouble, and it seemed to be sticking to him like tar. And he hadn't even left the station yet.

By the time Dan boarded the train again, the engines were building up steam and the train was beginning to inch forward. He paused beside Mrs. Wilson and Annie. "Your carryall has vanished, but you have four crates in the third car from the end of the train. Is that all?"

Annalise nodded, relief washing over her face.

"Thank you, Mr. Miller," she said.

"Dan," he corrected.

"Mr. Miller," she repeated.

He shook his head and moved to the rear of the car where the rest of his crew had settled in.

Stubborn, she was. She'd accept his help, but only because she wasn't as steady on her feet as she needed to be. Even then, she'd do it on her terms.

"Thanks for the help, Red," he said as the train rolled slowly away from the station. He had to put this in perspective. These women were not his responsibility. The sooner they learned how difficult their journey would be, the better. Looking around at the other passengers, he noticed that their expressions seemed to indicate expectations just as high and just as impossible. They would soon learn the difficulties ahead, and so would he.

Still, the excitement was contagious. Dan had to admit it. He'd hated to leave his mother so soon, but at least he was away from his father's business associates and their wheeling and dealing. A few weeks in their company made him even more certain than ever that a future in high finance was not for him. Marrying into one of their families would ensure his involvement. He didn't even want to think about that. Yes, there was something appealing about the West; it would be a greater challenge than he'd expected, but he liked challenges—he thrived on them.

If he accepted the reports of the construction people he'd consulted, he'd need three hundred men, or more time than he had, to complete the forty-two miles of track. He wasn't fooling himself; the weather could double all his calculations. He'd heard tales of having to blast the ice

and snow to get to the ground. And if the Indians continued to be a problem, he'd have to triple his estimate. But
somehow, he'd get it done.

In the beginning, he'd told himself it was because he
couldn't let his mother lose her home. But it was more
than that. He had to prove he could do something real,
something he could see through to the end. In a war, the
end was never truly a victory. One man had little to do
with the outcome. And sometimes a man was called a
coward for trying to play his small role to affect it.

Building the cattle spur from Cold Springs to Laramie
was his future. On completion, he could claim personal
victory far away from Wall Street. He would save his
mother's home and he'd no longer be just Teddy Miller's
son. He would create his own identity.

Now that they were actually leaving, he admitted that
he was worried. The undertaking was fraught with potential for failure. He wished he had the confidence he'd seen
in the maid called Annie. She was strong, a woman dead
set on getting wherever it was she was going no matter
what got thrown in her way. She wasn't asking for help; she
was giving it, seeing after her mistress who was expecting
a child.

And there was Red, ready to be Mrs. Wilson's de-
fender, an apparent man of honor. Honor was a powerful
thing.

Half an hour later, with the windows closed and the
stove roaring at full blast, the smell of cabbage, garlic, and
unwashed bodies permeated the car. Traveling as a working man was a necessity for Dan, but at that moment, a
Pullman car would have been very welcome. Perhaps he
should have waited until he reached Chicago to take on
his new persona. He wondered how Mrs. Wilson was
faring.

And her maid.

———

Annalise leaned her face against the window. Between streaks of soot she could see the squalid houses belching out smoke, looking like snails with hiccups. Inside, the railcar was full of passengers. She wondered that anyone was left in the state.

A crosscurrent of conflicting emotions held her in its grip. As a physician, she knew that she hadn't been badly injured, but she couldn't tamp down a swelling in her stomach that felt like sour yeast. It matched the swelling in her head. And she couldn't be certain that any of her feelings came from the fall.

Finally, the slow-moving cars moved beyond the outskirts of Brooklyn. The din of conversation dropped. Wise decision or not, she'd done it. For the second time in her life she'd left everything that was familiar to her for an unknown future. This time wasn't any easier than the first. Before she'd even gotten on the train, someone had tried to rob her. Suppose she was making a mistake?

She appreciated that Daniel Miller had checked on her crates, but from now on, she had to take care of herself and Ginny.

"Are you sure you're all right?" Ginny asked.

"I'm fine. Stop asking," she said more sharply than she'd intended.

But Ginny's face was already drawn into a concerned frown that said she didn't intend to follow Annie's instructions. "Why did you let Mr. Miller believe you're *my* maid?"

"Because it's best. If my father searches for us, all he'll find is that a Mrs. Wilson left with her maid. My father won't know who that is, but if Robert is looking for you, he will."

Ginny stared out the window for a long time before she spoke. "Annie, I . . . I've been thinking. What if Robert never intended to come back. What if he just wanted to get away from . . . me? Then, I've caused all this mess for nothing."

Annalise took Ginny's hands in her own. "Listen to me, Ginny. This is my choice. Somewhere out there, in the West, there are sick people who need me. We just have to find them. Now, I don't want to hear anything else about it. We're going west!"

The reassurance sounded a bit overly positive, even to Annalise. Her head still pounded. The seats were hard and the stove wasn't producing enough heat to keep the coach warm. Annalise didn't know who she was trying to convince, Ginny or herself. It was cold and she was scared.

They'd lost some of their clothing, but at least the thieves hadn't gotten their tickets. Still, there'd been precious little money left, and she'd expected it to go for other essentials, not on the purchase of clothes. At least she still had her grandmother's watch; it was pinned on her bodice. She pulled her hand from beneath the blanket and reached for the purse hanging from her wrist.

Suddenly time stopped. No sound touched her eardrums. No words left her mouth.

The purse was gone. The locket was gone and so was all their money.

"Annie, what's wrong? Annie!" Ginny was shaking her arm.

"Nothing . . ." Annalise lied. "Just a headache." There was no point in frightening Ginny. There was nothing she could do about it anyway. There was no going back, and she wouldn't ask her father for help. What was she going to do?

From where Dan was sitting, Annie was in clear view. He could see those night-dark eyes, too stoic, too concerned. Whatever her trouble was now, he didn't need it.

They wouldn't reach Chicago before tomorrow, and he hadn't had much sleep the night before. On his last evening in New York City, he'd stopped in on three different social gatherings in one final attempt to find the elegant woman in the emerald green dress. He'd played the role of his father's son and heard every new get-rich scheme being bandied about by the financial elite. But nobody knew his lady of the night.

Absentmindedly, Dan reached inside his jacket pocket and touched the silver bead he'd found at the top of the stairs after she'd run away. He'd finally decided that she must be married. That was the only answer. She could hide behind a masque that allowed her to flirt with anyone she chose without fear of recognition. Otherwise, someone would have known her.

He'd thought leaving New York would put an end to his fascination. Perhaps time would do what distance didn't. If the memory of one woman wasn't enough, now he had another one prickling his conscience. Annie. Annie with no last name was an annoyance he couldn't seem to dismiss. Well, she'd just have to get in line. He had real problems. If his father and the others were to recoup any of their investment, Dan had better get his mind on what he was here for.

Building a cattle spur.

"Hey, boss," one of his newly employed men called out. "Some of us are getting up a poker game. You want to play?"

He didn't, but it was time he started being what he was supposed to be, a real railroad man. "Sure," he answered, "maybe I'll get lucky."

Annalise watched the men pull a box into the aisle and lay out their cards. They had a long night before them, and she needed to rest. As she listened to the men start their game, she thought she might see a way to replace her stolen money.

Annalise smiled and closed her eyes.

6

Over the edge of his cards Dan watched Annie fight sleep, until she could no longer. Once she closed her eyes, she was gone. Shortly after she dropped off, the conductor came through collecting tickets and fares. The maid never knew it when her mistress retrieved the tickets and handed them over.

It was what she did afterward that caught Dan's attention. She looked inside the folder, took out the bills stuck inside, and counted them. The counting didn't take long. Then Mrs. Wilson began looking around, frantically searching for something she obviously couldn't find. A look of total dismay crossed her face.

It couldn't be Annie's carryall; the woman already knew that was missing. Then what?

Money. Annie's money purse. Mrs. Wilson's money. Annie must have been carrying their funds. He replayed the scene when Annie was attacked. He remembered that the thief took Annie's wrist and shoved her over the rail. The purse was what the pickpocket had been after, not the tickets. And he'd been successful. The horrified look on Mrs. Wilson's face confirmed it. Damn!

Dan had already figured out that Annie had made up a tale about looking for her mistress's husband, to cover up something much more serious. "He mustn't stop us," she'd said when she was half unconscious. Who mustn't stop them?

He watched as Mrs. Wilson unfolded the other blanket and covered Annie, brushing her dark hair away from her face with unmistakable concern. Who were they running from—or to? What was in those heavy crates? Who was Mrs. Wilson? A better question was, who was Annie? And, why did he care so much?

Though he played cards with only half a thought to his game, he won as much as he lost before they finally quit. He'd never been much of a gambler, but being one of the men was important to his plan. He intended to live and act like a construction boss.

Throughout the night, Annie slept, oblivious to the other occupants of the car, to the cold, or to the needs of her mistress. If Dan slept, it was fitfully.

At one early morning stop, Dan got off the train and sent a telegram to his father. At the next stop, he picked up a pot of coffee and a loaf of bread along with his father's response. *No report of any missing woman, with or without maid.* It was the next line that stopped him in his tracks: *Take care. Somebody asking questions about CP Spur.*

Why would anybody ask questions about the spur? As far as he knew, only his father's associates stood to lose or make money over the Cold Springs line. Only they knew he was going west to build it. Dan made his way back to his seat and held up the coffeepot to Red, who was awake. "I brought us something hot. I think there are cups in one of the knapsacks."

"I'll look." Dan's new assistant reached behind the stack of bedrolls in the corner. One fell over. There was a yell.

"Get your hands off me, bucko."

Dan turned around. "What's going on, Red?"

"Lemme go or I'll yell again."

Red drew back his hand, rubbing it vigorously. "You bite me again and you'll have something to yell about."

"Go soak your head."

Dan had heard that yell before, back on the dock in Brooklyn. He skirted the seat to confirm his suspicions. Red was hanging onto the ragamuffin who'd caused Annie to fall.

"Looks like we have a stowaway, boss," Red said.

Dan studied the small figure who was punching the air furiously. He put down the pot of coffee and the bread, then took the boy's skinny arms in his hands and pulled him forward. "Be quiet, son. Nobody's going to hurt you."

The boy stopped struggling.

"All right, let me have the lady's money purse."

"I ain't got it."

"Let's just see what you do have. Empty your pockets."

Minutes later they had the tin cups Dan wanted, two cakes of bread, a pair of scissors, and some dried fruit. But no lady's purse.

"What's your name, boy?" Dan asked.

"Name's Joe."

"What's your last name?"

"Don't got one."

"Well, Joe," Dan said, "I think you owe the lady an apology. I want you to take a good look at her face. See what you did to her?"

The boy's eyes widened. "Hey, now. Wait. I didn't hurt no woman."

"No, you didn't, but your partner did. Where is he?"

The boy looked frightened now. "I ain't got no partner. He's just somebody—somebody I knew."

"You worked together to steal this lady's money, didn't you?"

"No, sir! I ain't took nobody's money."

Dan felt the boy flinch beneath his grip. He loosened

his fingers and saw the purple smudges of old bruises. "Looks like you've been close to trouble before. I think we'll just let you apologize to the lady, and then we'll turn you over to the stationmaster to see that you get taken to the police station."

"No, sir! Ah, please. I ain't got no money. You done found everything I got. Just let me go." His voice trailed off into a sniffle.

"Well," Dan hedged. "Let me hear how good your apology is. Then I'll decide."

He dragged the boy down the aisle to Annie's seat. He intended to throw a scare into him, then let him go.

He glared down at Annie's face. It was turning blue over one eye and the scratches still looked raw and painful. She was sleeping, but he knew she was going to be sore when she woke, and hungry, too.

As he stood there, she began to stir, flexing her shoulders and moving her head gingerly back and forth before finally opening her eyes.

"Annie," Daniel said softly, "we caught your pickpocket."

It took a minute for his words to register. "How?"

"Seems he decided to go west with everyone else."

"Did he . . . I mean, are you sure?"

"I'm sure. He had his pockets full, but nothing of any value." He looked at Joe and pushed him forward.

"I'm sorry, lady," Joe said desperately. "Please, don't send me back. He'll kill me for sure."

Annalise blinked her eyes and took a good look at the boy. There was something odd about his arm. She pushed up his sleeves. Next she feathered his dirty brown hair away from his forehead. "You've been beaten."

"No, it's okay. Please."

"It's not okay. Straighten out your arm."

He tried, winced, and gave up. "It won't go straight no more."

Annalise nodded. "It's been broken and it healed crooked."

"Yes'm."

Ginny had been silent, up to then. "What's your name?" she asked.

"Name's Joe."

"Your family?" Ginny asked.

"Never had no daddy. My mama died last year."

Annalise had lost her mother and her brother, but she'd always had her father. "And you've been living on your own since? How old are you?"

"Old enough. And I've been doing okay. Till now."

"Why did you hide on the train?" Annalise asked.

"Heard you all talking about going out west and thought I'd give it a try," the child said, swallowing hard. "Please, lady, don't send me back."

He was small, undernourished, not more than ten years old, she'd guess. And he was scared to death. Annalise took a good look at Daniel's stern expression and knew exactly how he felt. "I'm hungry," she said. "I'll bet you are, too. Do they serve food on this train, Mr. Miller?"

Daniel nodded. "It just so happens that I have a pot of hot coffee and a loaf of bread here. Do you drink coffee, Joe?"

Moments later, Annalise had cleared a space on the bench beside her, and settled the reluctant Joe by the window.

"Here's the coffee," Red said, holding the pot. "Do we have any sugar, Mrs. Wilson? I've a fancy for some sugar in my coffee."

"I got sugar," one of the passengers offered. "I'll be glad to trade for some."

Before Dan knew what had happened, the child was drinking sweet coffee and invited to join Annie's traveling party.

Dan protested. "Annie, this boy is a thief."

"He's a child and he's hungry. How can I not take him? Mr. Red, please see that Joe gets some bread to eat with his coffee."

"And me, too," Ginny insisted. "I'm hungry enough to eat up New York City and take a bite out of Brooklyn."

Suddenly, Joe and Ginny and Red were sharing the breakfast Dan had brought on board, leaving him and Annie to sit and watch.

"All he needs is somewhere to belong," Annie said.

But you aren't prepared to feed yourself, he wanted to say. You have a pregnant mistress in your care. And now you're taking in a pickpocket. But he said nothing. It was not his business, and he already knew it would do no good. She would do what she wanted anyway. But he did wonder what she'd do next. And he wondered what she'd already done that had sent her into hiding.

"Listen to me, Annie," he finally said. "I know you have a big heart, but I don't think you have any idea what you're getting yourself into."

"And you do?"

He had to shake his head. For all his big talk, he was as ignorant about the future as he'd accused Annie of being. "No, but you haven't even reached the frontier yet and look what's already happened. You've been hurt and you've lost your . . . carryall. You don't stand a chance where you're going without a man to look after you."

Annalise might have agreed with him until he said that. He sounded like her father. Only she knew how close he was to the truth. But saying they couldn't make it without a man made her furious. They'd come this far. If her plan worked, they wouldn't have to return. And—she bit back a smile—she'd have the last laugh. She might not have all the answers, but she had a good mind. And nobody was going to tell her ever again that she couldn't do what a man could.

"We don't need a man," she said.

"Maybe not, but your mistress is going to have a child soon. Suppose she needs help?"

"We'll manage. I know more about medicine than most—doctors," Annalise said, holding back a smile.

The woman was impossible. "That could be true," Dan agreed. He thought of his mother. "I've seen what doctors do. You'd be better off with a gunfighter."

Annalise bit her tongue to keep from arguing. If she said anything at all, she ran the risk of giving herself away. "For an educated man, you're pretty narrow-minded."

"What makes you think I'm an educated man?" Dan asked curiously.

"Aren't you," she finally asked, "an educated man?"

"I'm just a railroad boss," he said.

"No, you're not just a railroad boss."

"And you're not just a maid. Are you? How'd you get down on your luck?"

He thought she was some poverty-stricken relative. She liked him thinking that about her. It helped her disguise. "You're right," she admitted.

"Mrs. Wilson is fortunate to have you," Dan said.

Annalise shook her head. "Luck is undependable. A person has to make her own. If you'll excuse me, Mr. Miller, I'll have to make arrangements for a ticket for Joe. Joe, you stay with Mrs. Wilson and Mr. Red." She placed Joe's hand in Ginny's. He shook it off, caught sight of Dan watching, and picked it back up.

Dan studied the boy. There was something about him that didn't quite fit. His instinct was kicking in, and instinct was a quality he'd been accused of honing to the limit. He wondered how Annalise could finance a growing boy, a pregnant woman and soon, a baby.

Later, as the train pulled out of the Philadelphia station, Annalise wondered the same thing. She'd used most of the money she had left for Joe's ticket. Since her purse had been stolen, all she had left was the watch that had belonged to her grandmother. It wasn't worth much. She started having second thoughts about her plan.

Still, she had to try. She had to earn some money, and the only one with money was Dan Miller.

Keeping Joe occupied turned out to be difficult. He was more interested in hanging out with the men than with her and Ginny.

By late that afternoon, the train was halfway to Chicago. The workers had started another poker game in the back of the car. The crowd of onlookers grew, along with the ribald comments and good humor.

"Hey, watch the language," Dan finally said, concerned that the men might offend the women on the train. "Let's call it quits. I can't afford to float any more loans to you men."

"It's no fun anyway, looking at all these ugly mugs, Boss," Red said good-naturedly.

Another man came up with a suggestion that Dan didn't want to hear. "If the boss won't play, let's find another way to liven up the party. At the next stop I'll get us some whiskey."

"No!" Dan's answer was quick. "If you want competition, I'll play."

"I'll play," young Joe said, "if one of you gents will give me a stake. I'll go fifty-fifty with you on whatever I win."

"Sit down, Joe," Ginny said. "Suppose you lose?"

"I won't," he declared. Behind his palm, he confided, "That's another thing I learned from my friend—how to win. Give me an hour and I'll pay you back for the ticket and make enough for our food."

Annalise took a deep breath and stood. "No, Joe. This time, I'll play."

Joe grinned. "Hey, that's good. I'll coach you. You just bat your eyes and joke with 'em. When we get through, they won't know what hit 'em."

"No, you won't," Annalise said, as she threaded her way through the onlookers. "Is a lady allowed in the game?"

"Do you know how to play poker?" Dan asked. He'd wondered what she'd do next, but he hadn't expected this.

"I've played a few hands of cards in my day," she answered.

"Playing with the butler and the coachman isn't the same as playing with these outlaws," Dan warned. "Or maybe—" he gave her a curious look and considered the possibilities, "—you learned to play poker somewhere else."

She returned his glance with a challenging one of her own. "Maybe I did."

"Smile," Joe coached. "And look helpless."

"Are you sure?" Dan asked. "I mean, you could lose."

Annalise felt Joe poke her in the back and decided that maybe the boy was right. She could use all the help she could get. With her best impression of a flirty smile, she said, "But it would be such fun."

"If she runs out of coins, she could play for kisses," one of the men suggested. "That way it won't matter who wins. If she takes the hand, I'll give her a kiss. If I take it, she can give me one."

Batting her eyelashes was harder. "Oh, dear. I really wanted to play for money. Of course, I'll have to put up my jewelry for the first hand." She unpinned the watch and held it out.

Dan struggled to keep from laughing out loud. He didn't doubt that Annie, with her dark dancing eyes, could play cards, but her sudden flirtatious manner was a new side to the maid, and he was enjoying it.

One of the workers rose, gave Annalise a bow, and offered her his seat. "Come on, doll," he said. "You can play my hand. I'll even stake you to some coins."

She tried to hide her look of relief. "Why, thank you, sir. I'll be sure to return them with interest. Are you ready to deal, Mr. Miller?"

She saw that Dan had a worried expression on his face. He thought he was going to see her lose. She hoped he was ready to be surprised.

"I'm ready, Miss Annie. You want to name the game?"

"Let me think." She rolled her eyes upward as if she were trying to remember a name of a card game.

"You got 'em going," Joe whispered behind her.

Annalise ignored him and went on, "I think the game is called blackjack." Annalise knew that was the game; her fellow students even called her Jack's Lady. From the time her brother had taught her to gamble, she'd had a natural talent for the game. In medical school it was a means of forcing the other students to accept her equality, particularly when she won their beer money which she later returned. Then, she played cards with the hospital patients, using their bets as a means of being accepted as a doctor. When she won, they had to let her treat them. She didn't lose often.

Tonight she needed to win, and the only way she was going to do that was by ignoring Dan Miller.

"Would you care to cut the cards?" he asked.

"I don't think so. I trust you."

Joe growled. "I don't."

Dan dealt one card facedown to each of the three men, to himself, and to her. "What do you say?" he said and waited for the man to his left to respond.

The player threw out some coins. "Just so I can stay in the game."

The next player added money and raised the first bet without even looking at his hand.

Finally they were down to Annalise. "Well, I guess I ought to look before I throw my cards in, oughtn't I?"

"Look!" Joe whispered. "I'll tell you what to do."

Tightening her face muscles so that nothing would give her helpless-woman attitude away, she peeked at her hole card. She'd drawn a ten. Before Joe could speak, she added her money and raised the bet.

Dan covered her raise and gave the first player a king and watched him throw in his cards. The second player drew a six and stayed.

The next man folded.

Annalise drew an eight and tried to look worried.

Back to Dan again. His card was a seven. "I'll stand. What you got, darlin'?"

She turned over her hole card. "Eighteen out of twenty-one. I think that means I win."

Dan pretended not to mind when she won the first hand, but it was soon obvious that he wasn't accustomed to losing. He loosened his tie and unbuttoned his shirt. She smiled.

"The game is getting a little hot." He ran his fingers up and down the edge of his shirt, teasing her with his movements. "Are you sure you aren't a professional card player instead of a maid?"

"I've played before, but only with friends," she said demurely as she won the next game.

"Oh? Male or female?" he asked lightly.

She gave him a pouty look. "Mr. Miller, I'm not certain women ever have male friends, do they?"

This time there was no concealing Joe's snicker.

"They're either husbands," Annalise went on, "or brothers, or—" she lowered her voice, "or maybe both."

"You left out one category, Annie."

"Oh? And what would that be?"

He leaned back slowly as he said, "Lovers."

Joe's snicker turned into a chortle.

Annalise swallowed hard and glanced down at her pile of money. She couldn't say her flirting had anything to do with her winnings, but she'd gone too far to stop now. Besides, she was enjoying the interchange. "It *is* getting warm, isn't it?" She pushed her cape away so that she could unfasten the high collar of her travel dress.

Dan folded, and she won two of the next three hands before she began to wonder if he were somehow letting her win. Joe had given up his coaching spot at her back and now sat at Annie's feet. The other players dropped out, content to watch the match between Dan and Annalise. Red was the last to disappear from the circle of watchers. Annalise glanced over her shoulder and saw him sitting beside Ginny, who was talking to him shyly in the corner. That worried her, but there was nothing she could do about it now. Perhaps he was only being kind.

Dan, too, watched the exchange between Red and Mrs. Wilson. He couldn't blame his employee; Mrs. Wilson was the kind of woman men naturally took care of. At least she wasn't fighting Red's efforts the way Annie had fought his.

Annie was a puzzle. He watched the way her spiky lashes fluttered up and down over eyes that darkened to a shiny black when she wore a serious expression. He knew she was no ordinary dance hall girl; she'd never submit herself to a man unless she chose to do so. But what was she?

Dan had never thought too much about physical beauty; the women in his life were always attractive although they didn't always interest him. Annie wasn't beautiful, but there was something about her, an inner fire that made her vibrant and attractive.

And she was smart, too.

And she won again.

The men watching looked at each other in amazement, sat back, and began to laugh. Annalise made neat little piles of her winnings. She didn't want to leave the workers broke. They had to have money, just as she did. Still, she had over a hundred dollars in front of her. At least they'd eat.

"I think it's time for me to quit," she finally said. "I don't want to take all your money."

Dan nodded, then asked, "By the way, what did you decide?"

Annalise gathered her winnings and stood up. "About what?" she asked.

"Me. When I asked you who you'd played cards with, you said friends and brothers. Then you stated that women never have male friends, only husbands and brothers. I guess you have to put me in the third category."

She didn't have to ask what that category was; she remembered.

Lovers.

By the time they arrived in Chicago's Water Street Station, Annalise's pockets were filled and she was gathering up the men's IOU's. Those who were low on money offered to work off their debts with physical labor.

Dan watched her return to her seat. The way he figured it, she could probably build his railroad spur with those IOU's. As far as being a lover, he could see where there might be merit in that. He gave her a long look, then smiled and fastened the buttons on his shirt.

She nodded and fastened her own buttons.

He allowed himself one last observation. For the most part, she'd kept her hands beneath her cloak, but he'd seen enough to know that she hadn't done much physical work. Maybe, just maybe, he and the other players had been tricked. Maybe Annie *was* a well-educated cardsharp who created a cover to mislead her victims. She had taken Joe in with little concern. Mrs. Wilson? He had no answer there. Nothing matched. Who was this mysterious lady, and what was she up to?

The telegram waiting for him in Chicago came from his father.

COUNTING ON YOU, SON. LUCY RIDDENHOUSE,
LENORA FRY, AND ANNALISE SINCLAIR ALL
GOOD CHOICES FOR BRIDE. MOTHER HAVING
TEA WITH EACH.

7

—❧❦—

Mason Clanton looked at his partner with an accusing stare. "This was never about getting cattle contracts for our meat packing plant, was it, William? Ruining Teddy Miller was your priority from the beginning."

"You're damned right it was. I've been waiting to ruin him for a long time."

"Why do you hate him so much? What did Miller ever do to you?"

"The son of a bitch cost me my reputation. Because of him, I lost my business, and the woman I was engaged to married someone else."

Mason shook his head. He'd known that William Russell was a bitter, determined man when he'd taken him in five years ago. He single-handedly turned the small Clanton Meat-Packing Company into the largest in Chicago. But this new side to the man was disturbing. "How'd he do it?"

"During the early part of the war, I got a contract to sell cattle to the Army. Teddy's firm supplied the Army with weapons and other goods. But he wanted it all. Tried to buy me out. I refused to sell. Suddenly Teddy's son goes to work for the President and the Army cancels my contract, said my meat was rotten before it got to the troops. Because of Teddy Miller, I was put out of business. Now, I'm going to get even."

"And how do you plan to do that?"

"Seems he and his little group—I call them Teddy's Rogues—are going to build a railroad cattle spur on that land they expected to sell to the Union Pacific. We're going to stop them. When they're busted, we're going to take over the spur, and then I'll take Teddy Miller's house. He's going to know what it feels like to lose everything."

"I know about the mortgage you hold on Teddy's house, but how do you plan to get hold of the spur?"

William smiled. "A tribe of hostile Sioux Indians are camped right where the line goes. We'll let them get rid of the Indians, endure the winter weather, and then fail because of all the future accidents."

"Accidents? How can you be certain they'll have accidents?"

"Because I've already arranged them."

All the way back to her seat Annalise could feel Dan's eyes on her. The other card players were ribbing him about losing to a woman. It hadn't appeared to bother him, but she suspected that he covered his dismay with his teasing.

"Was Dan right?" Joe asked as he followed Annie down the aisle.

"Right about what?"

"Are you some kind of lady cardsharp? Is that what you're going to do out west?"

"Of course not. And don't wake up Ginny."

"That's not what Dan thinks," Joe whispered. "He's right. I've seen a lot of poker players, and you're a natural."

"I just got lucky," she protested, allowing herself a smile of satisfaction.

Joe grinned. "Yep, you skunked 'em good, and you vamped 'em good, too, and you didn't even need to do that."

"I didn't vamp anyone. I wouldn't know how to vamp a man."

Joe was grinning from ear to ear. "Reckon it just comes natural to some. How much did we make?"

"I made enough to get us where we want to go, if we're careful."

"Well, if you need me to help you with anything else, you just say the word."

Annalise realized what Joe was suggesting and reproached him immediately. "Joe, you are not to steal anything. Do you hear me?"

Joe dropped the blanket he was carrying on to the floor between the rows of seats, pretending not to hear Annie. "I'll just sleep down here."

"Do you understand what I just said?"

"Yes, ma'am. I heard every word."

Annalise settled back in her seat, and thought about the last exchange between her and Daniel Miller. She just couldn't get him out of her mind.

She glanced toward the back of the car. All the lamps had been extinguished except for the one held by Daniel Miller. He caught her gaze as if he'd felt her watching him. The nod he gave her was unmistakable, but the wink that followed had to be a reflection of the light as he blew out the flame.

The car went dark. Annalise's breath caught in the huge lump in her throat, temporarily cutting off her air supply. Dan Miller's contention that she was a gambler wasn't nearly as threatening as his suggestion that he might be a lover.

In the darkness, Annalise folded her winnings into a

handkerchief and poked it into her bodice. Nobody would steal this money unless they undressed her to get it.

Undress. Daniel Miller's eyes had undressed her during every hand of the card game. She'd known what he was doing. She'd fought the tension he created by reminding herself that she'd probably seen more naked men's bodies than he'd seen women's. But there was a difference between considering a naked body as Dr. Sinclair and as Annalise, the vamp.

She'd never had to separate the two until Dan Miller came into her life. Until she'd danced with him at the ball. Until she'd touched knees with him for two hours while playing cards. Until he'd loosened his tie and unbuttoned the top of his shirt.

Physical attraction between a man and a woman was not part of her medical training. The body and its responses had always been measured by sickness and wellness. Nobody ever mentioned sensations of heat, shortness of breath, or weakness in the limbs when a person was perfectly healthy.

Joe's voice, a mere whisper, interrupted Annalise's thoughts. "Don't suppose you'd like to share a bit of the loot, would you? I mean, at the next stop, I could get us something to eat besides coffee and bread."

"At the next stop," she said sharply, "we're going to get you a bath and some clean clothes."

"Ain't no cause for you to go spending money on a thing like that," he argued. "Just get dirty all over again."

"Nonsense! A clean body is a healthy body. Cleanliness is next to godliness."

"Yeah, well, I'm thinking that being godly might just be out of place where we're heading."

It was cold and wet and foggy when the train stopped in Chicago. Red pulled his green cap over his eyes and blended into the crowd of departing passengers. His in-

structions were to go to the Wet Dog Tavern, where someone would contact him. His purse would be filled with
more coins and he'd be on his way again. So far, it had all
been too easy. He swallowed back the pang of guilt that
nagged him by reminding himself that the money wasn't
for him, and that if he could have gotten it any other way,
he would have.

Dan Miller seemed like a good man, a fair man, though
Red wasn't sure he could pull off building a railroad with
only eight crew members. But he'd have to hand it to the
man, he had a way with words and people, too. He'd willingly taken on the chore of protecting the two women and
their adopted ragamuffin, and Red respected him for that.

As a person, he was friendly and easygoing. He even
laughed when Annalise beat the socks off him in poker. It
was the other woman that caught Red's attention, the
quiet, less confident one. She hadn't acted superior. But
no matter how friendly she was, she was a lady, and he was
a common cook. Or he would be, once he learned something about it. The lie he'd told to get the job still stuck in
his craw.

The wind was blowing in gusts now, pelting all the travelers with icy cold. He hoped that Dan was seeing to the
women. Red would have to make up some excuse for his
disappearance. He couldn't afford to get fired.

Red spotted the sign for the tavern just ahead. He
ducked in the doorway and paused, waiting for some signal. A man sitting in the corner gave him a nod and Red
sauntered casually over and took a seat.

There was no greeting. No handshake. Just a rough
question. "What have you learned, Irishman?"

"Not much. The boss is a man that keeps things close to
his vest. It's gonna take a wee bit more time."

"You're not getting paid to take a bit more time."

Red stood. "If you're unhappy with me services, we can
be ending 'em. I'll not hold you to the deal."

"Not so fast, Irishman. You took our money. The man I

work for won't like that. And what he don't like don't live. Understand?"

Red inhaled sharply. They weren't going to let him off the hook. Desperation had forced him to make a decision he was beginning to regret. He hadn't asked questions. Now he was committed, not to Dan Miller who had offered him a real future, but to this low-class little man with his beaver hat and fur-trimmed coat. He wasn't much different from the rich landowners Red the lackey had left behind in Ireland. For now, he had no choice. Keep the job—keep both jobs. "I understand."

"Just remember, I'll be close by and I'll expect you to keep me informed."

Red nodded. He had to make them believe that he would follow through on the job. He'd tell them what they wanted to hear. That would keep him alive, while he figured out what to do.

His contact handed him a bag of coins and disappeared into the smoke-filled room. Red thought about it for a moment, then exchanged one of the coins for a loaf of bread and some cheese, which he divided into two parcels. A pregnant woman needed food, and he wasn't sure Mrs. Wilson was eating enough for two.

Back on the train, Red dropped one of his parcels of food on Annie's empty seat and sauntered back to his own. Dan was studying his paperwork. "Once we get across the Mississippi, our timbers will be waiting for us in Boggy Gut."

"And how far is that?" Red asked, watching as the women and Joe took their seats. Ginny had picked up the parcel and was looking around. Her question about its origin went unanswered, but when she opened it, her eyes went straight to Red and she smiled.

He returned the smile and opened his own. "Care for some food?" he asked Dan.

"No, thanks. Bought some from a vendor. Tried to buy

the ladies something to eat. I think Mrs. Wilson would have accepted, but Annie refused. She said thank you but that they couldn't take anything from me."

Red bit back a smile at Dan's miffed tone of voice, but he couldn't resist saying, "Guess she didn't feel that way last night."

Dan's wounded grimace turned into a smile. "Didn't seem to, did she?"

"That's the way with a woman," Red observed. "When she wants something from you, she drags out her feminine wiles. Didn't think either one of those two had any."

"Just goes to show you how wrong you can be about a person, doesn't it."

Red chewed on that fact for the next hundred miles. When they reached the Illinois side of the Mississippi River after midnight, he still hadn't figured out what he was going to do.

Annalise and her crew were the first ones off the train. She led Ginny and Joe behind a stack of supplies in back of the ticket office and waited, hidden from view.

Now, an hour later, everyone had disappeared, leaving them alone in the dark. "I guess we can come out now," Annalise said, holding onto Joe, afraid he'd run off and find Dan and Red.

"Well, I should hope so. Annie, I'll tell you, I don't feel a bit good about hiding behind this ticket office. Now we're all alone."

"Don't be such a goose, Ginny."

"I am a goose. It's pitch dark and I'm scared."

"So am I," Annalise admitted. "But, Ginny, we're going to have to be alone sooner or later."

"Maybe, but I'd rather it be later, Besides, it's nice having . . . one of Mr. Miller's men doing our lifting and carrying, and generally looking after us."

"We can do without *one* of Mr. Miller's men. We have

Joe," Annalise said, more confidently than she felt. "He's a strong boy. He'll carry anything you need."

"Yes," was Ginny's quiet reply, "but he's a boy. He finally admitted, he's only ten years old. Personally, I prefer the protection of a man."

Ginny pressed her hand against her back. "It looks like this is as far as the train goes. What do we do now?"

"Yeah," Joe echoed wearily, "what do we do now?"

Annalise was beginning to regret her attempt to separate them from their rescuer. Even if Daniel Miller was driving her crazy, she had to think of Ginny who, in her advanced condition, needed a place where she could rest. She forced herself to sound optimistic. "Our crates are stored inside the depot. So, now we find a place to spend the night."

"And then what?" Joe asked. "I'm used to finding a place out of the wind, but I don't think Ginny will fit under a porch or in a stable. I think we need Dan."

"Or a policeman," Annalise said.

"A policeman?" Joe was gone before Annalise considered what effect her careless remark might have on him.

"Wait, Joe, I meant we'd ask for his help." But Joe had vanished. "I'll go after him, Ginny."

"No! Don't leave me here in the dark."

Annalise stopped. A sudden feeling of being watched rocked her more than the biting wind. On top of everything else, with her nerves strained to the breaking point and her confidence freezing into a solid sheet of thin ice, she suddenly wanted to drop the blankets she was carrying and run back onto the train.

"It's okay, Mrs. Wilson," a familiar masculine voice observed. "Head toward the light up ahead. Red and Joe are coming this way. Red will get you to shelter."

Annalise gave a dejected sigh. So much for separating herself from Dan Miller.

Ginny picked up her steps, moving ahead to meet Red. Annalise turned around, swaying slightly from fatigue.

Dan stepped out from the side of the depot, holding a lamp. "Where have you been, Annie? We've been looking for you."

Dan didn't know whether he wanted to hug or spank her. He didn't know what she'd been up to since everyone else left the train, but she looked half frozen, and more exhausted than her mistress. "You need to get to bed. The ferry will be leaving at six A.M."

"Ferry? I don't understand."

"Didn't they tell you the line stops here?"

"No, the ticket agent just said this was the cheapest fare out west."

"It is, because we have to take the ferry across the river to the logging camp. Once the timbers are loaded, we'll pick up another train. Then, we won't be more than a day out of Omaha." She just stood staring at him, as if she were too frozen to speak or move. "Let's go, Annie," he said gently. "I'll help you."

Why was he doing this? "Look, Mr. Miller," she finally said, "the poker game was a mistake. I'll never do that again. I'm sorry I won your money, and I'll repay every cent of it—as soon as I can."

"And how do you plan to do that?"

"I . . . I'm not certain yet, but I do have skills with which I can earn money."

"You mean other than gambling?"

"Certainly!" she snapped, then realized that she should say no more and avoid his questions.

"I can't wait to find out what." Dan held up the lamp and took her arm. "You come on, let's get out of this wind."

"Yes," she said between teeth that weren't totally chattering from the cold. "I have to find us a place to stay tonight."

His lips spread into a wide smile as he started down the platform. "Don't worry, that's all been arranged."

"But, I can't afford—much."

"Why not? I can't wait to see those other skills. You can

use them to pay for these accommodations and save your winnings."

Annalise picked up the pace. "Doesn't look like there's much here," she said, peering into the darkness.

"There isn't."

"Then where are we going to spend the night?"

His answer was short and direct. "With me."

8

When Annie saw their sleeping quarters, she realized that Dan had been teasing her when he'd said they were spending the night with him. What he meant was that they'd all have to share the attic, a drafty second-floor room over an old inn. Later she learned that the inn was originally a trading post for ships traveling the Mississippi. Now railroad passengers paid for space on the floor in front of the fireplace to warm their tired bodies and get some sleep before continuing their journey.

After a sorry meal provided by the owner's wife, which Ginny didn't attempt to eat and Joe did, they were provided with worn blankets and shown to the attic.

"I'm sorry," Dan said as they looked with dismay at their quarters. "It was this or the floor downstairs, and I thought you'd prefer the privacy."

"Yes, but what about you?" Annie asked. "I thought . . ."

He grinned. "You didn't think I meant we'd be spending the night together literally, did you? I mean, it's a bit too public, wouldn't you say?"

"Mr. Miller! Don't say things like that in front of Ginny and Joe. What will they think?"

Ginny spoke up. "I'll think that I'm going to bed, and I don't care who sleeps up here so long as I don't have to move before noon tomorrow."

"Sorry, Mrs. Wilson," Dan apologized. "The ferry leaves at six o'clock."

Ginny groaned. "Somebody wake me," was all she said.

"Where will you and Red and Joe sleep?" Annie asked, feeling guilty for her ingratitude.

"Downstairs with the others. At least there's a fireplace. You can have our blankets, too," Joe said, laying his on top of the others. "I'll go downstairs with the . . . men."

"I don't think that's a good idea," Annie said.

"He'll be all right with us," Dan said, and left the room, closing the door behind him.

Annie helped Ginny to the floor and covered her with both blankets. She had her cape; that would be enough. Besides, she doubted that she'd sleep anyway. The door didn't look too strong, and she'd seen the way some of the men had looked at her and Ginny.

Six o'clock would come soon enough, and once they were over the river, they'd be in the West. Then she remembered their crates. The stationmaster had agreed to store them until tomorrow. Unless she made arrangements now, they could miss the ferry. Without her medical supplies, she'd be helpless. She paced back and forth, searching for a solution.

None came to mind. There was nothing to do but go back to the depot and see if she could rouse the stationmaster and have the crates delivered to the ferry tonight.

Ginny was already sleeping when Annie picked up her cape, wrapped it around her, and slipped down the back stairs and out the door. Big wet flakes of snow had begun to fall. Annalise pulled her cape around her face and felt the warmth of her breath trapped inside its folds.

She moved quickly along the boarded sidewalk, hugging the shadows as much to keep out of the wind as to keep out of sight. When she reached the railroad station she ducked around the back, coming up to the side nearest the ticket window. She didn't have to rouse the agent; Dan already had.

"You're welcome, Mr. Miller," he was saying. "I'll send your message. Just let me read it and make sure I have it right. You want to say, *Stop searching. I'll find woman myself.*"

Annalise felt her heart drop to the pit of her stomach. He was looking for a woman. What did that mean? She couldn't think. In a panic, she whirled around, retracing her steps, then stopped. She couldn't go back to the inn without knowing what she and Ginny were going to do. She had to think, and she thought better alone.

She bent her head and walked into the wind, keeping the lights at the edge of the river in view. She could hear the current slapping the posts in the water, but there was nothing comforting in the sound. Everything seemed to be pushing against her, telling her to go back.

A flat-bottomed boat as big as a house bobbed in the water like a cork on a fishing pole. An apron circling the center structure was already being packed with goods. Lamps inside a middle room sent a wavering slash of light into the darkness. On the upper level was a second, smaller balcony around a smaller room. At the front of the structure the antlers of some very large animal pointed the direction the ferry would take.

A round man, wearing a navy blue jacket and cap, was fingering a railroad watch on a long chain and puffing on a stubby cigar. "Howdy, ma'am. Captain Wally here. What can I do for you?"

"Captain Wally, I'm Anna—Annie. My mistress, Mrs. Wilson, asked me to inquire about crossing the river. There are two adults and one ten-year-old child."

"Oh, yeah, you're them people traveling with Dan. He said you might sidle off down here. Your passage been took care of. Just be here at daybreak. Unless the storm gets worse, we'll shove off then."

"Storm? Will it be safe?"

The ferry captain blew into his hands, trying to warm them. "Course it will be. I usually make this trip twice, morning and afternoon."

"Are there that many people?" she asked. Then the solution she was looking for slapped her in the face. He said he made the trip twice a day. They didn't have to catch the ferry at dawn.

"Not always. The working crews come through here and lots of them settlers. Cheaper fares."

Workers. He might know Robert. "Don't guess you've ferried a worker named Robert Wilson, have you?"

"Could have. Don't ask names. What did he look like?"

Annie couldn't answer that question. Ginny never described Robert to her. It could wait until tomorrow. "Never mind. Captain Wally, I have several crates of goods stored in the train depot. I didn't know when I left them there that we'd be leaving so early. I wonder if you—"

"Say no more, little lady. Your crates are already aboard. A red-haired fellow with a little green hat made the arrangements for Mr. Miller."

"But I'd rather not go at daybreak. The lady I'm traveling with is with child, and she needs her rest. We'll take the afternoon ferry."

"Suits me," he agreed, "but Miller seemed to think you were going to take the logging train to Omaha. Never know what time it'll leave, or when the next one will come along. Don't think two ladies want to be stranded in Boggy Gut to wait. No lodging."

"But you said you made two trips a day."

"Usually, but a lot depends on Rosco Thurmon. He owns the ferry and his house is on the other side of the river. If he comes over in the morning, we go back in the afternoon, even if he's the only passenger. Never know what he's gonna do."

"Who's Rosco Thurmon?"

"Rosco owns a logging business, and the rail spur from Boggy Gut to Omaha. The railroad runs pretty much like the ferry; it goes when he wants it to go. He's filthy rich."

Annie glanced down at the hem of her travel dress, wet and frayed. "And I'm just plain filthy."

Captain Wally laughed. "The logging camp wasn't named Boggy Gut for nothing. It's mostly black mud and piles of timbers. Except for Rosco's mansion. Built himself a fancy house over there, just like one he saw in Chicago. He thinks he's a gentleman. He ain't. Fancy houses don't make an old pirate into a man of quality."

Maybe not, Annie thought, but she remembered her father and decided that money went a long way. Annie couldn't imagine a man building a mansion in a place called Boggy Gut. The name conjured up a bad picture but conditions were even rougher than she'd imagined, and she'd brought Ginny out here into the midst of hardship and misery. For what? Had she truly done it to find Robert, or had he been her excuse to search for a place where she was valued?

Dan Miller was an even bigger question. Why was he looking for a woman? Could that woman be her? If so, she might have fooled him with her shameless flirting and her poker playing skills, because Annalise Sinclair and Annie had no more in common than Annie and Dan Miller. From the looks of the house his family lived in, they could afford to buy their own railroad. Why was he going out west as a construction boss on a train that stopped at Boggy Gut? It didn't make sense. The likelihood that two members of the wealthiest families in New York City would end up in this place was slim to none.

Yet they had.

The daughter of Roylston Sinclair as a lady's maid.

The son of Teddy Miller as a construction boss.

"So, if I'm to make certain I get on the train to Omaha, I'd better be there when it leaves," Annie said.

"Yep!"

There was no use discussing her crates or their ferry ride with the captain. She'd take it up with Dan Miller—tomorrow. Excusing herself and promising to be there at first light, Annalise started back to the inn. The wind was swirling the snow around now so fiercely that she couldn't see. Soon she realized that she'd taken a wrong turn. She should have reached the inn by now. Shading her eyes with her hands she searched for lights.

When a large black shape suddenly appeared before her she screamed, tottered, and almost fell.

"I've got you," a man said.

"Turn me loose," she yelled. "My husband is waiting for me. He'll tear your arms off."

"I'd hate that, Annie. Without arms I couldn't hold you."

"Daniel Miller! You scared me to death. Why are you . . . following me?" she asked, covering her relief with anger.

He drew her even closer. "Joe saw you leave, and I thought that you'd gone outside to . . ." his voice trailed off lamely, "but when you didn't come back I was afraid you might have gotten lost."

"I almost did," she admitted and for a long moment she allowed him to hold her, as she nestled her head beneath his chin, and curled her hands into tight little fists against his chest.

Dan took a deep breath in and exhaled. "Your hair. I know that scent. Have we met before?"

She gave a dry laugh. "We've never met, Daniel Miller. How could we? I'm just a maid and you, you're a—" she cut off her words, lest she give herself away. A maid wouldn't know who Dan was. Instead, she raised her eyes. "Thank you for rescuing me again, but I'd better go now."

Dan didn't let her go. He couldn't. She could feel the rapid beat of his heart and she was puzzled. He'd held her before, at the ball, and that had turned her insides into bubbling mush. But that night he was holding a woman he believed to be his equal. Now he was reacting the same way with a woman he thought was a maid. And she was responding to him now just as she did then. Her confusion momentarily stilled her.

"I want to kiss you, Annie."

"Why?"

"I wish I knew." Dan lowered his face, his lips only a breath away from her forehead, then her nose and finally her lips.

Annie parted her lips beneath his, allowing his tongue to touch hers. His hands released her, slid beneath her cape and pulled her even closer. She was crushed so tightly against him that she could feel his muscles throbbing. She felt a rush of panic and gasped. Just for a moment she wanted to give in, to kiss him back.

"Please don't," she said, breaking the kiss.

"Why? You want to be kissed."

"No, I don't. Why are you doing this? I'm just a maid and you . . . you're probably already . . . married or promised and I'm . . . I'm not available."

He gave a light laugh. "You think I'm married? Would that matter?"

"Of course it would matter! I mean, I—I don't know. I just don't think you're what you seem."

There was an imperceptible jerk in his grip. "And neither, my lovely, are you."

"What do you mean?"

"I mean you're much too polished to be a lady's maid. I'm having a hard time believing you're some soiled dove heading out west to open up in one of those movable hell-on-wheels railcars that follow the railroad laborers to fleece them. Tell me, Annie, with no last name, who are you, really?"

Her heart skipped a beat. He'd determined what she wasn't. Could he know the truth? No, there was no way he could connect a down-on-her-luck maid with Dr. Annalise Sinclair. "I'm just an ordinary woman, heading west," she said.

"An ordinary woman? I think not. I do believe you're a woman who's running away from something in her past. You're afraid."

"Nonsense!" She tried to pull away. "I'm not afraid."

"Then why are you trembling?"

She angled her head and raised her eyes to meet his. In the darkness there was a fluttering veil of white drawn between them that concealed whatever she might have seen. Still, she felt the overwhelming maleness of him, and as the air between them arced with tension she searched for a way to turn that heat off. "Why are you trembling, Mr. Miller?"

He wanted to shake her, to force her into submission, to diffuse this wild current of desire that held them in its grasp. His voice went low and deadly. "Damn you, woman. I'm not immune to you."

"What does that mean? Am I some kind of disease?"

"I'm beginning to think so. Don't you know what you've done to me with your sashaying around, giving orders, getting into one mess after another?"

"No, I don't."

"You've made me think about you instead of what I'm supposed to be doing. I can't allow that to happen."

She was silent for a long time, standing in the darkness with the falling snow cloaking them in robes of white. Finally she said, "Then I suggest you stop thinking about me. I can take care of myself."

Dan swore. "I've tried. I have a railroad to build. And the last thing I want is a woman in my life."

"That's good, for the last thing I intend to be is a woman in some man's life."

"Tell me, Annie," he asked huskily, "what are you running from?"

"I'm not running from anything, except men like you. I'm running to the future, one I choose."

He clasped her tighter and swore. "Annie, you can't do this. You may think you can gamble and use your 'other talents' to survive out here, but it won't work. You . . . you deserve better."

Annie wasn't cold anymore. Dan's words warmed her; his genuine concern melted the last of her control, and she had to hold onto every ounce of resolve not to slide her fingers beneath the rough texture of his jacket and feel the chest that vibrated with the beat of his heart.

They stood for a long time before Daniel finally said, "I know I'm going to regret this, Annie, but I'm going to kiss you again. I have to."

This time his kiss was hard, demanding, lusty, and she felt her lips open willingly beneath his assault. Ruthlessly he plundered her mouth, demanding, taking. She could do nothing but surrender to the flare of heat that he'd ignited.

She'd never known a man's kiss before Daniel Miller's. How could she ever have understood the intensity of her physical response? Her breasts tingled. Her loins felt as if they'd been branded with a hot iron. Her blood seemed to roar through her veins.

Then, just as she felt she might explode, his kiss softened and changed into something hesitant, tentative, wondrous. He pulled away, one hand leaving her back and sliding up her arm to her neck, then her chin. "How about that?" he whispered, his mouth only inches away from her lips. He caressed her neck with his thumb, stroking it between the buttons of her travel dress. "You're so tiny, so fierce. I know it sounds crazy, but I feel as if we've done this before."

Annalise drew in a sharp breath that caught in her throat. "Why would you think that?"

"The way you taste. The feel of your lips." He shook his

head and studied her. "Maybe it's just that you remind me of someone else."

Why didn't she pull away? Why didn't she jerk herself out of his arms and run back to the inn? Because, with every ounce of her being, she wanted him to kiss her again. "I'm a maid, Dan. I'll bet you've kissed a lot of maids you didn't know, in a lot of mansions."

"No, I haven't." He slid his arms beneath her cape and pulled her closer. "I haven't kissed anyone I didn't know . . . except—"

She felt him stiffen. He was confused, and she couldn't let him remember. But how was she to stop him when she couldn't get away? For a moment she swayed, then she shook herself, drew back, and did the only thing she could think of. She socked him in the nose.

Dan gasped. He saw stars and felt a gush of warmth. He let her go.

"Damn it, Annie, you hit me!"

"I did, and if you ever—do that again, I'll do worse." He suddenly heard a shout, someone calling his name, over and over. "Dan! Dan, are you out there?"

"Annie," he said, then more urgently, "Annie! Someone is coming." He felt moisture on his upper lip and reached for his handkerchief.

The light of a lantern penetrated the darkness. "What happened to you?" Red asked, catching the blood-flecked white handkerchief in the light.

"I slipped and fell," Dan said. "Gave myself a nose-bleed."

"On what?" Red asked, looking around suspiciously.

"On a limb that broke in the storm. Are you ready to get back to the inn, Annie?" he asked, taking her by the arm. "Daybreak comes early."

"I can walk by myself, Mr. Miller," she said, tugging her arm slowly away from him. "Please, let me go."

He stopped, allowing her to move away from him. "Shine the light for Annie, Red. She's a little unsettled."

"Did she fall, too?"

"I—think she did."

"Well, that's what you get for wandering about out here in the dark. You could have gotten into real trouble. I've been looking for you for half an hour."

"Too bad you didn't find us sooner," Dan remarked.

9

Ginny was waiting anxiously when Annalise entered the sleeping room.

"Where have you been, Annie?"

"I . . . I've been down to the river."

"Is something wrong?"

Annalise stood in the light of the candle Ginny was holding, eyes wide, heart racing. Her lips felt swollen. Her mind was in turmoil.

"Annie, what's happened?"

Annalise forced herself to focus on Ginny's worried expression. Whatever had happened, it wasn't something she could share. "Nothing," she finally said. "We have to be at the river at daybreak. Go back to sleep."

Ginny studied her. "Are you sure you want to go on with this, Annie? We could go back to New York. I've already told you, I'll tell my father what happened and face the consequences."

Annalise considered Ginny's suggestion that they go back home. She couldn't do that. She wouldn't admit defeat. She had to prove herself. If she could just stay out of Dan Miller's arms and focus on the task at hand.

"No, Ginny. We came out here to build a new life for ourselves. We aren't giving up. Now, let's get to sleep. By the way," she asked as she lay down, "what did Robert look like?"

"Robert?" Ginny repeated softly. "He was big and dark and . . . Oh, Annie, I'm having a hard time remembering."

"I don't understand. How can you forget someone you've . . . been with. That changes you forever, doesn't it?"

Ginny sighed. "I don't know, Annie. I guess that sooner or later you realize that what you're feeling and expecting isn't the same thing he is."

"You mean Robert didn't feel something for you?"

"At the time, he did," Ginny explained. "It's just that men seem to feel that way often."

Annie thought about that. "And women don't?"

Ginny's voice dropped, "I didn't think so, Annie. I thought that when you loved someone, it went on forever. Now, I don't know. Maybe women are more like men than they think."

"Have you ever struck anyone, Ginny?"

"Struck? As in spank a child?"

"Not exactly. I was thinking about socking a man."

"No, but I've wanted to," Ginny admitted.

Long after Ginny fell asleep, Annalise lay awake. To say her very being had been rocked once again by her encounter with Dan was an understatement. He'd seemed to react just as strongly to her when she was his snowbird as he did when she was his maid. Would she know the difference between his kiss and that of another man's? She thought she might, and that scared her. He couldn't know who she was, not yet. Fighting him and her father would be more than she could handle. Though her father had given her a chance to succeed, he hadn't expected her to leave New York to do it.

Earlier, she'd glossed over Ginny's predicament by

deciding that all she needed was to find the man who'd left her with child. Once married, Ginny would be settled. But if Ginny had such powerful feelings about Robert, why couldn't she remember what he looked like?

Annie could still see Dan's face in the light of Red's lamp, and she remembered every single feature on it, especially his nose, where she socked him one. She'd never be able to look him in the face again, nor would she ever forget it. Yet they would be on the ferry together in the morning. Until they crossed the Mississippi, there was no way she could avoid him.

Annalise turned from side to side, seeking relief from the physical aftermath of the storm Dan Miller had built inside her. Nothing helped.

"Annie?" Ginny whispered. "You've been talking with Mr. Miller, haven't you?"

"I . . . saw him, yes."

"Is he the reason you're jerking about like a cat with fleas?"

"No! Yes. I don't know. I guess he is."

"It's hard, having those feelings, isn't it?"

Even though their status had changed, she couldn't talk about this with Ginny. All she could answer was, "I don't know."

"I'm sorry I got all this started, Annie."

"You didn't start it, Ginny. I did, a long time ago when I decided I wanted to be a doctor. I refused to give up. It's done now. We can't go back to what we were before. Too much has happened, and we've both changed. We just have to go forward. Go to sleep. Once we get to Omaha I intend to make certain that we never see Dan Miller again."

"Sometimes, Annie, I think things are meant to be and nothing we can do will stop that."

"Go to sleep, Ginny."

As Annie tried to sleep, she thought about Ginny's words. She didn't want to accept them. She had to stop the response she had to Dan Miller and put out the fire once and for all. When she decided to become a doctor, she'd closed everything out. And, she'd do it again. She had to do it again.

The ferry didn't leave at daybreak. It finally lifted anchor and left the dock around noon. The trip across the river was scary. Ginny stayed far enough away from the edge so that her stomach didn't churn with the waves. Joe clung to the rail and relished every minute of the trip.

Dan Miller entered the storage area where Ginny and Annie were waiting. "We'll be docking soon, Mrs. Wilson. Annie."

Dan studied the women and frowned. "The docking is simple enough, but moving you across the mud to the plank sidewalk will be a mess. As much as I hate to say it, ladies, you're going to have to take off those shoes. You'll freeze, but at least you'll have something dry to put on your feet when you get through the muck. Joe, I want you to—"

"We'll manage fine, Mr. Miller," Annalise said, moving up beside him. Recalling her vow the night before, she ignored Dan and began moving their things into one pile, until she caught sight of Joe.

"Joe, what's that bulge in your pocket?"

"Nothing . . . I ain't—don't have nothing in my pockets."

"I think you'd better empty them," Annie said, ignoring the eye-widening shock still across Dan's face.

Annie watched as Joe pulled out a pouch of tobacco, a chunk of something wrapped in a scrap of cotton, and a pair of red knit socks.

"The kid pinched me socks," Red said, "and my tobacco, too."

"Ah, I wouldn't a' kept them," Joe said. "I just wanted something to keep my hands warm." Sheepishly, Joe handed the socks to Red, then turned and climbed over the goods stored inside and disappeared from sight.

"Are you going to just stand there, Mr. Miller?" Annie asked. "If so, I wish you'd move a bit to the side." She brushed by him and started toward the outside. "Come along, Mrs. Wilson."

The engines began to slow and the boat shuddered.

"Annie," Dan said, following her, "I don't think you understand what's involved from here on out. You're two women alone and you'll be in a logging camp."

"And I don't care what you think, Dan Miller. I intend to get where I'm going, and I'll take care of any trouble ahead."

Annalise felt the lurch of the boat's bow hitting the dock, as the engine came to a stop. They'd made it. Until now she hadn't been certain that they would. So far they'd survived losing their money and extra clothes and crossing an angry river in a storm.

What she hadn't escaped was Dan Miller.

Yet.

"Let's get off the boat," Annalise said. "We've got a train to catch." And she still had to mail the letter to her father. She'd put it off as long as she could. But after what she'd heard last night at the depot, she couldn't be certain that Dan wouldn't eventually give her away. She wouldn't tell her father where she was yet, just that she was safe. By the time her father got her letter, she'd be gone.

Glancing behind her, Annie caught sight of Dan's odd expression and admitted that safety was relative. She'd have been a hell of a lot safer in New York City than out here.

Joe caught up with Ginny and Annie as they made their way down the ramp. Annie shivered. She was as cold as the icy water they'd just crossed and, once she viewed the muddy ground, she regretted that she hadn't already bought boots for Ginny.

"Oh, my goodness," Ginny said in dismay. "Annie, I don't know about this."

"Don't worry, ma'am," a male voice reassured her. "I'll get you to dry land."

Red, who was standing behind them, made his way around Ginny and lifted her effortlessly. It was obvious to everyone that Red's progress through the muck took longer than it should have. "Hold on, Joe," he called over his shoulder, "I'll be back for you."

"You gonna pick me up like some swooning woman?" the child asked incredulously. "I don't think so." He stepped off the plank into the mud and, marched as firmly as he could to the wooden sidewalk beyond.

"Wait, Annie," Dan called out from the boat. "I'll help you across."

"I'll get myself across," she said, and started down the plank. Somebody yelled behind her as a keg broke loose and rolled down, catching Annie from behind. She tripped. When she tried to catch herself, all her weight came down on her right ankle. It folded beneath her, and she stepped forward into a bed of black mud that enveloped her boots and held on for dear life. As hard as she tried, she couldn't put any weight on her injured ankle. She was trapped in the middle of a mud hole, standing on one foot with Red, Ginny, and Joe watching.

And Dan was behind her. She could feel his presence even before he spoke.

"Annie, wait. I'll help you."

"I'll help myself."

As he sloshed past her, he stopped. "Of course you will. You don't need anybody." He glanced down at her dress, now fringed in black mud. "I know that experiencing Mississippi mud is awe-inspiring, but you might want to get a move on, otherwise, you're going to be run over from behind."

He tipped his cap and moved on, leaving Annalise firmly stuck where she stood.

In all of her twenty-four years, Annalise Sinclair had never been so angry, nor felt such humiliation as she did now. Here she was, trying to get herself and her little band out west, and she couldn't even get out of the mud.

She felt tears gathering behind her eyelids. "You'd better not cry," she told herself in a stern whisper. "What kind of doctor will you be if you can't manage a little mud?" Though her ankle was screaming in pain, she forced herself upright.

"Annie, look out!"

Later she would have to admit that it was her own foolish pride that did it, that and one overzealous pig anxious to experience the richness of the mud. She couldn't blame the captain, nor the hands who were carrying the crate, nor the animal who crashed through the slats of his cage and escaped, hurtling into Annie and slamming her face-down in the mud.

Three days ago, she'd fallen down a ravine at the Brooklyn station and covered her face with scratches. Now she painted it with thick gooey mud at Boggy Gut. From this day on, she would never again worry about how she looked. A sprinkle of laughter broke out, then was swallowed immediately. Annalise tried desperately to get up. The pig dug in. He was better at moving in the mud than she.

"I'd give you a hand," Dan said, "but I know you want to do this yourself."

Annalise lifted her head, ready to spit nails, instead of the half-frozen mud in her mouth. She wiped her mouth on her sleeve, smearing the dirt even more. The pig oinked as he burrowed into the muck, drew back, and shaking himself, flung fresh mud across the face she'd just wiped. He oinked again.

Annalise couldn't hold back. She began to laugh. She'd done this to herself, now she'd laugh at herself. *Pride goeth before a fall, foolish woman.* Carefully, with deliberate movements, she forced herself to stand and learned another painful truth. She'd definitely sprained her ankle when she tripped. Laughing now to cover her pain, she first pulled one foot out, staggered forward, then pulled out the other.

The pig squealed.

Joe cheered her on.

And the crowd clapped.

Finally she reached the end of the mud and planted her good foot on the plank sidewalk, then caught hold of a pile of rails and pulled herself forward. She shook her head, slinging ropes of mud everywhere, including Dan Miller's face. One way or another she intended to make it down the platform to where Ginny was watching with her mouth agape. "Thank you for your offer, and you're right about the quality of Mississippi mud. Maybe I'll take lessons from that pig."

"I'm sorry, Annie," he said, concealing his urge to laugh. "I would have helped you but you wouldn't let me."

"That's right. I may have had the bad luck to choose the same train you're on, Mr. Miller. But, just so you know how I feel, if I have to wade through every mud hole from here to Wyoming, I'll get there. By myself."

Standing as stiff as a starched crinoline, Annie limped down the sidewalk. "Now, Annie," Ginny began, "we don't want to be foolish. Mr. Miller and . . . his men have been very nice to us—"

"My pleasure," Red interrupted. "I'll see to the rest of your things."

"Thank you," Ginny said, smiling at Red.

"Forget it!" Annalise said at the same time.

Ginny turned toward Annalise and frowned. She pursed her lips, paused for a moment, then smiled. "Annie, you're a mess. I'll find us a place to clean you up, then I want you to get me some new clothes, and boots. If we're going to be western women, let's go all the way."

Annalise felt her jaw drop. This was her old friend, Ginny, her personal maid, talking to her as if she truly were the lady and Annalise the servant. Gritting her teeth, she could only nod.

To make matters worse, Dan began to scrape the mud from his face and flick it to the ground. His lips crinkled at the corners, then began to shake. Finally he burst out into a belly laugh.

"Ah, Annie. First you give me a bloody nose, and now this. I have no doubt you'll survive the West. But will the West survive you? As much as you drive me crazy, I can't imagine you not being on your own."

To his credit, he didn't offer to help her. He didn't suggest a place for them to stay or inform them of the train schedule. Instead, after watching Ginny head up the walk toward the few ramshackle buildings that made up the infamous sawmill town of Boggy Gut, he headed back to the steamer to make certain his goods were unloaded. The picture of Annie and the pig sharing the same mud hole made him chuckle. She'd gotten out on her own and even if she was walking a little oddly, she'd get where she was going. She was just the woman to do it.

Time enough later to deal with *"just"* Annie and his reluctant admiration for her. If only he could figure out who she really was and where she was going. Once he was unloaded he'd better check for another message from his father.

There was a new telegram, assuring Dan that his mother would not be out calling on any more prospective brides. That was a relief. More than ever, Dan was certain that none of the women wealthy enough to meet his father's requirements would be as strong or as appealing as Annie. He wondered what she'd look like in a ball gown and feathered masque.

Then he shook his head and chuckled. Annie as an ethereal snowbird? No, Annie was a woman who could smear mud all over her face and come up spitting fire.

Fire was what a man needed out here. Snow? He'd left that behind in New York.

Ginny quickly learned there was no hotel in Boggy Gut, only a washhouse, the train station, and a trading post.

"Sorry, Annie," she said, "there are no private baths. But the lumber camp washerwoman will put up a sheet and give you the use of one of her tubs for a fee. She'll wash you and your clothes. While you're doing that, she'll dry your boots on top of her stove."

"Fine," Annie agreed. She'd do anything to get off her ankle and out of the clothes that were beginning to freeze on her body. Her lips were turning blue and her teeth chattered. "Take me to her."

Ginny frowned, started to speak, then turned and headed around behind the building, Joe in close pursuit.

"A tent?" Annie said.

"Hey," Joe piped up, "it's better'n some. Lots of people do the wash out in the open. At least in here, the fire and the hot water warm the air."

Annie made her way inside the tent, making no attempt now to conceal her injury.

The proprietor was a black woman with white teeth and a bulging lower lip filled with shredded tobacco. "Come on in here, honey," she said, pulling back a sheet draped over the line. "What's wrong with you?"

"I'm afraid I sprained my ankle."

"You po' thing. You set down here on the stool and get them clothes off. I got soapy water. Hot soapy water, make that hurt go away. Where you been anyhow?"

"She and a pig wanted the same mud hole," Joe said. "The pig won."

"Hush up, Joe," Ginny said sternly. "Why didn't you say you were hurt, Annie?"

"And let that gloating buffoon think he's got to take care of me? It's nothing."

"I think it's something. Take off your bodice, Annie." She knelt to unhook the strings of her boots.

"Don't do that," Annie said. "My ankle will swell and I won't be able to get the boot back on."

"And if you don't take them off, your foot will freeze."

Joe kept fidgeting. "I think I'll go help Red unload our supplies," he said and dashed out of the tent.

"You stay right here," Annie said, "you're next in this tub."

But Joe was already gone.

Ginny pulled off the first boot, then gently removed the other. Annie's face creased in pain but she didn't complain. The rest of her clothes quickly followed and were tossed into the wash pot. The mud had splotched her white chemise, turning it a dingy gray.

"I think we'd better just get you into the tub with your drawers on. While you're washing, I'll go over to the store and get more clothes for you and some boots for me. Do we have any more of your gambling money left?"

"Oops! The money." She reached inside her chemise and pulled out the handkerchief filled with her remaining gambling spoils. "Hang on to this."

"I will. We can't waste it," Annie warned.

"Annalise Sinclair, I've been looking after you since you were twelve years old. Why are you worried about me doing it now?"

"That was different. Now you're expecting a child."

"That's right, but I've been an invalid long enough on this trip. I'm fine. And don't worry about Joe, Red will look after him."

It wasn't easy, but between the washwoman and Ginny, they got Annie into the tub. She sat there a long while, not thinking, just letting the hot water soothe her body.

"Put your head back, ma'am, and let Pearl see to you," the black woman said, drawing her fingers through the strands of Annie's hair. "You sho' did mess yourself up."

"Now you've done it, you've wet my hair and it's freezing out there." Annie's words would have been uttered in anger if she hadn't been so comfortable enjoying Pearl's pampering.

"Don't you worry none. I'll get your hair dry. You just slip out of them drawers and lay here while I wash 'em."

"I don't think I can move."

"Then just heist up your bottom and I'll pull them off."

Too tired to argue, Annalise complied, leaning her head back into the hot water, watching the smoke from the fire escape through a hole in the top of the tent. As crude as it was, this might be the last hot bath she'd get for a long time. She would allow herself, just for a moment, to feel the gentle warmth of the wash water soothe her body.

A moment was all she had.

"Everybody decent in there?" The voice of her tormentor called out, but he didn't wait for answer. "There's been a change in plans."

Before Annie could move, he'd entered the tent, his large body hovering over her.

It was too late to cover herself. She scooted lower in the tub. "Don't you ever knock?"

"Can't recall ever knocking on a wash tent before," Dan said in a low voice.

"A gentleman would turn his head," Annie said, in a voice just as tight.

"But you've told me that I'm no gentleman." He leaned closer. "There's a spot of mud on your face. I'll get it for you."

"Don't—" she choked, then called for help. "Pearl? Will you hand me a drying cloth?"

"If you're calling the proprietor, she's gone to fetch more wood for her fire. I'll get one for you."

Annie couldn't just ignore Dan. She opened her eyes. What she feared was true. The water was no barrier to Dan's vision. At least she was still wearing her chemise. But it was stuck to her like a second skin and was very revealing.

"Dan, just because I let you kiss me last night—"

"You kissed me back."

"You're right, I did—but I shouldn't have."

"You're right. You shouldn't have. I shouldn't have. I'm still not certain why we did."

"That doesn't mean that we're going to . . . that I'm going to . . ."

"I know you're not," he said softly, wondering what in the hell he was doing as he leaned even closer. "I never expected that you would. Just close your eyes."

"Why?"

"So that I can get the mud out of your hair and off your face." Every muscle in her body tightened. If she'd moved, she would have shattered into a million pieces. Daniel Miller laid his fingertips on her forehead, and she almost did.

10

—⚯—

The air rushed out of Annalise's lungs, and time stopped. The touch of Dan's fingertips was something out of a delicious, forbidden dream, one from which she tried to wake and couldn't. His fingers moved across her forehead and behind her neck, lifting her head and lowering it into the tub of water.

As he stroked her skin, she sensed the power of those hands, newly roughened by his labor along the journey. Holding her head with one hand, he separated the strands of her hair one by one, sluicing them into the soapy liquid. The ever-present kernel of heat at the base of her spine intensified, turning into a ripple of fire that ran down her spine, settling between her legs.

"Ah, Annie, your skin is so soft. I like touching you. I like it too much," Dan said.

"Don't talk," she said. As long as he didn't talk she could just lie in the warm water and float. She didn't have to think about where they were going or what would happen. He let go of her neck and used both hands to hold her, gently massaging her scalp. His breath was light, coming in warm little pants against her forehead. The water slapped against her ears like the purr of a kitten. Annie couldn't hold back a shiver. Startled from her state of semiconsciousness, she shook her head and pushed back against the side of the tub, forcing his hands away.

He slipped them to her shoulders. "Are you cold?" he asked, kneading tightened neck muscles, reaching lower and inward.

"Yes," she lied. From the moment Dan Miller had touched her, she'd felt as if he'd put her into a hypnotic state, his fingers lighting her on fire. That phenomenon was a mystery she couldn't explain. She was learning that there was more to the physical side of the human body's reaction to stimuli than she'd ever been been taught. Although she'd always championed knowledge, she feared this learning experience.

"Relax, Annie."

"How can I, when you're . . ."

He knelt beside her, allowed his hands to move across her collarbone and downward, pausing for a moment, then brushing the buttons on her chemise before finally sliding between the buttons to cup her breast. The fire below flared, and she tightened muscles that rippled deliciously with the movement. "Oh!" she whispered and tried to swallow the moan that came with the word.

Her attempt failed and the sound escaped her throat. Her lips parted. "Dan?"

Then his lips found hers. Her protests formed her mouth into a receptacle for Dan's tongue. His hands left her breast and caught her arms, digging into them. Then his mouth changed, softening into a heartbreakingly slow kiss that soothed the whirling emotions that racked her. Finally, he stopped and pulled back, staring at her with a look as stunned as her own must have been. Annalise took a deep breath, then, marshaling her strength, pushed him away. "What are you doing?"

"I'm making a total fool of myself, I think."

"Did you come here for a reason?" she managed to croak.

Dan blanched and moved reluctantly away from the tub. He had come here for a reason, if he could just remember what it was. If he could erase the pounding of his heart and force his attention away from the half-nude woman whose nipples had turned into dusky rose beads pressing against the transparent wet fabric covering her upper body. With sheer willpower, he emptied his mind of consuming desire and replaced it with whatever reason he could still claim.

Through a throat so tight he could barely speak, he said, "Yes. I came to tell you that there was some kind of problem and the logs won't be here until tomorrow. Looks like we're going to have to spend the night."

"Spend the night? Where?"

"Don't worry. I've found a place."

She started to argue, but after her last attempt at independence she decided it was wiser to accept his help. "I hope it's better than the last one."

"Actually, it's a mansion. I think you'll like it."

She sighed. "I appreciate your help, Dan, but I wish you'd discuss things with me before you make plans. I may not be doing such a good job of it, but I'd like to think I'm taking care of myself."

She still insisted on making her own way. He couldn't resist. "And you came to this conclusion before you fell in the mud hole or after?" Dan grinned and rubbed his fingertips across the scratchy beard he'd started to grow. "Don't fight me, Annie. Think of Ginny and Joe."

"I wonder where they are?" she said, ashamed that she'd forgotten them so easily.

"I met them heading for the trading post. They ought

to be done. I'll go fetch them and come back for you. We're invited to dinner with our host."

"Dinner? With who?"

"Mr. Rosco Thurmon, the owner, mayor, and richest man in Boggy Gut."

"Oh, no!" Annie thought of her wet clothes and sat up. When she realized that she'd exposed herself to Dan, she slid beneath the water again. "Find Ginny and tell her to . . . never mind, just send her back here."

Dan found Ginny, told her Annie needed her, and went back to the ferry to make certain all their goods had been unloaded and stored in the shed which served as a make-shift depot. Red and Joe were moving the last of their personal goods onto the dock.

"You find the women, Boss?"

"I did. Annie's in the tub and Mrs. Wilson's at the trading post. Are we all done here?"

"All done. Think I'll do a little trading myself."

Dan smiled. "You mean you're going to check on Mrs. Wilson, don't you?"

"That, too."

"I'll go with you, Red," Joe said.

Recalling Joe's past history, Dan decided a trading post was not the place for a boy to be with an itch to trade. "I think I'd rather you stay with me, Joe. While Ginny's buying all of you some new clothes, you and I are going back to that washhouse to get you cleaned up."

All color drained from the boy's face. "Get me cleaned up? No way!"

Dan grabbed Joe by the collar, giving him no opportunity to escape. "Have to do it, boy. We're having dinner with a very important man. You don't want to disgrace Annie and Mrs. Wilson, do you?"

"Ain't gonna do that, 'cause I ain't going to *dinner* with nobody."

The boy was bordering on complete panic. "Whoa here. What's wrong, boy?" he asked. "You never had a bath before?"

"Sure I had a bath. I just never had one in a washhouse with people watching. And I ain't going to now."

Dan heard Joe's sniffling and realized that he was choking back real tears. He squatted down and turned the boy to face him. "Let's talk about this, Joe. You can tell me. What's this really all about?"

"You promise you won't be mad at me?"

"I promise."

"And you won't tell on me?"

"I won't, but Mrs. Wilson and Annie have taken you in, and if your problem is serious, maybe you need to tell them yourself. Be a man, Joe."

"That's just it," Joe said in a squeaky voice. "I ain't a man. I ain't even a boy."

Dan took a long look at Joe. It finally made sense— what had been bothering him all along. "I'll be damned. You're a girl."

Big blue eyes, still swimming in tears, looked balefully at him. The tears had streaked his—her—face so that she looked as if she were a stage actor wearing makeup.

"You're a little girl."

"Ain't so little."

"Don't say ain't," Dan corrected automatically. "What's your name?"

"My name's Joe."

"I mean your real name."

"It's Josephine," she finally said. "My name's Josephine and if you tell anybody I'll . . . I'll run off and you'll never see me again."

Dan stood up, shaking his head. "Why? Why have you pretended to be a boy?"

"It was the only way I could live," she said with such despair that Dan felt her pain. "Women don't count for much. Men treat 'em bad."

"Not all men," Dan corrected.

"No, but I never met none like you and Red, till now. Please don't make me go back, Dan. I'll do whatever you want."

"Let me think. We'll figure it out. That doesn't change anything about the bath, mind you. But I'll keep your secret for now, Josephine."

"Holy hell, Dan. If you go 'round calling me Josephine, I'm sunk."

"All right, for the time being you're still Joe. Now go help Ginny with her packages while I find our transportation to the mansion."

"What mansion?"

"The one where we're going to spend the night."

Joe started backing away. "I don't think so, Dan. I'll just stay with Red and the other men."

"Not anymore, Joe. You're a girl, remember, and that isn't proper."

"But I ain't no different than I was this morning. Nobody knows."

Dan looked Joe square in the eye and said, "I do."

"What was that all about?" Red asked as Joe whirled away from Dan and headed toward the trading post.

"Just a slight change in . . . plans," Dan said. "See if Mrs. Wilson needs any help with her packages, then go check on our crew. I have to find Mr. Thurmon's carriage."

"Why? Did he lose it?"

"No, he's sending it to transport us to that house up there." He focused his eyes on the trees in the distance.

Red followed his gaze and swore. "Well, would you look at that. Can't believe I didn't see it. The owner must be a leprechaun. Only an Irish spirit could conceive of such a castle."

"I don't think our host is Irish," Dan said with a wry smile. "But he might be."

Made of timbers instead of stone, the house was a cross between a castle and a Victorian mansion. It was big and gaudy and about as out of place as red satin at a funeral. But it was a house that could offer the women a proper place to sleep and good food to eat. And Dan knew how tired Ginny must be.

"Can't wait to see the carriage he travels in," Red said, as he headed for the trading post. He met Ginny and Joe, their arms full of parcels. "Let me carry those," he said to Ginny. "They're too heavy for you, ma'am."

"Nonsense," Ginny replied, "Joe's helping me. Besides, I'm sure you have work to do."

"Yes, ma'am," he agreed, reluctantly. "I guess I do." His eyes lingered on her a while before he headed toward the trading post.

"That man's sweet on you, Ginny," Joe said under her breath. "Whatcha gonna do 'bout that?"

"Why . . . why, nothing. What can I do?"

"You mean because you're a married woman?"

"I'm not . . . I mean, I can't."

Joe gave her a long look and a nod. "That's what I figured. You ain't married, but you can't tell nobody on account of the kid. Annie and Dan got something going but they won't tell nobody because—well, ain't nobody give me no good reason for that yet."

"Annie has her reasons, Joe. She'll explain herself when she's ready."

"Humph! I just hope Dan ain't moved on by the time that happens. Speaking of moving, we'd best get on to the tent 'fore Annie comes looking for us in her altogether."

Annie and Pearl were waiting behind the makeshift curtain Annie had insisted on after Dan's visit. She was surprised to find that Ginny had bought her a day dress of simple gingham. She had little choice but to wear it, given that her travel dress was beyond help.

"Why'd you bring a dress?" she asked crossly as she tugged it over her head. "I'd rather have had some of those men's trousers. Makes more sense in a place like this."

"You're going to have dinner with a rich man, Annie. You ought to look like a woman." Ginny gave Annie a sharp look, after seeing the swollen ankle and Annie's pained expression when she tried to stand. "Besides, I didn't think you'd get those boots back on tonight. But maybe these will work." She stepped outside the curtain and held up a pair of flat shoes made of soft leather.

"What's them?" Joe asked, as Ginny handed the shoes to Pearl.

"They're Indian moccasins. The trading post owner said there are still a few Kickapoo Indians around here. They make things to trade for goods."

Annie slipped her foot easily into one, grimacing as she tried to put on the second. "If I'm going to walk, I'm going to have to bind this ankle." She looked at Pearl, who was hovering in the background. "Do you have a strip of muslin I could buy?"

"Sho 'nough, honey and you can borrow a blanket till we get your clothes dry. You just stick your leg out and I'll wrap it up."

"No, I'll do it." Annie took the muslin and laced it snugly around her foot, extending the binding halfway up her calf. It was tight but not too tight. She hoped it would give her enough support so that she could walk.

"Hey, there's a carriage out here," Joe called out, "one of them fancy ones."

With Ginny's arm around her waist, Annie took a deep breath and stood, gingerly testing the injured ankle. "Ahhh!"

"Don't try to walk, Annie," Ginny said, her face creased with worry. "Red will carry you."

"Red will not carry me. It isn't broken. I will walk."

And she did. Choking back a groan every step of the way. How on earth was she going to do this? By nightfall, her ankle would be even more painful. And she'd brought it all on herself trying to prove that she could do anything herself, needing no one's help. After a few steps out of the wash tent, she gave up on that idea and, after making certain that Dan wasn't around, allowed Red to lift her into the sleek black open carriage that awaited them.

"Oh, my," Ginny said. "Are you sure I'm supposed to go, Annie?"

"We're all expected. Get in, you silly goose. Red, can you get our carryall from the ferry?"

"Sure, Annie. Once I deliver you, I'll bring it back up."

"Ah, Ginny," Joe said, "if there's anything left over—from dinner—could you stick it in your pocket and bring it to me in the morning?"

"Get in, Joe. You're coming, too."

"Oh, no, ma'am. I ain't going to no fancy house to no *dinner* party."

"Yes, you are," Dan said, approaching the carriage from the other side. He was carrying a parcel that he stuck under the seat. Then he climbed in beside Annie. "Get aboard, Joe, our host is waiting."

"Ah, no!"

"Yes," Dan said in a tone that said he was not to be questioned or disobeyed. Joe looked helplessly at the women, then scrambled up beside the driver. "Just as well you sit up there," Dan observed. "Until we get you cleaned up."

"I'm fine," Joe growled.

Annie refused to look at Dan. Partially because she couldn't face him after the intimate scene she'd allowed in the tent, but also because she knew he'd see her pain if she moved. She was glad she was wrapped in a blanket.

"So, what kind of man builds a mansion out here in the middle of nowhere?" Ginny asked.

"A rich man who needs something to spend his money on."

"How come he's putting us up?"

"I think it's because he doesn't get much company. I'm told he lost his wife and he gets lonely."

"I can understand that," Ginny said.

"By the way, Ginny," Dan said, "I've inquired about your husband, Robert, and I'm sorry to say, nobody knows anything about him."

"Thank you, Dan. I'm beginning to think something must have happened to him."

"What will you do?" he asked.

"Annie will—"

"Accompany her," Annie interrupted, "—until we're certain of that. And then we'll . . . look around for a place to settle. I hear the West offers opportunities to . . . everyone."

"Providing they have skills," he said. "I'm sure you will find a place to use yours."

"Yeah!" Joe called out. "Think the old boy's up for some poker?"

The carriage hit a bump, knocking Ginny off balance. She reached out to brace herself, taking hold of the first thing she could, Annie's leg.

Annie let out a yell, scaring Ginny, whose following scream set off the horses. The carriage careened wildly until the driver got them under control.

"Annie, that's your hurt ankle? I'm so sorry." Ginny's face grew white with concern.

Annie swallowed hard and forced herself to answer. "I'm all right, Ginny. Stop fussing!"

It was Dan who helped Annie back into the seat and straightened her blanket. "What about your ankle?"

"It's fine."

"What about your ankle?"

"I sprained it when I tripped over that keg. It's just a bit swollen."

Dan pulled back her skirt and gasped. "Driver, stop the carriage! The lady needs a doctor."

The carriage came to a rolling stop. The driver peered

back. "I'm sorry, suh, but ain't no doctor in Boggy Gut. She ain't fixing to have that baby right here, is she?"

"Not me," Ginny protested, "it's Annie. Her ankle."

The driver looked helpless. "Maybe if we get the lady inside, Mr. Rosco will know what to do."

Annie looked up. In front of them was probably the ugliest house she'd ever seen.

"Will you look at that?" Joe said. "It's beautiful."

With lions at the posts, huge stone gargoyles at the eaves, and intricate cutwork trim in between, the house overwhelmed the eyes.

"Oh, my!" Ginny said. "This is something."

"Yes, ma'am," a booming voice pronounced. A large heavyset man with a bushy beard and dancing eyebrows came forward with outstretched arms. "I'm Rosco Thurmon, the timber king. Welcome! Welcome to my humble mansion. Get out and come in."

Ginny's eyes and mouth fell wide open. She blinked twice, then cleared her throat. "Eh, thank you, Mr. Thurmon. This is a very . . . interesting place."

"That it is, little lady. Washington, get back there and help the lady into the house. Can't you see she's in a delicate way?"

"Yes, suh."

"Get down, Dan. Reckon you can help the other one. Kid, you hold the horses."

Before any of them could protest, they were swept inside the house and Rosco was still talking. "Letty!" he turned toward the end of the hallway where a beautiful white-haired woman stood. "Our guests are here. Show them up to their rooms. Let them rest or do whatever women do, then we'll have an early dinner. Dan, let's me and you have us a little toddy. It's good for the soul."

Ginny looked at the steps and back at Dan. "Can you bring Annie up, Dan?" Ginny asked, turning to their host to explain, "She sprained her ankle, Mr. Thurmon."

"Show him where to put her, Letty, make sure Mrs.

Wilson is comfortable, then bring Dan to my study. You can get lost in this house," he explained.

Annie didn't argue. She would have had a hard time getting an argument in. Apparently Mr. Thurmon had learned the art of conversation wherever he learned architecture. Any other time she would be amused. Now, she simply leaned against Dan, wondering how other travelers ever survived this cross-country trip. And she hadn't even reached the wilderness yet.

Suddenly she raised her head and looked around. "Joe, where's Joe?"

"Don't worry about the boy," Rosco said. "Last time I saw him he was sniffing. Looked like a bird dog getting a fix on a covey of quail. Then he headed toward the back of the house. That's where the kitchen is. My guess is that by now he's found it."

"Please God, let's hope that's all he found," Annie said. "This place must be a paradise for pickpockets."

Mr. Thurmon looked startled. "Madam! A pickpocket wouldn't dare enter my house."

Annie groaned.

Dan gave a knowing laugh. "Don't worry, Annie. I think your troubles with Joe may be about to come to an end. Or maybe, they're just beginning."

11

—❦—

Mason Clanton stood in his office, overlooking the new Clanton Meat-Packing Company holding pens—empty holding pens, the fences buried in mounds of snow for two days. He wasn't given to romantic foolishness, but there was something airily beautiful about the reflection of moonlight on the empty stockyards. The dark earth glowed with the intensity of the light, reminding him of a feather-stitched patchwork quilt. The fence lines produced the same effect of cross-stitched squares. He was oddly captivated by the sight.

A sudden gust of arctic wind swept across the lake and broke the picture, scattering the snow and blinding his view. The city of Chicago had shut down this February. All their cattle had been sold, and their customers were still demanding for more beef.

At least, the new year looked bright. Investors in the new Union Pacific Railroad crowed about the future. The East and West would soon be connected. People *and* cattle would ride the rails. The politicians took the credit for making expansion possible for the nation. He wanted to laugh. Progress was always the result of money not people. And, since William Russell had become a partner, he had enough of it to make certain that Clanton Meat-Packing would lead the way to expansion and be the first to benefit from the progress.

William's plan to ruin Teddy Miller and take over the Cold Springs cattle spur would mean more profits for the packing plant. They'd get all the cattle from the ranchers in the North, and they'd get the shipping fees as well. Mason craved wealth as much as the next man, maybe more, but he'd never sanctioned William's plan to cause deliberate accidents on the job site to bankrupt Teddy Miller, take over the spur, and evict Teddy from his home. But William was a hard man to dissuade once he made up his mind. Mason heard William's steps come up from behind, and he turned to face him.

"What did you hear from your man inside Teddy Miller's crew?" Mason asked.

"Not much yet. No point in making our move right away. We want them to get the work started, use up their cash and supplies before we step in and take over. Of course, I've arranged a few little things to delay them, build the pressure, and cause more anxiety."

"Like what?" Mason had to ask, though he wasn't certain he wanted to know.

"Well, there was a small incident on the logging site."

"Incident? What kind of incident?"

"Just a little delay at a place called Boggy Gut. Nothing like a little frustration to sweeten the pot."

"You know I don't like the idea of physical harm," Mason said.

William Russell looked at his partner. Weak men disgusted him. Mason had no idea how lucky he was. Of course, he had the money and the packing plant, but it had been William who'd anticipated the future and started planning for it. He'd enlarged the facilities and the holding pens, set up a New York broker who already had more orders than Clanton Meat-Packing could fill.

"Nobody's been hurt." *Yet*.

"And Miller?" Mason asked. "What makes you think he's going to take this lying down?"

William frowned. "By the time he figures it out, it'll be too late. This time, he's backed himself into a corner. Still, he's being uncharacteristically quiet. I don't like that. It makes me suspicious. It isn't like Teddy not to blow his own horn."

Mason looked pensive. "Maybe something's wrong. What happens if the spur doesn't get built at all? I can't see how that would significantly change our expansion plans. What do we care how the cattle get to us? We still slaughter enough of them to be the biggest plant in Chicago."

For now, William saw no point in telling his partner that he already had tentative agreements with the ranchers, and that the spur would belong to *him*—not Clanton Meat-Packing. That information would come later.

"Teddy doesn't have a choice. He thinks it's the only way he's going to save face."

"And recoup his money," Mason added dryly.

"That, too. But looking like a fool is worse for old Teddy." William laughed. "He has no idea how bad it's going to get."

Mason shook his head. "The whole thing worries me. We're taking a big chance by building more pens and making promises to deliver cattle we don't even have. Suppose this all blows up in our face?"

"It won't. Trust me, Mason, it won't. I won't let it. I can't fail. Teddy Miller will lose."

A thousand miles away, Annalise Sinclair was sitting against the headboard of a canopy bed Cleopatra might have slept on, if she'd been fond of ruffles, lace, and purple velvet. Her sprained ankle was propped up on a mountain of satin pillows so slick that Ginny had draped a drying cloth on top of one to keep her foot from slipping off.

"Does it hurt?" Ginny asked.

"A little," Annie lied. "When our carryall gets here, I'll take something to ease the pain."

Ginny put her hand to her back and groaned. "Oh, boy, this child is determined to stretch my innards with its feet. Next time I take a train ride I'm not bringing anybody with me."

"Oh, Ginny, I'm sorry. I should be taking care of you, but instead, you are taking care of me."

"Annie," Ginny said, looking her friend straight in the eye, "You work for me, remember? Be quiet and get some rest."

"Only if you go and lie down, too."

"I don't want to leave you."

"Then I'll just get up and walk some of the pain out," Annie threatened and started to slide to the side of the bed.

"No! You stay right there and I'll go. If you need me, my room is just up the hall, the one with the roses on the door."

Annie shook her head. "Roses on the door?"

"I know. Did you take a look at yours? You have violets."

Annie rolled her eyes. "Where's Joe?"

"He's with Dan. Dan says you're not to worry. They'll both see you at dinner."

"I don't think I like the sound of that," Annie said. "I don't trust Joe. This house is a temptation that I'm not certain he can resist."

"You want me to get him?"

Annie looked at her old friend and knew she was almost at the edge of exhaustion. "No, don't worry. It looks like I'm going to have to rely on Mr. Miller—again."

Ginny started to the door. "You know, Annie, that's not

a bad thing, relying on a man, especially when you care about him."

"Stop talking foolishness, Ginny!"

"I don't think it's foolish," she said softly. "You and Dan Miller make more sparks than the firebox on the train. I don't know what happened last night by the Mississippi, but your lips looked thoroughly kissed to me. Since then, the air practically vibrates when he's around you. And don't you deny it."

"I . . . I don't know what you mean."

"You do know what I mean. And I know what you're feeling. It's the way a woman feels about a man when they want to lie with each other. It's normal."

Ginny was right. When Dan looked at her, she felt like she'd been singed. And it didn't go away. Slowly, she spoke, feeling her way into unknown territory with her question. "Did you feel that way—about Robert?"

Ginny hesitated. "Yes . . . and no! It was exciting, being wanted. He had such big plans for our future. He told me we'd have our own house. I should have known better, but I was lonely."

"I know about making plans, Ginny, about wanting something so bad you can taste it. I let my plans take over my life so that I forgot about you."

Ginny walked back to the bed. "Annie, I think it's time we faced the truth. I'm not going to find Robert."

"Nonsense," Annie snapped, "of course we're going to find Robert. We may have to search every railroad camp from here to California, but we'll find him."

"You don't understand." Ginny touched her stomach and continued. "I'm not so sure I want to."

Annalise was silent. She thought she knew the answer to her next question but she had to ask it. "You don't want to find Robert? Why?"

"Because I don't have feelings for him anymore."

"It's Red, isn't it?"

Ginny's reply was an anguished "I think so."

"Oh, Ginny." Annalise pulled Ginny down beside her and caught her hands. "Does Red know?"

"I'm not sure. He thinks I'm married and he's an . . . an honorable man."

"Has he—did he—"

"No, Annie. He hasn't touched me. What are we going to do?"

Annalise had no answer for her. When she'd first started out it had seemed so simple. Find Robert. Find a place to set up her practice and notify her father where she was. Now, she was beginning to see that by concealing the truth to avoid marriage, she could hurt Ginny.

"I don't know, Ginny. Maybe I ought to tell Dan who I am, stop pretending."

"No! Not yet. Dan would tell your father and Mr. Sinclair would come after you and then you'd have to give up being a doctor and take a husband. No, we'll just go on as we planned. When you get your office and hang up your shingle will be soon enough to tell the truth. I've made a big mess of my own life, I won't ruin this for you. Not after all you've done for me. Promise me, Annie!"

"But you might lose Red."

"I won't," Ginny said with a secret smile. "Women know about these things. Just like you know about Dan. You just won't admit it yet."

"I can't think about that, Ginny." But the truth was, she'd thought of little else. He infuriated her at the same time he excited her with his touch. What was she going to do with a man who paid no attention to her wishes, and who kept kissing her silly? At some point he'd leave to build his railroad and be out of her life. Was that what she wanted?

"I don't know, Ginny. I've spent my life learning to be a doctor. I don't know how to be a woman. I think being a doctor is safer."

Hours later, Ginny stepped back and looked at Annie in the mirror. "You look beautiful, Annie."

Ginny had styled her hair into a froth of curls, pulled up and caught with a green ribbon that cascaded down the mass of loose dark hair brushing her shoulders.

"I don't know why you're going to all this trouble," Annie grumbled. "I've never been beautiful."

"You were beautiful the night you went to that New Year's ball."

For a moment that night flashed back in her mind. She could almost hear the music as she and Dan Miller whirled around the floor, the colors of the evening coming alive again in her memory. "But I was wearing a masque," she whispered. "Nobody knew what I looked like."

"Too bad. You may be the best doctor in the West, but you need to stop hiding behind that. Annie, you're still a woman."

"How can I forget it? Dan Miller keeps reminding me. Don't you see, Ginny, he's exactly the reason I can never marry. Men never think women can be anything except a wife. Quit fussing. You're going to a lot of trouble for nothing. I can't even walk. How on earth am I supposed to have dinner with anybody?"

Ginny smiled. "You don't eat with your feet, Annie. It's Dan you're scared of."

Annie groaned. "You're right. I'll just ignore him. I'll forget about manners and dinner. I'll lie up here in this purple coffin and . . . die."

There was a knock on the door.

"See who that is, Ginny, and if it's Dan Miller, tell him he's too late. I'm dead."

But it wasn't Mr. Thurmon or Dan. It was Letty, the housekeeper, delivering Annie's carryall. "Mr. Thurmon asked me to bring this to you and tell you that if you're ready, he will send two housemen to bring you to the table."

Annie sighed. "I'm as ready as I'll ever be, or I will be by the time they get up here."

As soon as Letty left, Annie asked for the carryall. The bag they'd lost at the Brooklyn train station contained all their clothing, but she was lucky; the bag they'd found contained a little laudanum. She selected a packet of the pain medicine and directed Ginny to mix half of it in a cup of water, then changed her mind. "No, use the whole thing. If I'm going to get through this evening, I'm going to need it all."

By the time she'd swallowed the liquid, two uniformed housemen had arrived with a velvet-bottomed straight chair. They moved Annie to the chair and carried her out.

"What about you, Ginny?" Annie said. "Aren't you coming?"

"No. Letty is bringing a tray to my room. Don't be angry with me, Annie, but if you don't want to deliver this baby on the train, I need a good night's rest in a real bed."

"Oh, Ginny. Forgive me. I'm being selfish. You go to bed. I'm sure—" she started to say Dan, then changed it, "someone will help me."

As they moved down the stairs, Annie caught sight of herself in a mirror. She decided that she'd been more right in comparing herself to Cleopatra than she knew. Even if her gingham dress wasn't grand, she had her escorts and her throne. All she needed was a barge. "Antony," she whispered under her breath, "look out."

Her throne was a match to the chairs around a table that could have comfortably seated thirty. The two housemen slid it into the empty space to the host's right.

"Good evening, Miss Annie," Rosco said. "You look lovely. How is the foot?"

"It's my ankle, and it's still a bit painful," she lied gallantly, wishing she had some guarantee that the pain medication was going to work. Dr. Sinclair had dosed lots of patients, but this was her first personal experience with the pain medicine she'd taken. "Where is Mr. Miller?"

"He'll be along momentarily. He's escorting our other guest."

That made no sense to Annie. What guest? Then Dan appeared in the doorway. There was someone with him, but Annie's eyes stopped on the man she'd sworn to ignore not ten minutes earlier, and refused to move. Neatly shaved, boots polished, he was wearing the same black frock coat he'd worn the night of the ball. And he was even more handsome.

Annalise Sinclair, don't do this! She forced herself to look at the person holding his arm. A girl. A girl with a short, uneven haircut. She was small, young, and obviously uncomfortable.

"Evening, Dan," Rosco's voice boomed. "Bring your young friend in. Now we have two charming ladies for dinner."

Daniel fought a smile as he started forward. There was only one problem, his guest planted her feet and refused to move.

"Come on, sweetheart," Dan coaxed.

"Holy hell, don't call me sweetheart. And let go my arm!" She jerked away and, had it not been for Dan's quick response, she would have run out of the room.

And then it came to Annie where she'd seen that hair before. Then it had been a dirty brown. Now it was the color of pale caramel, silky almost. It couldn't be. Annie planted her good foot on the floor, caught the table, and forced herself to stand. "Joe? Is that you?"

"Not anymore," Dan said pleasantly. "From now on, it's Josie. And Josie is going to sit down before she gets sent to her room. She doesn't want to miss all this good food, does she?"

Dan gave Josie a firm push into her chair and a look that warned her not to move. Then he came back around the table to help Annie sit. "Seems our Josie had been doing a little pretending."

Annie was speechless. "How'd you find out that Joe's a girl? I can't believe I didn't know."

"Let's just say that cleanliness is not only next to godliness, it's also a powerful revealer of truth."

"But, Joe . . . I mean Josie, you're so pretty," Annie said, still stunned. "Why did you pretend to be a boy?"

" 'Cause being a boy is easier."

Annie started to argue, then realized that Joe—Josie—had discovered a truth that Annie had also learned. Life was simpler for men. Her gaze slid to Dan and he was watching her.

"Maybe," Dan said, "but I'm glad you're girls. Where's Ginny?"

"She's having a tray brought to her room," Annie answered. "Where's Red?"

"He's with the rest of the crew. They're staying with our supplies."

"Well, since we're all here," Rosco said, picking up his napkin and tucking it into his shirt collar, "let's have a toast. Pour the wine, Washington."

The carriage-driver-turned-butler filled their glasses, stopping at Josie's with a question in his eyes. "Fill her up," Josie said.

"With water," Annie instructed.

"Ah, shoot! If I gotta do this, I don't see why I can't do it all. I ain't never made a toast."

"Because you're a young lady," Dan said gently. "When you get to be an old lady, like Annie, you may have wine. In the meantime—" He lifted his glass and waited until she'd lifted her water glass. "To luxury and fine company in the wilderness."

They all drank. Rosco laughed. "This ain't the wilderness. You ain't seen wilderness yet. Washington, bring the food."

Dan took Josie's napkin and laid it in her lap, whispering under his breath. "Remember, just do what I do."

Annie couldn't believe she was simmering about being called old. All he needed was to add two words, ugly and maid. *Ugly old maid.* For now, she needed the wine more than she needed to chastise Dan. She emptied her first glass quickly, hoping it would do what her medication hadn't, ease the pain. When Washington refilled her glass, she took another sip.

Moments later, a hot creamed soup was placed before them. Dan took a spoon and smiled. 'This is very good, Mr. Thurmon, as good as anything I had in Europe. Where'd you find a French chef?"

"Ran into him down in New Orleans. Cooks them fancy things good, but I had to tell him that we like plain foods—not so much wine and spice."

Annie sipped the soup. It was good and it was heavily laced with wine. She was content to let the men talk, leaving her out of having to make conversation.

"What do you think of my little town?" Rosco asked.

"I'm impressed. But I'm curious. How do you get the timbers here?"

"We cut them up north, then use oxen to drag them to the creek and float them down."

"After all the rail building, aren't you running out of trees?"

"Trees aren't the problem, it's getting them to the line. Costs them construction people an arm and a leg."

Dan groaned. "I can attest to that. I'm curious, Rosco, what happened to delay my timbers?"

"Funny thing about that. The creek got blocked by a fallen tree and the logs piled up. Something happened to the new man I hired who was supposed to keep it clear, and by the time we found the problem, there was a logjam. Sorry about the delay. I hope it didn't cause a problem for you."

"Well, every delay is a problem," Dan said, frowning.

That was the first clue Annie had that Dan might be anxious about the delay. "Does that kind of jam happen often?" she asked.

"No, never happened before. Another peculiar thing about that tree falling. My foreman said it had been sawed off at the base."

"You think it was deliberate?" Dan asked.

"Don't know what else to think."

The chef served pork with mushrooms, boiled turnips, and Indian corn. Annie picked at her food, continuing to sip her wine. Josie said nothing, but emptied her plate several times. When that course was done, Dan leaned over and whispered in Josie's ear. Her napkin suddenly appeared, along with two biscuits and a chunk of meat.

About that time, Annie realized that her ankle had finally stopped hurting. In fact, she felt remarkably good. "The food really is delicious, Mr. Thurmon," she said. "And your house is lovely. Don't you think the house is lovely, Josie? Now that you're a woman you should appreciate lovely things like this."

"Sure, it's *lovely*. But I like the sawmill better," Josie said. "It's a lot more useful."

"You're right, little lady."

"Don't call me little lady! I may be a girl but I don't have to be no lady."

Rosco nodded. "You may change your mind one day. I didn't always have a house like this, Josie. When I was a boy, I lived from pillar to post. Don't mind saying, now and then I did a little pilfering—just to eat. Now, when I find what I want, I buy it," Thurmon said. "What else am I going to do with my money?"

After they'd finished a generous helping of dried apple pie, Rosco summoned the cook. "Please fix up a plate of goodies for the little lady," he said, giving Josie a wink. "In case she wakes up and wants a midnight snack."

"Thank you, Mr. Rosco," Josie said. She paused for a minute, then asked, "You reckon you'll have any more leftovers tomorrow?"

"I'll just bet we will, and it would be good if you'd take them along when you go. My help's getting too fat."

"You think I could go now, Dan?" Josie asked.

Annie frowned and blinked her eyes. "Go where?"

"Back to the train, with Red and the men."

"You will not," Annie said, attempting to stand once more. "Oops. Not a good idea," she said, collapsing backward. "Mr. Thurmon, you'd better use some of those trees to fix this floor—it's rollicking like a pig in a mud hole." She giggled, then went silent and frowned. "We ate pork tonight. It didn't come from a real pig, did it?"

Rosco looked puzzled. "A real pig?"

Josie dropped her napkin filled with food into her lap. "Did the pig come in on the ferry?"

"The pig came from the pigpen behind the smokehouse. Why?"

Josie smiled. "Ah, nothing. It's just that Annie fell over a pig and—"

"I did not," Annie protested. "It deliberately pushed me. Still, it didn't deserve to be roasted."

Dan realized too late that Annie was tipsy. "It couldn't be the same pig, Annie. Mr. Thurmon's cook wouldn't have had time to prepare it. You need to rest your sprained ankle, Josie. Come along. I may need your help."

"Last time I went to help you, I ended up in a washtub and a dress. No, thanks. I'm going to bed." With that statement, Josie was gone.

"Don't wake up Ginny!" Annie called after Josie. "And what do you need Joe—Josie—to help you with?" Annie demanded of Dan as he rounded the table. "I can get upstairs on my own. Just head me in the right direction."

She pivoted out of the chair, took a step, and collapsed into Dan, who leaned over at that exact moment and let her drape herself over his shoulder like a sack of flour. He looked ruefully at Rosco, who was grinning from ear to ear. "Good night, Mr. Thurmon," he said, and as Annie began to squirm, slapped her smartly on the rear. "Be still, woman." He started up the stairs.

"You hit me."

"Now we're even."

"Put me down, Dan Miller," Annie demanded.

"Annie, you can't even walk."

"Don't want to walk," she said with a giggle. "I want to dance. Will you dance with me, Dan?"

"I don't think you're in any condition to dance, Annie. You're going to put on your nightclothes and go to bed."

"Don't have any," she quipped. "They got stolen by that pickpocket, or someone else."

"What have you been sleeping in?" Dan asked, telling his mind not to even think about Annie's answer.

His mind was as disobedient as Annie, and just as responsive as the rest of his body.

12

— ✂ —

Inside the bedroom, the lamps were lit and a fire was crackling. The bedcovers had been turned down, and a nightgown Annie had never seen before was lying across the foot of the purple coverlet.

"Dan, put me down."

He slid her forward, catching her in his arms to lay her on the bed. Annie looked up at him and smiled. "Am I a woman tonight, Dan?"

"Oh, yes, Annie. You're definitely a woman tonight."

She smiled, coquettishly. "Yes." She slid her arms around his neck and locked them. "I'm Cleopatra. And you're Antony."

"I hope you don't plan to do away with me."

"Nope. I feel too good to do anything bad. I think . . . I think I want you to kiss me." She puckered her lips and closed her eyes.

"Annie. Annie. This is not a good idea."

Her grasp around his neck tightened.

He knew kissing Annie was a mistake, just as it had been twice before. He was a man on a mission; the railroad—not a woman—was his future. No, he decided as he lowered his head; kissing Annie was not a good idea at all. There was a sense of déjà vu as his head dipped and his lips captured her willing ones. She twisted her body until she was pressed against him, her heart beating against his chest.

He slid away from her mouth, whispering as he planted kisses across her face and neck. "Annie, we need to get you out of this dress," he said, sitting her on the bed.

Her bemused "All right" accompanied the unbuttoning of her bodice and sliding it from her shoulders.

Until then Dan could have backed away, until he saw pert breasts with tiny hard nipples that said she was as aroused as he.

"No fair," she said. "If I have to take off my clothes, you have to take off yours."

"Annie, I can't do that."

"You need help? I'll call Washington." She opened her mouth.

"No! Shush! I'll do it." He expected her to change her mind. She didn't. Maybe, if he followed through she'd come to her senses. He sure as hell had lost his. He removed his boots and unbuttoned his shirt.

"Annie, I think I'd better stop here," he said. "Let's get the skirt off and you can sleep in your petticoat."

"Not wearing one," she said, giggling. "Guess I'll just have to sleep naked."

Dan groaned and started to turn away.

Annie leaned forward and caught Dan by the waist of his trousers. "You can't go and leave me, Dan Miller. You take care of me, remember, and tonight I need care. I think I may be about to faint."

"Annie, you've never fainted in your life."

Annie whispered, deliberately making her voice too

soft to be heard. "Dan . . ." She flung herself dramatically back across the bed, and moaned. "Oh, Dan!"

Dan dropped down beside her, leaning close to her lips. "What's wrong, Annie?"

"Not a thing," she replied with her lips curling into an expression of pleasure, "except you're too far away from me."

With one quick move she'd pulled him over her.

"Dan," she whispered, feeling his arousal pressing against her lower body. "You're still wearing your clothes."

Before he knew what she was doing, she pushed him to his back and unbuttoned his trousers, allowing his erection to spring free. "I've seen men before, but I never saw anything like that. I mean they always had covers in the presence of ladies." She turned to her side. "The ones I've seen before weren't so big." She smiled.

He almost smiled back. She was some minx, pretending to be so innocent, when he already knew that her past was slightly shady. She'd been the one who bragged that she had "special skills" in addition to her poker playing ability.

"May I touch it?" Her fingers tentative at first, then grasped it tightly, moving her grip up and down. "It's very hard. I . . . wasn't sure."

She was studying him minutely. He felt as if he were livestock being sold at auction, until she grinned and lifted her gaze to his face. Dan groaned and caught her hand. "Don't do that, Annie."

"Why. Did I hurt it?"

"No, but I wouldn't do too much touching, Annie," he gasped.

"All right. And it's very big, isn't it? I'll just hold on while I kiss you."

"No . . . not that exactly. But—here, let me show you." He pushed her back and touched her breasts, ringing her nipples with one finger, slowly, repeatedly. Beneath his touch she began to squirm. Then he kissed her breasts, taking one nipple in his mouth as his fingers moved down.

Annie gasped and moaned. He pulled on her breasts with his mouth, rasping his tongue across and beneath, then moving to the other. His fingers reached the soft downy hair below, and lowered into the moisture of her womanhood, where he touched and rubbed until she began to move in earnest.

"Dan . . . Dan . . ."

"Not yet, Annie."

She gave a moan of protest, reached down between them, and touched him again.

"Annie, are you sure? You've had too much wine. I don't want you to wake up in the morning and regret this. Do you know what you're asking?"

For a moment she stilled her movement. Her body felt as if it were flying. She knew she'd had far too much wine. That and the medication had taken away all her ladylike reserve. But she could never say she didn't know what she was doing. What she could say was that she wanted to be with this man. Until she got past whatever force drew her to him, she'd never be able to go forward without him.

"Teach me to be a woman, Dan."

There was no turning back. She was right, she wasn't wearing a petticoat, only her chemise and drawers. Once they were gone, he had one knee between her legs and felt her clamp her thighs around it, her moisture sleek against him. He'd thought to wait until she was ready, but he couldn't. She was so tiny, so tight. He didn't want to hurt her so he willed himself not to move, allowing her body to know his. Then he discovered a stunning truth: She'd never been with a man before. That stunned him. He tried to withdraw.

But Annie was having no part of that. In one swift move, she locked her arms around him and lifted her hips, driving him inside. And he was lost.

Dan had thought he'd known women before, thought he'd felt every sexual emotion a man could feel. He'd been wrong. This was more than just a physical response; she was melting into him, merging every inch of herself with every inch of him. He tried to hold back, to wait for her. His efforts were unnecessary and unsuccessful. Annie cried out, and her body began to writhe. Her fingers dug into his back. Her legs tightened around his and pleasure exploded through his body.

Then he collapsed over her, supporting himself with his elbows as he gazed down at this woman who knew what a man looked like but had never been with one.

She was smiling.

Dan studied the curve of her face, strong, classic, happy. He kissed her, loved her now with soft touches and little words he'd never thought to use. Finally, fearful of his weight crushing her, he started to withdraw.

"No," she said. "Not yet."

"But you're so tiny," he said, "you're injured and you need to sleep now. Tomorrow, you'll be very sore. It isn't good to—"

She clamped herself around him. "It's good to me. Never in my whole life have I ever felt anything so good. If I sleep, I'll wake up and this will be over forever." Her eyes flew open. "Is it hurting you, our staying like this?"

He laughed. He was already as hard as he had been before they reached her bedroom door. "It isn't hurting me, Annie."

"Good. I'm glad." She reached up and tugged his head down to her breasts. "Start again, please. But don't take too long."

He didn't and she didn't. That time or the next.

The fire was out and the sky was gray with morning light when Dan slipped from her bed and dressed. He knew he'd crossed a line from which he couldn't retreat, but when he leaned over Annie one last time and saw the soft shadows of her lashes against her cheek, he felt something powerful, something he wasn't certain he was ready to feel, something all too real.

"Morning, Dan," Red said, giving him an odd examining look as he walked up the platform toward the log train. "You get much sleep?"

"Enough."

"The logs came in last night. They're loading them on the car now. They're wet, so they'll weigh more."

"Did you hear what happened?" Dan asked, glad to have something to focus on other than the reason for his lack of sleep.

"Only that there was a logjam."

"An intentional logjam. Somebody cut down a tree that fell across the creek and trapped the logs."

Red frowned. "Why would somebody do that?"

"If I didn't know better, I'd think it was a warning. Somebody is trying to tell us something."

"I hope not," Red said in a strained voice. "I really hope not. You don't suppose they'd do anything to the train, do you?"

That thought caught Dan by surprise. "They? Who in hell are they?"

Red looked troubled. "I'm not sure. But I'm worried. More about the women than us."

Dan sent a questioning glance at the man who was becoming a friend as well as a valued employee. "The women? Or Ginny?"

"Ginny is a fine-looking lass, I'll admit. And I'm a sucker for a woman carrying a child, God knows. My ma carried enough of them. There were twelve of us, nine who lived."

"Are they back in New York?"

"No, but they're the reason I came to this country, to earn money to send home to Ireland."

"And still you threw in with me, knowing I couldn't pay you normal wages?"

"I thought it was a good gamble. My da never had a chance at anything more than working in the mines. When he was killed, life was hard for my mother and the little ones. Sometimes a man takes a chance because he has to. Just like Mrs. Wilson and Annie. That's why I have a soft spot in me heart for the women."

"You know, Mrs. Wilson probably won't find her husband. You could have a chance there."

"Sure, and I've got one of the little people in me back pocket." Red frowned. "No point in thinking about that. She's out of my class."

Dan shook his head. "I'm not so sure about that. Sometimes things don't work out like you plan."

"What about you?" Red asked. "Don't mean to pry, but Annie, that Annie looks like a firecracker. I don't know if any man could ever conquer her."

Dan thought about the Annie of the night before. "Red, a smart one wouldn't try. Besides, she's got some kind of plan and I don't think she's going to let anything or anybody get in her way."

"I can't think that she's that keen on finding a husband. If she is, I don't know why she isn't taking a look at you."

Dan's eyes widened in disbelief. "A husband? Annie?"

"Hard to believe. Ginny wouldn't tell me all of it, but that first day, when I asked Ginny what they were doing, she said they were going out west to find her husband, and that Annie had promised her pa if she couldn't find a place where she's needed in a year, she'd choose a man and marry."

Dan swallowed hard. Could he have misunderstood Annie's motives? Was she searching for a husband for herself? If so, he'd just spent the night giving her a reason to think he would be a good choice. He didn't know whether he was more rattled over that or over imagining someone else being with Annie as he had. He hurried toward the train, leaving Red behind in his wake.

"Hey, what'd I do, Boss?"

"You just explained something to me, Red. Something I should have figured out and didn't."

"Well, that's good. But there's another thing about me I need to tell you, before you find out that I'm not what you think."

"Not today. I can't take any more confessions right now. Whatever other truth you think you need to share—hold on to it."

Two hours later a rested Ginny, a beaming Josie, and a subdued Annie appeared at the train. Annie was limping painfully, and she was moving very slowly, but at least she was moving under her own power. She hardly glanced at Dan as she climbed on the train and took her seat.

"I'm sorry your ankle is still so bad," Ginny said. "Why didn't you let Mr. Thurmon's men help you?"

"It's not my ankle, Ginny, it's my head. It feels like someone is playing a base drum in the middle of it, while some street entertainer is tap-dancing behind my eyes."

"If you'd let me have some of that wine instead of trying to drink it all yourself, you wouldn't have a hangover," Josie said.

Ginny's eyes widened. "Wine?"

"It's not the wine, Ginny," Annie protested, "it's the medication. I think I took too much."

Josie was shaking her head. "Hangover, Ginny. Believe me, I've seen enough of 'em."

Ginny didn't comment. Instead, she left the train, filled her handkerchief with snow, and came back inside. "Lean your head back, Annie."

"Don't shout!"

Ginny smiled at Josie and laid the ice pack over Annie's eyes. "I'm sorry your evening ended badly, Annie," she said.

"You don't know, Ginny," Annie whispered. "You wouldn't believe me if I told you. If I die between here and Omaha, notify Father to come for my body."

Ginny bit back a laugh. "What do I tell him you died of?"

"Being a woman," Annie said. She groaned, caught the ice in her hand, and turned her face to the window.

By the time they left the log train in Omaha and boarded the Union Pacific, Annie had recovered from her ankle injury and her hangover, and had resolved never to be alone with Dan Miller again.

She blamed her bizarre behavior on the medication and, though she wouldn't admit it to Ginny, the wine. To herself, she was more honest. She'd known what she was doing. She could have stopped Dan and she hadn't. But she had no intention of letting anything like that happen again. It appeared that Dan Miller was of the same mind.

Finally, they reached Cheyenne.

Smoke plumed from buildings. A circle of smutty tents huddled together like beggars. "Cheyenne, the newest 'hell on wheels' capital of the railroad," one of the passengers said as the train pulled into the snowbound little town.

Josie, back in her boy's clothing, had her nose pressed against the window. "I've heard people talking about 'em. Dance halls and gambling. Don't know how they just pick up and move like they do—say, Annie, you sure you don't want to get off and pick up a little more money?"

"I do not, and you'd better not get out of my sight, Joe—Josie. The only thing I want to know is whether or not they have a doctor."

Josie looked worried. "Annie, is there something

wrong? You been acting peculiar ever since the night we spent at the mansion. You sick, Annie?"

"The doctor's not for me, Josie. It's Ginny who could need her."

"Her? Are there lady docs?"

"The best doctors are ladies," Annie snapped, feeling sabotaged by her own sex.

Ginny spoke up. "I'm thinking Josie's right, Annie. You haven't been yourself. Maybe we ought to have you checked out."

"I don't need checking out, Ginny. I know what's wrong with me."

Ginny gave her a troubled gaze. "I'm wondering if you do."

Later, Ginny left the train briefly, then returned with news. "Josie, they're adding a fancy Pullman car behind ours. It belongs to the Casement brothers. They're the ones building the railroad. They're bringing some visitors out to see the site. You can watch so long as you don't go out of the car."

Once Josie moved away, Ginny leaned forward. "Annie, they have a doctor in Cheyenne. I haven't questioned you before now, but I'm concerned. I don't know what happened back at Boggy Gut, but Josie's right. You're acting very strange."

Annalise felt a flush of color on her face, and groaned. The frequent rise of her heart rate was becoming a familiar occurrence, one she seemed to be unable to control. She knew what it meant.

"Look," Josie called out, "there's Dan."

"Mr. Miller," Annie corrected. She didn't have to be told he was on the platform. She didn't have to look to know. She might be avoiding him, but her body was on constant alert and it knew his presence long before her eyes found him. For once there was nobody on their car except her, Ginny, and Josie. She hoped Dan didn't get on.

"Ah, Annie. Nobody calls him mister. He's just Dan."

Just Dan Miller, son of one of the richest men in New York. He was as much "just Dan" as she was "just Annie." He looked even more dangerous now than he had the first night she'd seen him. Remembering that night was safer than reliving the night he'd spent in her bed. He hadn't shaved since they left Boggy Gut, and the dark shadow of a mustache rimmed his mouth.

"Howdy, Dan," Josie piped through the window she'd cracked. "You getting off the train here in Cheyenne?"

"Nope, my stop's just ahead. How about you?" He allowed himself to look at Annie for the first time in days. "I understand it gets pretty rough from here on out. You could stay here in Cheyenne, and I could ask about Robert and send you word."

"Thank you, no. We're going on to Laramie," Annie said.

"And what do you think you're going to do when you get to Laramie?"

"Why, I'm going to . . ." But she couldn't get the words out. Why was this so hard? Why couldn't she tell him she was a doctor in search of patients?

She hedged. "Mrs. Wilson and I have considered that very question. The answer depends on a number of things. I—we'd appreciate your inquiring about Robert, but we've given up on finding him."

"Annie . . ." Dan began. "About that night—I don't want you to misunderstand."

Ginny took those words as her cue to leave Annie and Dan in private. She grabbed Josie by the hand and pulled her to the next car.

"I never meant to . . . I mean I thought . . ."

Annie looked as if she were holding on by a thread. "I know what you thought and I don't wish to discuss it," she said, lowering her voice. "I make my own choices and I live with my decisions. Please! Go on and do whatever it is you have to do and forget about us."

"That would be my choice. I have an obligation to do a job, and my life doesn't include a woman or a—wife. But

Annie," his voice turned suddenly tender, "believe me, there's no way in hell you and Mrs. Wilson and Josie can manage this alone."

"That's what my father said. He was wrong, too. Men never think women can get along without them, do they?"

"Men hope they can. Then they hope they're wrong."

13

They'd been traveling for more than a week. Annie was beginning to feel guilty about leaving New York without telling her father that she'd gone. By now, he'd have learned that she never went to the summer cottage. She hated feeling like a coward. She wouldn't have acted so secretively if she'd thought she could convince Roylston Sinclair to let her go. It was time she took responsibility for her actions and let him know where she was.

Tearing up her letter, she left the train to send a telegram instead.

SORRY I LEFT WITHOUT TELLING YOU. KNEW YOU'D
STOP ME. HAVE TO TRY AND FOLLOW MY DREAM.
KNOW NOW I CAN'T BE A DOCTOR AND A WIFE.
LOVE, ANNIE.

Reboarding the train she let out a deep sigh and hoped she'd done the right thing. He'd know she was in Cheyenne. He just wouldn't know she wasn't going to stay there. Either he'd send someone after her, or he'd let her try. She was banking on his doing what he'd always done: let her succeed or let her fail—on her own.

The track from Cheyenne to Laramie ran through banks of snow towering fifteen feet, held back only by the snow fences. Annie felt a little like Alice in Wonderland, hurtling down a rabbit hole with no idea of what world waited at the bottom.

In spite of the huge mounds of snow, the train moved on. Night fell fast now, and everyone slept. Annie was the only one awake when the sound of the train's wheels on the track changed. She sat up and peered out into the darkness. Beyond the jagged edge of the distant mountain an almost full moon hung, fat and pearl-colored in the sky.

With its light, Annie could see a sliver of mirrored reflection below. It took her a moment to understand that they were on a bridge, over a gorge. The water was iced over and, swept clear of snow by the wind, it served as a prism. She suddenly heard a muffled explosion followed by an unmistakable creak, and felt a skip in the train's movement. The skip came again, and the wheels turned even more slowly, as if the engineer were trying to tiptoe across the bridge without waking it. From somewhere behind in the darkness came a low rumble. The engineer picked up speed. The faster the train moved, the more unsteady became its gait. The skip turned into a hiccup. Something was definitely wrong. Annie felt alarm rise inside her.

"Ginny! Josie, wake up!"

Josie woke instantly. "What's wrong?"

"I'm not sure. Gather up all our things. Quick!"

Seconds later, the train jolted. A loud snap preceded the sound of buckling metal. In the next few minutes confusion reigned. Annie reached for Josie and held her tight. Ginny screamed. Josie was jerked out of Annie's arms and slid under the seat. Then the forward movement of the train stopped.

"We'd better get off," Josie said, scrambling out and tugging on Annie's arm. "Hurry up!"

Annie grabbed a carryall and a blanket. "Out the front."

"What's happening?" Ginny asked, falling in behind Annalise. "Where's Red?"

Annalise threw the blanket over Ginny and inched her way toward the door. "I don't know. We must have hit something. Move slowly. I think we're on a bridge."

"Oh, good," Josie said. "We hit something on a bridge? What? A giant snowflake? Where we gonna go?"

Annie wondered the same thing when she stepped out onto the platform and down, testing the wooden beams that made up the foundation. Where she stood seemed steady, but behind her, lanterns were being lit, and soon enough she could see a hint of the problem. A portion of the wooden trellis had collapsed, and the last car was hanging perilously off the end of the bridge, dangling in space.

The engine and the passenger cars had made it across. As far as she could tell, the main body of the train was heavy enough to support the weight of the dangling car for now. How long the bridge would hold was a different question. Behind their car was the Pullman car carrying visitors to the construction site. Dan's passenger car appeared to be intact, but she couldn't be sure. The last car, whichever one it was, appeared to be perilously close to the abyss.

She said a silent prayer of thanks that their car was at the front of the train. If they'd been farther back, they'd have been knocked about like the rest of the cars now forming a pattern of chicken feet in the snow.

The rest. She caught her breath. Where was Dan? "Come on, let's get to safety," she said.

"What about Red?" Ginny asked, frozen where she stood. "I won't go without him."

"Ginny!" Annie caught her friend's shoulders and shook her. "We have to go! Think of your baby."

Shaking off the horror of what had happened, Ginny turned reluctantly away. Annie caught Josie just as she was about to slip past them to the site of the trouble. "Help me, Josie. We don't know that the rest of the bridge isn't about to go. We have to get Ginny to safety."

Josie took one look at Ginny and she didn't have to be urged again. "They're okay, Ginny. You know Dan and Red always come out all right. You lead the way, Annie. We'll follow you."

Reluctantly, Ginny turned. Testing each step, they crept past the engine toward the icy embankment. The timbers beneath their feet were treacherous. Every step released a crackle of ice.

"I think I'm glad I can't see," Ginny said, the chattering of her teeth almost drowned out by the sound of debris now falling into the darkness below.

Inch by inch Annie led them across to the ridge at the other side, feeling her way to a rocky alcove where Ginny and Josie would be sheltered from the worst of the wind.

"Cover yourselves with your blankets and wait here," Annie said. "I have to see if anyone is hurt."

"You may need some help, Annie," Josie said. "I'll come with you."

"No. What I need you to do is look after Ginny. For once, don't argue." Reluctantly, Josie nodded and crouched down next to Ginny.

Halfway across the gorge, Annie heard a rumble, followed by a crash and a terrifying scream of pain.

"Stand still!" Dan shouted.

Annie heard his voice and let out the breath she'd been holding. Dan was safe.

"Everyone get off the front of the car," Dan directed, "one at a time, and make your way to the other side."

"We can't leave Red," someone called out. "He's hurt."

"Red?" Annie swallowed hard. Dan was all right, but

Red was hurt. Ginny had probably heard. She could only hope that Josie could convince her to stay put.

Forcing her way past the two special guests of the railroad, Annie took a quick look at the passengers and directed them to the alcove on the ridge on the other side where they'd be safe. They didn't argue. She hoped her medical supplies were where they could be reached. She'd be useless without her equipment.

Finally Annie reached the end of the bridge. Several men were holding lanterns, throwing light on the coupling between two of the supply cars, one still on the track and the other dangling in space.

Caught between the two cars was Red, his face taut with pain, his leg twisted between the coupling and the track.

"Red," Annie called out. "Don't move until I can get to you."

"Annie, go back!" Dan ordered, tugging her arm as she attempted to slide through.

"Let me go, Dan. I have to help him."

"You can't. His leg is broken."

She glared at him. "I can help him. And if you don't let me go I'll break your leg and you can learn firsthand what I'm capable of."

Annie jerked away from Dan and stepped gingerly on the rails until she reached Red. Kneeling beside him, she felt his leg. "He's right, Red, it's broken. Where else are you hurt?"

"Nowhere else," he gasped, pressing his lips tightly, trying to hold back another scream. Then, "At least not that I can tell, darlin'. It's so damned cold out here I could be missing me nose and I wouldn't know it."

"We'll have you out of here in no time, Red," Dan said from behind.

Annie turned her head "Can we get him out?"

"It's only a matter of releasing the last car and lifting him up at the same time," Dan said confidently.

Annie didn't have to be told that it had to be timed just right. There was the danger that the weight of the men releasing the car could make the bridge go, and Red would be dragged over in the crash.

"I think I can pull myself up," Red said, "if someone will lift my leg."

"We need a small man, who is quick on his feet," Dan said. "Any volunteers?"

There were none.

"I'll do it," Annie announced, crawling forward.

"No, I'll do it," Dan said.

"We need you to lift," one of the men said. "Let the woman do it. She weighs less."

One look at Annie's face told Dan that he wasn't going to stop her. "All right, but someone tie a rope around her waist. If the track goes, we can pull her in."

The man who'd overruled Dan found a piece of rope and handed it to Dan, who looped it around Annie's waist. "You don't have to do this," he said to Annie.

"Yes, I do," she said. "This is the first thing I've been certain of since we left New York. I know what I'm doing. Now tie the rope."

He didn't ask any more questions. "All right, then." He finished the knot and stepped back. "One man will stand on either side of the rails to help lift Red. Annie, you take his leg. As soon as I give the signal, you men pick him up. I'll release the pin and we'll let the last car go."

"Before you do that, Dan—where are my crates?"

"Don't worry. They're in this car. Whatever you're carrying is safe."

"But your timbers—all your supplies are in the last car," Annie said. Dan didn't reply. The car had to be released from the rest of the train in order to free Red.

"I'll order more," Dan snapped. "Are you ready, Red?"

"I'm ready."

"Then, let's move him. On the count of three."

One of Dan's men stationed himself on either side of

the coupling. Dan straddled the tongue and Annie crouched beside him.

Red was breathing heavily. "If it starts to go, Annie, forget about me and run like hell."

There was a sharp creak and the car jolted forward another inch. Red cried out in pain.

Teeth clenched, he raised himself on his hands, moving up enough so that the two workers could catch his shoulders. As they lifted, Red couldn't hold back a scream. Annie caught his leg, ready to straighten it. There wasn't enough room. The car had to be disconnected first. Red groaned again and passed out from pain.

Annie held her breath.

Dan caught the pin. "Ready. Set. Go!" He released it. The car in the rear rolled back. The tongue attached to the car in front lifted, releasing Red's leg, and the rescuers jerked him out. Annie held his leg as they scurried awkwardly toward the bank on the other side.

The timbers and rails clattered into space. The bridge swayed and the next car teetered, the end hanging over the edge. Once the rescuers made it across, Dan untied Annie's rope and turned back.

"Dan, wait." Annie picked up a lantern and started toward him. "Where are you going? Leave it alone, Dan. Wait until daylight."

"I can't, Annie." He picked up a lantern. "I have to check the cars, make certain that everyone is out."

He was right and she knew it. At any minute that last car could shift and bring down the bridge, pulling the rest of the train into the chasm. With that car went all her medical supplies.

Red's leg. Annie had to have those supplies to set his leg. She caught Dan's arm. "I'm going with you. I have to have my crates, Dan."

"Don't be foolish. You're not going to be killed over a few clothes."

"Not clothes, Dan. Medicine. Bandages. I have to have

my supplies to treat these people, beginning with Red's leg."

He stared at her. "Who are you, Annie?"

"I'm someone who can help," she snapped, giving him a shove. "If I'm going to take care of Red's leg, I need those crates."

"I'll get them," he said. "Wait here, or I'll use that rope to tie you in place." Satisfied that she'd heard him, he disappeared into the darkness.

She didn't think he'd hesitate to tie her up, but she didn't have time to argue. The passengers needed to be checked and Red—Red! Ginny would be scared to death.

"We'll help Dan," several men said, and followed him.

Fifteen minutes later she'd confirmed that Red's leg was the worst of the injuries. He was slipping in and out of consciousness, the pain more than he could bear. The small amount of laudanum she was carrying wouldn't be enough. If Dan didn't get her medicine, she'd have to set the leg without painkillers.

Seconds later, the grinding of metal ripped the night like a long unearthly scream. The bridge seemed to bend. Then came an eerie silence as the last car fell, hitting the water with a crackle as it broke the ice and splashed into the river below. The timbers creaked. The rest of the train swayed. And then it was still.

A low clapping gave way to a roar of cheers from the bank behind her. The passengers knew they had survived an encounter with death.

Dear God. Where was Dan?

His lantern had disappeared.

For the first time, Dr. Annalise Sinclair forgot about the sick and wounded. There was such a pain in her chest that she couldn't breathe. She had to know that Dan was all right. She had to know.

She started toward the spot where she'd last seen him, feeling her way past the engine toward the end of the train. "Dan! Where are you?"

From the darkness came his answer. "I'm coming. Get back, Annie. This bridge could twist and the whole thing could go at any minute."

She kept going.

Then she met him. He was safe. Her heart pounded with relief that he hadn't been thrown into the water below. His hands were behind him, holding one of her crates. For a moment she almost flung her arms around him. "Are you all right?" she asked.

"I'm fine. Red? The others?"

"Red's in a lot of pain. The engineer and the conductor are moving the passengers to a place out of the wind. I think they're all right. What about the men riding in those last cars?"

"So far as we know there weren't any back there but I don't know," Dan answered. "Until daylight there's no way we can even get down there to see—if then."

When they reached the bluff, Dan and his helpers dropped Annie's crates. By the light of a lamp, Dan studied the temporary camp they'd established under a section of rock where blasting had made a natural cave. The men were already attempting to build a fire with wooden seats and debris. Dan gave his nod of approval.

The engineer, his crew, and the railroad inspectors were conferring in a circle slightly away from the front of the engine.

"Annie, I'll talk to the engineer and find out what can be done about getting us in to Laramie. Can Red make it there?"

"The leg will have to be set before he can be moved," Annie said. "I'll take care of that. You men find a way to get us away from here."

"If you'll wait, I'll help you," Dan said.

"I don't need any help, Dan." Annie made her way toward the fire lighting the enclosure where the injured were gathered.

She had no difficulty locating Red in the makeshift

camp. All she had to do was look for Ginny. The maid, pinch-faced and worried, was cradling Red's head in her lap.

He was awake. "How bad is it, Red?" Annie asked, kneeling beside the Irishman.

"Not so bad, darlin'," he managed. "But I could use a belt of some stiff Irish whiskey."

"I'll give you something better to ease the pain," Annie said, riffling through her carryall for another packet of laudanum. Next, she pried open the crate with a piece of metal someone handed her and located her instruments and a brown bottle of chloroform. Annie turned toward the passengers standing around. "I'll need a piece of wood for a splint. Josie, can you find some blankets?"

Josie grinned. "Yeah, and I think I know where." She whirled around and disappeared into the darkness.

Once the fire was built up enough for a white-faced Ginny to melt snow for water, Annie mixed the laudanum and gave it to Red. "I'll need more light," she said. Soon a ring of lanterns circled Red, who had already begun to breathe easier.

Annie had assisted in the medical school surgery as often as she was allowed, but this would be her first real challenge. Under the best of conditions, she'd be nervous. Out here, she didn't even want to think about the possibilities of a failure.

Finally she was ready. Where were Josie and the blankets Annie would need to make a bed for the patient? She stood and turned. "Josie?"

"I'm coming," the little girl announced. "Somebody give me a hand with this."

The ten-year-old was pulling a feather mattress. "Will this do?"

"I don't want to know where you got it," Annie said, motioning to the onlookers where she wanted the mattress spread.

Annie and Ginny covered the mattress with a blanket,

and the men moved the Irishman to the hastily prepared hospital bed.

"Those of you with steady hands, take a lantern and hold it high enough so that the light covers the leg," Annie directed.

Opening the brown bottle, Annie poured some of the liquid on a cloth. She pressed it against her patient's nose. "Breathe in, Red. This will put you to sleep."

"Never much liked sleeping alone," he said in a tight voice.

"You're not alone," Ginny said. "I'll be here with you."

"That's all I need to hear," Red said as his eyes slowly closed.

This time the pounding of Annie's heart came from trepidation, not Dan's touch. She wondered what he thought about her now. This was what she wanted, what she'd come out west for. She wouldn't have picked such a spot to become Dr. Annalise Sinclair, but doctors rarely received their patients under ideal circumstances.

Her hands were shaking, her fingers stiff from the cold. The wind picked up, moaning across the opening to the rocky enclosure. The smoke from the fire was already making her eyes water. *You can do this, Annie. The conditions are not ideal, but you can do it.*

Red was beginning to breathe deeply. He was almost ready. Taking a deep relaxing breath, Annie flexed her fingers and picked up her scissors. She cut his trousers up to the thigh, exposing the wound.

There was a large gash just below the knee, but the bone didn't protrude. She examined the area once more. Good, the fracture wasn't complete. She'd set the fracture and then stitch the wound.

Red groaned.

Annie grasped the leg. Finally, total calm set in. She was a doctor. Dr. Annalise Sinclair had finally begun to practice medicine.

With one ear, Dan listened to the discussion of how the engineer intended to get the train and the passengers to Laramie as quickly as possible. The well-being of the passengers on the ledge was more pressing than the welfare of the men who'd been in the last car. With the other ear, Dan listened to Annie's quiet voice of authority.

"I need someone to hold his shoulders," she said.

"We have to telegraph the people back in Cheyenne," the engineer said. "Otherwise, we'll lose the next train, and more people will be killed."

"How many were in that last car?" someone asked.

"I'm not certain now," the engineer answered. "Someone saw a man inside when we left Cheyenne. He was carrying a bedroll."

"Who was he?" somebody asked.

Nobody knew.

The discussion went on, unidentified voices making nervous conversation. "We've been lucky. Other than the Irishman, the rest of us only have a few cuts and bumps."

"We'd better be quick," another said, stamping his feet. "We're going to freeze to death out here."

"Can we walk out?" Dan asked. The lack of any response was answer enough.

"What about the Irishman's leg?"

The answer Dan heard was chilling. "Well, it's like this. You'd better hope that woman can fix it, because there ain't no doctor ahead and unless somebody sprouts wings, we're gonna have a hard time getting back to Cheyenne."

Dan didn't want to hear that. He'd come to appreciate Red's loyalty and skill. He was a natural leader. The other men followed him. But more than that, Red was the kind of man you wanted as a friend.

Glancing over at the makeshift hospital, Dan saw that everyone was watching Annie silently. He started toward the circle of light. Then stopped to watch as well. With quiet authority Annie directed a passenger to hold Red's shoulders. Then grasping the leg around the ankle, she jerked it hard. The unmistakable crack signaled that she'd snapped the bones back into some kind of alignment.

In amazement, Dan watched Annie examine the leg, pressing here and there with knowing fingertips. In a medical bag, she located a packet of needles and thread. After washing the wound with her bare fingers and water from a pot on the fire melting the snow, she filled the gash with some kind of powder and stitched it up.

Dan was only marginally aware of the engineer explaining a plan to uncouple the last cars on the train and try moving the others forward. If the bridge held, they might be able to continue. Nodding his agreement, Dan watched Annie's face, furrowed in concentration. Finally, apparently satisfied that she had the results she wanted, she pulled back and wrapped the leg in muslin.

"Hand me the splints," she said, taking a pole someone had cut in half. Lining the pieces up on either side of the leg, she held them in place. "Bind it with the strips of muslin," she told Ginny.

"I don't know how," Ginny began. "What if I tie it too tight?"

"Just tie it. Once it's steady we'll swap places and I'll finish."

Ginny followed Annie's instructions. The two women bound the leg and laid it back on the mattress. Annie let out a deep breath and leaned back, massaging the back of her neck.

Dan watched. Annie was amazing. He'd seen enough to know that there were people who had a knack for settling broken limbs, but sewing a wound with the skill Annie showed came from more than just kitchen knowledge.

One of the watchers touched Annie on the shoulder. "Sorry to bother you, ma'am, but I think you'd better look at the kid's finger."

"Kid?"

Josie's eyes were downcast. She shuffled her feet, reluctant to come forward. "Let me see, Josie," Annie said firmly.

Finally Josie held out her hand.

Annie gasped. The end of her pointing finger was missing. "What happened?"

"It got pinched."

"Pinched how?"

Josie squirmed. "I just caught it in . . . in the—a door."

Annie knew she wasn't going to like the answer. "Which door?"

"In that fancy car. That's where I got the mattress."

"And how did that pinch your finger?"

"Well, I was thinking that Red would feel lots better if he had something warm and dry to wear."

"And?" Annie insisted.

"Well, there was this here robe, in a kind of a trunk." She held the fur-trimmed dressing gown out to Ginny. "The trunk had a heavy top."

Annie finished the story for her young charge. "And it closed on your finger, slicing off the end."

"Something like that. Don't worry, Dr. Annie, this finger ain't gonna slow me down. I been in lots worse spots."

Doctor? No wonder Annie never sounded like a maid. She'd told Dan she wasn't a gambler, but she'd been wrong. She'd bucked all the odds and trained to be a doctor. He'd bet she was about as appreciated as a doctor in New York as he'd been as a diplomat. But why was she out here? He looked at her curiously, but it was Josie he spoke to.

"Speaking of tough spots," he said absently, "I don't suppose you happened to see my gun anywhere, did you?"

Annie's gaze flew up to meet his. "You have a gun?"

"No, I had one. I didn't advertise it, but I didn't think it was smart to come to an unsettled area without protection. What about it, Josie?"

"Where would I hide a gun? Didn't even know you had one. I saw a man in a fancy hat in the car when you was off the train in Cheyenne. Maybe he took it."

"A man in a fancy hat?" Dan said, puzzled.

"Yeah, and his jacket had fur on the collar. Didn't look like no railroad man. Looked more like a peddler."

"Where is he now?" Dan asked, studying the passengers.

"Ain't seen him since Cheyenne," Josie said. "You want me to look for him?"

"Don't you dare," Annie said. "But I do want that dressing gown. I think you promised me you wouldn't steal again, didn't you?"

"Eh, yeah. What I said was that I wouldn't take nothing, lessen you told me to. You told me to get something to keep Red warm. That's what I done. If we put this fur robe on him, he'll stay warm a-plenty."

Josie expected to be chastised for her rather loose interpretation of Annie's instructions, but Annie couldn't bring herself to say anything. The child was tough, but beneath that rough exterior, she had a loving heart.

Dan helped Annie get Red into the robe. It was more elegant than anything a railroad worker would ever have worn. It was a gentleman's dressing gown, elaborately cut from velvet and lined with fur.

Dan could imagine Red's reaction to waking up and finding himself wearing it. But Josie was right. It would be warm, and it would cover his broken leg. "I expect the gentleman in question will be happy to lend it to Red."

"It was mine. He can have it," a strange voice called out. "Never liked the thing anyway."

Annie couldn't see the speaker but from the robe she decided that he was one of the guests of the railroad builders, occupying the fancy Pullman.

"Does your finger hurt, Josie?" Dan asked.

"Naw. Well, it's complaining some, 'bout like my stomach. Something to eat would sure make it feel better."

"Finger first, then food," Annie said, trying to ignore

Dan as she stood up. The doctor in her had taken over but the woman was still there. Briskly she used melted snow to clean the end of Josie's finger, then bandaged it. "The others need food and heat, too. It will keep them from getting too cold. Ginny, will you see what you can do?"

"Red?" Ginny said, torn between helping the others and staying with Red.

"He'll sleep for several hours."

"All right, folks," Ginny said. "Let's find out what we saved. Who has some coffee?" Moments later she had the passengers organized, and food supplies were being laid out to be shared.

Dan watched Annie. She shrugged her shoulders, swaying slightly from exhaustion. He held out his hand. She took it, and allowed him to draw her away from the others. "That was some piece of work, Dr. Annie. Why didn't you tell me?"

She couldn't avoid the question any longer. Both of them knew that the woman he laughingly called *just Annie* had never been a maid. She owed him no explanations, but they'd shared too much for her to lie anymore. She nodded. "You really don't know who I am, do you?"

When he shook his head, she said softly. "It's a long story and I think I'm too tired to explain it tonight. Tomorrow, I'll tell you everything, but for now, can you just hold me?"

He pulled her closer. He didn't know what would happen in the future but tonight, he couldn't refuse her anything. Questions could wait. Besides, she felt so damned good in his arms.

14

Mason Clanton studied the newspaper he was carrying and frowned as he walked into his partner William Russell's office. "The newspaper says the bridge between Cheyenne and Laramie is out."

"I know. The cattle buyer in Cheyenne wired me this morning. Too bad, isn't it?"

"You don't sound upset. Quite the opposite, actually," Mason said. "Is there something about the bridge collapsing that we should cheer about?"

"Yes, Mason. I'm always pleased when we're about to make money." William answered with a satisfied grin.

"How so? The railroad has to deliver our steers. If the bridge is out, we don't get our cattle."

"Until those beeves get to our pens, they still belong to Durant's cattle brokers. They have to feed them. If they die, it's their loss, not ours."

"But without beef, how will we be able to supply our customers?"

"Use your head, Mason. We'll supply fewer customers, yes. But the price will go up. We'll do very well."

"Any word on Miller's building crew's progress?"

"Not yet."

"Aren't you worried, William?"

"I'm not worried. Either Teddy's group goes belly-up before they finish and we take over, or it never gets built. Either way, we win." The man behind the desk rubbed his hands in glee. "I can't wait to see Teddy's face when he finds out he's lost everything—to me."

"He hasn't gone belly-up yet, William."

"Not yet. But he's feeling the pinch. That bridge went down and took his supplies with it."

"I guess I don't understand you, William. You want them to build the spur so you can take it, but you're happy they lost their supplies?"

"I'm very happy. Think about it Mason. Teddy will have to come up with more money to replace them. Where's he going to get it?"

"From you?"

"Exactly!"

"I hope you aren't underestimating the man," Mason said cautiously. "I'm your partner, and I don't look forward to suffering the result of his anger."

"The only person who will suffer is Teddy Miller."

At the site of the train crash, Dan's involvement in helping the engineer and his crew get the remaining cars righted saved Annalise from having to face his questions about her identity. "We'll talk when we get to Laramie," he said, and left her alone.

For now, convincing Red that he didn't have to be an iron man in the face of pain was impossible. Annalise finally decided that having Ginny comfort him was more to his liking, and a little pain meant a lot more comfort.

It wasn't until after she reexamined all the other passengers that she finally got back to check on Red, and found him wearing the pilfered dressing gown over his ripped trousers. He looked like a Russian czar, but he was warm and, thanks to a drop of laudanum Ginny had put in his coffee, he was resting. It was nearly morning when the conductor called out, "Get aboard!"

Dan was instantly in motion, directing the transfer of Red from his shelter onto the train. They'd rigged a pallet on the floor, in the place by the door where Josie had originally hidden.

Two cars were lost, and two others were temporarily abandoned because the limited crew and the bad weather prevented their realignment. Crowding two sets of passengers into the remaining cars made for noise and confusion.

Annalise didn't even suggest that Ginny leave Red's side. She'd decided that Ginny's affection for the Irishman was well known to the other passengers, and accepted. The knowledge that the woman they believed to be a maid was a physician was a juicier bit of gossip, but the passengers' gratitude and awe kept them from questioning Annie. All that was left was for Ginny to confess that she wasn't married.

That ought to keep Laramie buzzing.

Dan's reaction remained to be seen.

Their close call with death seemed to hit home with the passengers and all fell silent. Through the windows the watery light of day touched the rocks on either side of the track, brushing the peaks of granite with trails of white that glistened like tears on a stone face.

The train was moving, but Annie couldn't be still. Her mind raced with the possible consequences of the train accident. The aftermath could make or break her future. Had she set the leg properly? Would it heal well enough so Red could walk again? Her first real challenge as a doctor had come under the worst of circumstances.

Another dilemma kept hammering at her as well, a dilemma she tried unsuccessfully to push away. What about Dan? Before they'd crossed the Mississippi, she'd managed to put a certain amount of distance between them. Now, it was only a matter of time until he'd demand answers. She'd lied to everyone, not outright, but by omission, an act that had severely tested her conscience.

Dan might have wanted his men to think he was a regular worker, but he'd used his real name. And she knew that if she'd asked him, he would have told her the truth about who he was. It was her own determination to refuse any possible suitors that had led her to disguise who she was. And she knew, without being told, that Dan Miller would never approve of what she'd done.

There was a certain amount of relief that she could not control the outcome. Her father would know where she'd sent the telegram from and, once the bridge was reopened, he'd probably come after her. She'd known that was a possibility from the beginning. She could only hope that she'd proved her worth before he arrived.

Unable to sit still any longer, Annie stood up and threaded her way through the crowd and out the door to the platform between their car and the engine ahead. So far today, she seemed to have spent as much time on the connection link as she had inside. The icy wind slapped her face as if it were admonishing her impudence.

With Laramie just ahead she had to decide what she was going to do. Ginny didn't want to find Robert, and Annie doubted that they ever would. As for Josie, where she settled didn't seem to matter. And finally, if what Annie had heard was true, she'd found a place with no doctor. Annie watched her breath catch in the icy air like the steam from the engine's smokestack.

Ginny finally came out to stand beside her. "What's wrong, Annie?"

"You're always asking me that question." Her tone sounded harsh. She hadn't meant to rail out to Ginny. "I'm just having trouble sleeping."

Ginny pulled her blanket closer, drawing her shoulders

up to keep her neck warm. "Papa always said trouble was what happened when we told lies."

Leveling a sharp gaze at the woman who seemed to be gaining stamina at the same proportion she herself was losing it, Annie tried to reassure her friend. "Trouble? We have our supplies. Red is doing fine. And Laramie needs a doctor. What trouble?"

"Well, for starters, there's Dan Miller. Stop pretending that you don't care about him. He's a patient man, but he won't wait around for a woman who constantly puts him second."

"Second? Setting Red's leg is the first real doctoring I've done since I left New York. I've let Dan Miller . . . I mean, he's interfered in my life every day. Besides, he can't be interested in me, Ginny."

"Dan likes you a lot, Annie. I'm not sure even he knows how much. Both of you pretend you're not interested, then you end up together every time something happens. You've got him tied in knots and shooting steam. And you're—well, you're out here in all this cold and you aren't even shivering."

"That is the most ridiculous thing I've ever heard. I'm the last woman a man like Dan would want."

"Why would you say that?"

"I'm hard-headed. I'm not a bit frail and I already have a future carved out that doesn't include a man. I thought I had considered every possible problem."

"And nothing is like you thought it would be, is it?"

"No, it isn't."

"But you've found people who need a doctor, and I haven't heard a one of them say you shouldn't be treating Red because you're a woman. I'm ready to tell them that even though I'm having a baby, I'm not married. Why are you so worried they won't accept you?"

Annie turned away from Ginny. She leaned her head against the post by the opening at the top of the steps. "You're right. And you need to tell Red the truth. But you might want to wait a day or so. He's liable to be so happy that he'll break the other leg dancing."

"I hope so. Because I'm going to marry him. Now, what about your search for a husband. Seems to me you've got a good one, right here."

Annie turned away from the blur of white along the tracks. "I don't know. I never thought things would work out like they have. Everything has turned into such a muddle."

"Doesn't have to be a muddle."

"So, let's just say Dan might appear to be interested in me. Ginny, I know about a man's needs. Back in New York he probably wouldn't even notice me, but out here, he's just a man—alone."

"You met Dan in New York. He noticed you. Didn't he? When you came home from that ball you were turned inside out, and you still aren't over it."

"Well, yes. But I was wearing a mask. He didn't know who I was."

Ginny pursed her lips. "So, he didn't know, but he was interested and he still is. And he has plenty of other women on this train to choose from if he just wants to satisfy a man's needs."

That caught Annie by surprise. "Other women?"

"You're wearing blinders. No, that's wrong. You've wrapped yourself up in such a heavy blanket of responsibility you haven't even noticed the other passengers who got on the train since Omaha. They're people, not just patients. And a fair number of them are women."

Annie thought back to the throng of passengers she'd examined, the ones with cuts and bruises. Families, she'd thought, but she hadn't paid any attention to the number of women present.

"Don't worry, Annie, Dan's as blind to them as you were. Nope, he's yours for the asking."

"But I'm not asking. I can't. I won't. The last thing I'm interested in is a husband. Don't you understand? I'm a doctor and that's all I ever wanted to be and I'm not interested in a husband—or a . . . a lover."

"Uh-huh. And I'm going to be a virgin bride," Ginny said softly. "Where's it written that you can't love a man and be a doctor at the same time?"

"It doesn't have to be written, Ginny. I learned that lesson the hard way. Even my father knew. Men want nothing to do with professional women like me."

"You're wrong, Annie. I've decided it's all in how a woman handles a man. She's in charge from the beginning. I just didn't understand that before. You can have Dan if you want him. Would you take offense if I offered you a couple of suggestions?"

Annalise nearly swallowed her tongue. Six months ago, Ginny would never have said such a thing. There'd been a time when she was uncomfortable even calling her Annie. But somehow both things felt right, listening to Ginny and becoming Annie. Annalise Sinclair had been left behind somewhere between New York City and a mud hole in Boggy Gut. It was Annie who asked, "Suggestions for what?"

"Turning a lion into a pussycat."

"But I wouldn't want Dan to be a pussycat. I like him just the way he is. Besides, I don't want to be dishonest, ever again. It's too difficult."

Ginny shook her head. "Well, then, you're going to have to take the risk. If you want him, let him know."

"I don't know, Ginny. I just don't know. I've worked too hard for this to take a chance on letting anything get in my way."

"If you say so. But I'm thinking sometimes you ought to stop planning and just be. Better get some rest now. Tomorrow is just over that clump of rocks and we're both gonna need all our wits about us, and," she laughed, "maybe a couple of big sticks."

"Sticks?"

"To protect you. I'm thinking about all those men up

there, waiting to be examined by an unmarried woman doctor. What are you gonna charge for an office visit, Dr. Annie?"

At the Laramie station, Dan and his crew removed Red from the train by making a chair with their hands and carrying him down the steps to where the sheriff and the construction boss were waiting.

"I'm Will Spencer," the sheriff said. "Take your man into the depot until we can find a place for him. Anybody else hurt?"

Ginny stepped forward, acting as a spokesman for the group. "The rest of us were lucky, Sheriff. Red's broken leg was the only serious injury. Fortunately, we had a doctor on the train."

"Doctor?" The sheriff's attention focused on Ginny. "You've got a doctor on the train?"

Annie stepped forward. "Yes. Why?"

"Where is he? We really have need of him."

This time it was Dan who answered. "You're talking to the doctor, Sheriff. This is Dr. Annie . . . what is your name, Annie?"

The moment of truth had come. "I'm Dr. Annalise Sinclair," she said.

She cut her gaze to Dan and waited for him to say something. But his reaction was puzzled silence.

"You're the doctor?" The sheriff let out a sigh of dismay.

"I'm the doctor. What's the trouble, Sheriff?"

"I'm sitting on a powder keg here. Got a Sioux Indian with a bullet in his leg. But there's no way I'd ask a woman to get involved in that."

"Don't ask a woman," Annie said. "Ask a doctor. Where is he?"

"No. I won't do that to you."

"Why not?"

"He could die, and so would you." With that, Sheriff Spencer turned and walked toward the engineer. "Tell me what happened."

"Wait!" Annie called out. "I can help him."

The sheriff didn't stop.

"He's just trying to protect you, Annie," Dan said.

"I don't need protecting," she snapped. "I need patients. I need to practice medicine." It was happening all over again, the rejection. For the first time since Steven's death, she felt tears collecting in her eyes.

But it was Josie who stopped her, jerking her back to reality. "You ain't giving up, are you, Dr. Annie?"

Annie looked around, taking in the curious glances of all the people standing around, and the militancy of the members of her little gypsy band. Anyone who made any move to criticize her would be dealt with by Ginny and Josie. But not Dan. Dan had just come to the defense of the sheriff.

"No, I'm not giving up, Josie. Let's get unloaded and find us an empty building. We're going into the doctoring business right here in Laramie—if we have to doctor each other. About that examination fee, Ginny, it's going to be high. Now let's check on Red."

Dan followed her inside the depot and caught her arm. "Annie?"

"Yes?"

"I'm sorry."

"Sorry? For what?"

He started to answer, then shook his head. "It'll wait. I have to send a telegram. Then I'll help you look for a building."

A telegram? He didn't intend to waste any time contacting her father. "Thank you, but I'll do this alone. And you don't need to send a telegram. I'll tell my father where I am."

His look of confusion seemed genuine. "Your father? I

don't understand." Then knowledge washed across his face. "Sinclair. Annalise Sinclair. It's Roylston Sinclair you're running from?"

"Don't try to pretend you didn't know."

Dan's hand left her shoulder and moved up to cup her cheek. "Ah, Annie. I'm sure the bridge collapse is front page news. I was only going to let my family know that I'm safe. I don't know what your father did to make you leave New York, but if you want to remain lost, I'll respect your wishes."

That stopped her. She couldn't let him believe her father was some kind of monster. "My father didn't do anything—except ask me to give up medicine and choose a husband for my own good. When that didn't work, he tried to make me think he was in some kind of financial trouble that would suddenly be solved if I married a wealthy man. But I know him too well. That was just an excuse."

Dan's mouth fell open. Then he began to laugh. "You were asked to choose a husband to save your father's business?"

"Yes. That's what he said. The truth is, he knows how the public feels about women doctors, and he didn't want me shunned. That's why I came out here. To find people who need my special skills, people who don't care if I'm a woman."

"Oh, Annie." He put his hand on her shoulder. "You are some woman!"

She moved away. "No, Dan. I'm some doctor. And I only have eleven months to prove it."

"Thank God," Ginny said, "the whole truth is finally out. Though I was kinda getting used to being a lady. It's going to be hard to go back to being your maid."

"Ginny, you aren't my maid," Annie said. "From now on, I'm a doctor and you're a lady."

Ginny looked straight at Red. "An *unmarried* lady," she said.

"Unmarried?" The Irishman repeated, with a big grin spreading across his face.

"Unmarried," Ginny repeated. "I'm ashamed to say I was never married to Robert. Wilson is my name, Red. I'm not married."

"Hallelujah!" Red said jubilantly. "There's no husband. Hallelujah!" Then he looked down at his leg and frowned. "I mean, I'm certain a lady like you won't be unmarried for long."

He didn't see the disappointed look on Ginny's face. Annie knew what he was thinking. With a broken leg he might not be able to care for a wife and child. She didn't think Ginny would mind, but for now, that decision would have to wait. "I'll leave the supplies in your hands, Ginny," she said over her shoulder. "I have a telegram to send. Then I need to find a place for us to stay. After that, there's a patient who needs a doctor."

"I'll go with you, Annie," Dan said.

"Dan, I told you—"

"I know. You can do it yourself. Go ahead. I just thought that since we both have to send telegrams and find sleeping quarters, we could save time and do it together."

Annie finally nodded. She was tired of Dan's interference, but she was more tired of arguing. Here was where she'd open her office—somewhere. That thought buoyed her. At least it did until she'd finished sending her telegram, and stepped outside to take a good look at the town.

Rough boarded storefronts had been hastily nailed onto boxed framed huts, with cracks so wide that rodents could and probably did climb in to escape the bitter cold. Even the rats would have to take up mountain climbing to scale the drifts that swept up halfway to the roofs.

It didn't take long to determine that space was at a premium. Once the Union Pacific's chief officer, Dr. Durant, had decided to move the railroad roundhouse from Cheyenne to Laramie, he'd sent in surveyors to lay out the town. Every businessman they questioned told the same story. Overnight, the lots, owned by a dummy land company everyone suspected of belonging to Durant, had been snapped up at high prices. And the hell-on-wheels storekeepers moved in.

Raucous music and laughter spilled out into the frozen street. Workers, much the worse from a night of drinking, staggered from the saloons back to their makeshift tents.

"Look, there's a bank," Annie said, stamping the snow from her feet. "I'm going to ask in there. A banker ought to know about available space."

Dan agreed, opening the door to see a potbellied stove that was trying to supply heat with little success. "Warm yourself," he directed. "Let me inquire."

"Inquire about what?" a man wearing a sheepskin-lined jacket and gloves stepped into the small iron-fenced cage. "Do you wish to make a deposit?"

"Not just yet," Dan answered. "We're looking for space to rent."

"For what purpose, sir?"

"For a doctor's office, with living quarters attached."

The banker's response was a laugh. "Sorry, the only quarters in town with any occupancy available is the jail. But we're sure glad to have a doctor here," he said, holding out his hand to Dan. "Welcome."

Annie couldn't hold back a scathing comment. "From the looks of the drunken men I saw, the jail ought to be full. And by the way, I'm the doctor, not him."

"But you're a woman!" the banker said in astonishment.

"I certainly am. I'm Dr. Annie Sinclair. The gentleman is Dan Miller." She held out her hand. "And you are?"

"Dawson Harper at your service ma'am." He shook her hand, then quickly let it go.

"Fine. The service you can perform is finding me an office. There must be something other than the jail."

"Actually, the jail isn't empty. Normally it would be full of miners and workers, except for that Indian."

Annie held her hands over the stove and rubbed them

together. "Sheriff Spencer has an Indian in his jail? What did he do?"

"Attacked the workers laying track."

That got Dan's attention. "What happened?"

"Not much. His little band of Sioux are pretty pitiful. Black Hawk got shot. Pete Ross—he's the construction boss—brought him here. Foolish thing to do. Soon as that Indian dies, the rest of the Sioux will come after us."

"Why'd they attack the work site?" Dan asked.

" 'Cause they're scared. They've been sick. Most of the buffalo are gone, and they're about to be moved to a reservation."

"Sick? What's wrong with them?" Annie asked.

"Don't know. The sheriff won't let them come in here. Don't want to catch whatever they've got."

"Where's the jail?" Annie asked.

Dan was ahead of her. "I saw it. It's across the street. But I'm not sure this is a good idea, Annie. An injured Indian isn't the kind of patient you should be treating."

Annie's face grew grim. "I'm a doctor, Dan Miller. I treat the sick—whoever they are."

15

—❧—

Red had been moved to one corner of the jail, where he seemed more troubled than Annie would have expected. He continually apologized to Dan for what he'd done, as if he'd broken his leg on purpose. Ginny, hovering anxiously over him, was forced to keep him calm with laudanum. Josie was leaning against the bars, eyes wide, studying the Indian lying on the floor inside the cell.

"Unlock the door, Sheriff," Annie said.

"No, ma'am. I don't think that's a good idea. Black Hawk may just be playing possum."

"Open the door, Sheriff," Dan said. "You might as well, or she'll get an ax and chop her way in from the outside."

The sheriff shook his head, took the keys from the wall, and opened the cell. Annie pushed past him and knelt beside Black Hawk, touching his forehead with her hand. He was burning with fever.

"When was he shot, Sheriff?"

"Three days ago. Bullet's still there. Couldn't find anybody who'd dig it out."

"I will. Help me get him onto that bunk in there. Then bring the lamp closer. Ginny, you boil some water on that puny stove. Dan, go get my medical supplies."

"Yes, ma'am," the two men replied. Dan left the jail, and the sheriff took the wounded man's shoulders while Annie lifted his feet. The Indian groaned and said something Annie couldn't understand.

"What else do you need?" Sheriff Spencer asked.

"Nothing, until Dan—Mr. Miller—gets back with my equipment."

"I'll go help Dan," Josie volunteered.

"Josie!" Annie said in a voice that brooked no argument. "You're not going anywhere. Just sit down over there by Red and be quiet!"

By the time she'd removed the animal skin trousers the Indian was wearing and examined the wound, Dan had returned.

"Open the crate, please."

"Annie," he said warily, "are you sure you don't want to send for that doctor back in Cheyenne—just to give you a hand?"

She looked up at Dan, lips clenched tight; otherwise, she'd have spit in his face. Just when she thought he was beginning to understand, he turned into her father and questioned her competence. "You think I can't do this?"

"No. Of course not. I just don't want you hurt if something doesn't go right." His voice trailed off in the wake of the fury he was clearly reading on her face.

"I think you'd better go, Dan, before I use this scalpel to do something very painful to your body."

She turned away, her eyes watering so badly that she had to wait for a moment to clear them. "Will you remove the top of the crate, Sheriff?"

Will looked helplessly from Annie to Dan, then used a piece of metal standing in the corner to pry the box open. Annie reached inside and pulled out a packet. "Ginny, add some of this chemical to purify the water."

"Annie, I'm sorry," Dan said. "I never meant that I didn't think you were capable. I just—"

"I know what you meant, Dan. I'm a woman. If I were a man you wouldn't have questioned me. Please go. I don't need any distractions now."

"You're wrong," he said, "but I'll go—for now." He turned and left the jail. Two hours later, Annie had removed the bullet and filled the hole with healing powders and herbs. Once she was finished, she stood, weary beyond belief.

"Sheriff," she said, "since this is apparently the only available space in town, we're placing ourselves under temporary arrest."

"Sleeping in a jail ain't gonna be too bad," Josie said. "At least this time I'm on the outside of the bars."

Annalise lifted a tired eyebrow. "Why don't you find some food for our group, Josie? Some food we can *buy*." She glanced over at Red, sleeping with his head in Ginny's lap. The next few days would prove to Annalise whether or not she had the skill needed to heal the sick. So far a broken leg and a gunshot wound were her testing grounds. If Black Hawk died, she could be finished before she'd even started.

Black Hawk began to stir. Quickly she went back to her spot by his bed. "Try to be still," she said, knowing that he probably didn't understand her words. "I'll mix something for the fever."

"Medicine woman?" he asked.

"Yes, I'm a medicine woman."

"Great Spirit send." He swallowed the bitter liquid she'd prepared, then drifted back into his state of unconsciousness.

"You'd better hope the spirit is a friendly one," the sheriff said. "Miller was right. This man is the chief. If he dies, it'll take every spirit you ever knew to hold on to all that hair. I wouldn't like to see you without it."

"Neither would I," she admitted, drawing closer the

shawl someone had draped over her shoulders. The jail was a better shelter than her last hospital, but the wind still whistled through the cracks between the logs. For now, she needed rest. "Watch him, Sheriff. I'm going to take a quick nap."

First she checked on Red. His skin was cool to the touch. No fever.

"Annie, me girl, thank you," he said softly. "For so much more than just my leg."

"Thank you, Red. You're my first patient out here. Of course, you didn't have much choice in letting a woman treat your injury."

"If I'd had a choice, I wouldn't have objected," he said. "Where's Dan?"

"I don't know," was her crisp reply.

"He didn't intend to question your ability, Annie. He was just looking after you."

Annie shrugged her shoulders and rolled her head backward trying to stretch her tensed muscles. "Sooner or later he's going to understand that I can look after myself. He has a job to do, and so do I. He wouldn't argue with that if I weren't a woman."

"Maybe not. But I'm worried." Red looked very uncomfortable. "Those supplies he lost took all the money he had. Now that they're gone, I don't know what he'll do."

"His father is a very wealthy man. I'm certain two boxcars filled with railroad supplies won't be hard to replace."

Red shook his head. "Then why was he hiring his crew on shares? No, I don't think he has any more money."

That surprised Annalise. In spite of his overbearing attitude, she refused to believe that Dan Miller would take advantage of a man like Red by pretending to be broke when his father owned half of Wall Street. It didn't make sense. "That's hard to believe."

"I probably shouldn't say this, Doc, but he told me his mother's home and her well-being depended on the railroad spur. But I think it's even more than that. Dan is a man who walks his own way, and wherever he's going, he needs to prove he can get there by going it alone."

That sounded familiar to her. She understood that feeling all too well. But why would his mother's well-being depend on a spur line from cattle country to the Union Pacific Railroad?

Annie found a spot near the door and sat down, covering herself with a blanket. She knew that whatever Dan was doing was honorable and that he'd get it done. She'd stake her life on it. Why wouldn't he extend her the same courtesy?

Later, when Dan opened the door, he found Annie—no, not just Annie—Dr. Annalise Sinclair sound asleep. She was covered with a blanket, her head wrapped in a shawl, exposing only her eyes. She looked so vulnerable. For a long time he stared at her, disturbed by something that he couldn't quite identify. He still couldn't believe that her father and his father were partners. Why had he and Annie never met? One thing was clear; his mother couldn't have tea with Annalise if she'd wanted to. And it was also clear that Annalise Sinclair had another plan for her future that didn't include a husband.

As he watched, her dark eyes flew open, anxious with the kind of fear that paralyzes you, holding you in some dark area of the unknown. Slowly she sat up, sliding away from him, holding up her hand to ward off whatever emotion fed her surprise.

Dan's gaze met hers. Met hers and stayed.

He'd seen that kind of startled response before.

Where?

Annalise came slowly to her feet. "Is something wrong?"

"No. I hear you got the bullet out. How's Black Hawk doing?"

She moved over to the bunk and checked her patient. "He's alive, that's all I can say." She glanced around. Everyone was asleep, even the sheriff who'd been charged with watching Black Hawk.

"Will he make it?"

"He's very weak, but I think so," Annalise said, feeling suddenly awkward with Dan.

The sheriff jerked his head up and looked around. "Sorry, I must have dozed off." He studied Annie and Dan. "Not used to so much heat in here. Everything all right?"

"Seems to be," Dan said. "I wonder if you'd watch the patient a bit longer?" When the lawman nodded, Dan brought his attention back to Annie. "I'd like to speak with you, Dr. Sinclair. Outside, if I may."

Annalise let out a deep breath. She'd known this conversation was coming. "All right, Dan." She draped the blanket around her shoulders.

Dan opened the door and she followed him into the night. The sheriff must have been joking. The jail had been cold, but nothing prepared her for the blast of ice that swept down the street. She was almost blown off the crude sidewalk.

Dan grabbed her and held on. "I'm sorry. Maybe this isn't such a good idea. Come, let's find a place out of the wind."

Moments later they were standing inside a barn, or what was being used for one. Cows were lined up on one side of the long building, and horses on the other. The pungent smell of the animals permeated the air but their presence took the edge off the cold. Dan led her to the back corner where hay was stored.

Annalise pulled her blanket tight and leaned against the post on which the first stall door was mounted. "What did you want to talk to me about?"

"First, I apologize for trying to make decisions for you. But I don't apologize for trying to protect you. I'd hope that if I had a sister as headstrong as you, someone would be in her corner. Now that I know you're Rolyston Sinclair's daughter, I can understand why you felt you were being maneuvered. I've had the same kind of experience."

Annie leaned her head back, looking up at him in the darkness. Somehow the anonymity made it easier. "I'll bet nobody told you that you had to stop being a diplomat and choose a wife to save your father's business."

"You'd lose."

She heard what he said but it still took a few moments for it to register. "I don't believe you. Your father didn't demand that you choose a wife with money?"

"He did. Called me home from Europe for that very reason."

Annie was stunned. "Then why are you out here building a railroad?"

"Why are you out here setting up a medical clinic?"

This time they both laughed.

Annie finally caught her breath. "Even if I'd believed my father, which I don't, where in the world would I find a man who'd marry me and not ask me to give up medicine?"

"In a hospital, maybe."

Annie shook her head in confusion.

"I mean a sick patient."

"The only sick patient I know is Black Hawk, and I don't think marrying him would do my father any good."

Dan's "Humm" sounded serious. "Actually, not that it would ever happen, but marrying Black Hawk could do your father a lot of good."

"Why do I think I'm about to hear a Roylston Sinclair sound-alike message? What do you know about the Indians?"

"I've learned a good bit, asking around. The Sioux are a major obstacle to the Cold Springs Spur."

"And why do I care about the Cold Springs Spur?" she asked.

"Nothing, but you care about the Sioux or you will, once you find out they need you."

"Good. They need a doctor. I need patients. The Indians are people, just like anybody else."

"That's what I thought you'd say. They're not just like

everyone else out here. They're the enemy. You see, Black Hawk's tribe is small, but his Sioux have given the railroad plenty of grief and it could get worse. It didn't have to be that way, but there have been so many broken promises between the government and the Indians that it would take only a little disagreement to set off a war."

Annalise shivered, stamping her feet to keep them warm. "Politics don't interest me, Dan. Healing does. I think you're making too much of this."

Dan groaned. "Annie, please try to understand. Just like you, I'm only trying to help. I've had some success in diplomacy."

"Right now the only men I'm interested in are the rest of Black Hawk's warriors," she said. "He can't have been the only one hurt."

Dan took her hands in his, felt her resistance, but didn't let go until she stopped pulling away. "No, he wasn't the only one, but he was the only one the soldiers brought in. I think the sheriff is caught between his conscience and his duty. Saving the chief means the tribe still has a leader. The citizens of Laramie think it might have been better if he'd died."

"It's never better to die. I thought the West was a place where a person could be free. I'm beginning to wonder if the people out here are any better than the ones I left behind."

"There are desperate people everywhere. Black Hawk's attack was a last-ditch attempt to survive."

"Why would he attack the workers?"

"Durant brought in an excursion train with a car filled with investors who wanted to kill buffalo for sport. According to what I'm told, they slaughtered the animals. Just cut off their heads as trophies and left the rest."

Annie shivered again, but not from the cold this time. She was picturing the animals, the blood in the snow, the destruction. Then she turned practical. "Couldn't the Indians have eaten them?"

"They did. But so many of the creatures were killed that the Sioux feared for the survival of their food supply. Black Hawk finally sent a peace party to the car to plead with the men to stop."

Annalise understood the chief's desperation. "And the peace party? Were they hurt?"

"No, they were invited into the car, offered food and liquor. They forgot their mission as they became entertainment for the passengers."

"How awful for Black Hawk's men."

"That wasn't the worst thing. A passenger on the train had some kind of fever. Nothing serious for him, but the Indians took the sickness back to the tribe. Eventually, Black Hawk's daughter and two of his grandchildren died."

"Influenza. I've heard about the Indians dying from our diseases." She waited for Dan to continue the story.

"He attacked the next train of imbeciles who wanted to shoot buffalo. That's when he was wounded."

"I don't blame him," she said. "First we take their land, then we kill them with our diseases. I'd never condone murder, but there are times . . ."

"So you may have saved him for now. But I'm not sure what that's going to mean. I've got to build a railroad straight through their winter camping grounds. Will the tribe be grateful for what you did and leave us alone? Or will they remember what other railroad people have done to them?"

"I can understand your concern," Annalise said thoughtfully. "But I don't know what I can do to help."

"Well," Dan teased, "if you won't take Black Hawk as a husband, I'm going to try and reach the Bureau of Indian Affairs. Perhaps there is a way we can work out our differences peacefully. Until then, Annie, stay out of the Indians' problems."

Annie shook her head. "I'm not marrying Black Hawk or anyone else, Dan, and if someone asks for my help, I

have to give it. I swore an oath. No one seems to understand that."

"That's what I thought, so I've done some more inquiring. When the citizens of Laramie learned that you intended to stay, they saw the wisdom of giving you a chance."

"You did what?" Annie was outraged, and embarrassed
at her own reaction. "I'm sorry, Dan. I know I sound un-
grateful. I do appreciate what you did. I just wanted to—
never mind. Go on."

"I know it seems like I'm always interfering," he fumbled
for a way to explain without angering her even more. "But
if you start a war, my project could fail. The best way for
me to be sure there is no problem is for us to be on the
same team. Your office will be a big asset to the towns-
people and my workers."

"Are you telling me that you actually found *office
space*?"

"Well, it's not ready for patients yet. It's an old trading
post out at the edge of town. It has one large room with a
fireplace and a storage room downstairs. It's pretty run-
down but with a little work you can make do, and the good
part is, there are two sleeping rooms upstairs. Don't guess
you can put Red up there. You have to climb a ladder to
reach them."

Annalise was stunned. She was also very ashamed. Dan
Miller had done nothing but try to help her, and she'd re-
buffed him at every opportunity. That hadn't stopped him.
Why? She looked down, glad that he couldn't see her in
the dark. She brushed her wrinkled gown, stained now by
days of wear and the emergency situation they'd just gone
through. As a woman, she was a mess.

Pushing her hair out of her eyes, she forced herself to
look at Dan, his strong features becoming more distinct in
the shadows. "Thank you. May I see the building?"

"You may, but not until morning. There's no light and
we have no lanterns. You'll just have to trust me."

She didn't waver when she answered. "I do."

A long pregnant silence stretched between them. "Annie—Annalise—I guess I should call you Dr. Sinclair. I need to say something else."

Finally, the other shoe. She'd been waiting for it to drop. "It's all right, Dan. I forgive you. I told my father that you were responsible for me contacting him. I'm certain he'll find a way to offer you a reward. You can use it to replace your lost supplies."

"Replace my supplies?" There was confusion in his voice as he tried to make sense of what she was saying. "Listen, Annie. I don't think you understand. Your father and mine are partners in building the spur. Unless you know something I don't, Roylston Sinclair doesn't have any more money than Teddy Miller. They're both scraping the bottom of the money barrel. Though I'm not sure the other knows it."

She stared at Dan. "I don't know what to say. To think that one of the men my father picked out as a suitor was you."

"And my mother is supposed to be having tea with you, just to make certain you're a good candidate for me."

"Tea? Your mother is planning to have tea with me?" She looked down at her travel-worn clothing and laughed. "Somehow I don't think I'd pass inspection."

"I think you're wrong. I think she'd like you," Dan said, threading Annie's arms inside his jacket and pulling her close. "She'd like you fine."

"Dan, stop it. What are you doing?"

"I'm just trying to keep those surgeon's hands warm. You never know when I might need help. Black Hawk's tribe might not be as friendly as I'd like."

"Oh, I think they'll be friendly. Who knows, you might even find a Sioux wife. That ought to make your job easier," she said in a teasing tone.

"That's a problem I don't need. I'm beginning to think

that somebody other than Black Hawk doesn't want me to succeed."

"What do you mean?"

"I didn't think too much about it at the time, but my father telegraphed me in Chicago that somebody was asking odd questions about the Cold Springs Spur. There was the mysterious jam that held up my logs. Then the bridge gave way."

Annie gasped. "You don't think that was deliberate, do you?"

"One of the passengers thought he heard an explosion before the track fell. Until the sheriff can get down there in the daylight, we can't be sure."

Explosion. She'd heard something. Could Dan be right?

"What are you going to do?"

"I'll be heading out at first light. I want you to be careful."

"You're leaving Laramie?" She couldn't mask the alarm in her voice. Her voice spooked one of the horses, who let out a neigh of anxiety. She lowered her voice. "I mean, why? Where are you going?"

Dan's voice dropped even lower. "While I'm waiting for more supplies, I'm going to scout the site for the spur. I want to see the area myself. Somehow, I have to find a way to deal with the Sioux."

"You can't go out there, Dan. It isn't safe."

"Do I detect a little concern for me, Annie?" He caught her chin with his fingertips and tilted her face up to his. "Don't tell me you're worried."

She winced. "Of course I'm worried. What kind of experience do you have with Indians?"

"None, but I do know how to deal with men. That's what I was trained to do."

"But the people you dealt with during the war were civilized men. What if you're scalped? I don't know anything about treating that kind of injury."

He moved closer. "Could it be that you'll miss me? Tell me you'll miss me."

"I'm going to miss you," she admitted. "Who else is going to try to boss me around?"

"Nobody. I've put out the word that anybody who messes with my woman messes with me."

For days they'd hovered on the edge of this moment, this wanting. Now it had come. "But I'm not your woman—" she began.

He cut her off. "Oh, yes, you are. We crossed a country to escape from each other and here we are. Stop fighting it, Annie. I have." He put his arm around her and pulled her close. She tried not to let herself respond. The consequences were too dear. This time there was no medication, no wine on which to blame her behavior. She needed to know the things Dan was telling her. And she was grateful for his help in finding her a place for her clinic. That was true, but the possibility that she might never see Daniel Miller again scared her.

"Oh, Dan, be careful."

"That's better." He let his hands slide down her back and under her shawl until they rested in the hollow of her spine.

"Why, Dan? Why are you doing this? One of those other women on the train would be better for you."

"Ah, Annie, darling. Society might think so. But none of them fire my blood like you do. You don't have to feel the same way yet, but we'll work on that. Kiss me goodbye, Annie, for luck."

"No! I mean I don't believe in any of that nonsense." She felt a little giddy and tried to back away, but his hands refused to allow that, pulling her even closer. Annie moaned.

"Neither do I," he said, and kissed her anyway. She should have stopped him but she could only stand there, pressing herself against him. She wasn't cold anymore; her skin felt hot all over, like a patient with a fever. She'd tried to forget, to close out the feelings he'd awakened in her during that night they spent together. But her body refused to cooperate.

Even in the icy air she was warm, with the kind of heat that was more than just having his mouth on hers asking, demanding. There was a joy inside her that bubbled, and she wanted to cry out with the sheer wanting of something that she couldn't forget.

She wanted to dance again with Daniel. She wanted to lift her arms and fly out into the night. She wanted to laugh. Just once more, Annalise Sinclair wanted to be a woman.

All of the boundaries, the tall fences of reserve she'd resurrected, the rules and laws that were supposed to hold her in check, melted away and her hands left his shoulders and slid around his neck. She opened her lips. Was she still moaning? Or was it Dan? Did she draw him down into the straw, or did they both collapse because neither could stand?

Her bodice was open now, her body exposed to masculine lips that wandered hungrily down her body. He was touching her everywhere, marking every single inch of her. Unable to remain still, she slid her fingertips inside his shirt, feeling the familiar texture of his skin, drawing in the pure male scent of him.

Was this what her professors had called the life force? If so, now that she'd felt it, she couldn't understand how anyone lived without it.

"God, Annie!" Dan said, drawing back, breathing heavily in his attempt to find control. "I didn't mean to make love to you right here. I only wanted to talk, to explain."

"Explain this? I don't think you can." She caught his face and held it, taking on the role of aggressor as she kissed him as hungrily as he'd kissed her.

Dan didn't know where her kisses would have taken

them, for he'd lost all sense of time and place. But, somewhere between the unfastening of Annie's gown and his own trousers, he heard a voice, distant but insistent.

"Annie! Dan! Where are you?"

The voice became more frantic, so much so that Dan finally reined in his passion and pulled back. "Annie . . ."

"Hush, Dan."

"No, Annie, listen."

She grew still. "It's Josie. Something's wrong."

Seconds later she'd wriggled free, repaired her clothing, and was racing out into the night. "I'm here, Josie." Burning with embarrassment, she stopped and turned back. "Dan?"

"I'm right behind you. What's wrong, Josie?"

The child came barreling out of the darkness, crashing directly into Annie. "Indians. Lots of Indians. They're at the jail."

"The sheriff?" Dan asked.

"He's there, too. Said for me to slip out and find you."

"Let's go," Annie said, grabbing Josie's hand and heading for the jail. "Maybe someone else is sick."

Dan watched her run. Just like that, what they'd shared was forgotten. Annie the woman turned into Dr. Annie, and if he was going to keep up with her, he'd better button his shirt and move.

A dozen Indians, wrapped in bearskins and blankets, sat immobile on horseback along the front of the building. Their weapons were not a threat, but Dan knew the situation could change in a second if one of the railroad workers lining the walls moved.

"Let me go first, Annie," he said. "I may be able to reason with them."

"Don't be silly. The two of us are no match if they mean to harm us." She nodded at the Indians in passing, marching into the jail as if she were in charge.

"Thank goodness," Ginny said, valiantly trying to hold back her tears. "They want you, Annie."

Dan forced himself in front of her. "Why are you here?" he asked quietly, addressing the tall man standing beside Black Hawk. "Why are you disturbing your chief?"

"Chief lives. Chief say Medicine Woman made him well."

"Yes. Dr. Sinclair removed the bullet and saved Black Hawk's life, but," he added, trying to direct any future failure away from Annie, "but now his life is in the hands of the Great Spirit." Dan took stock of the situation. The sheriff was wearing his gun, but he hadn't pulled it. The Indian was armed with a knife but he didn't appear to be threatening anyone. What was happening here?

"This is good. Where is Medicine Woman?"

Annie stepped in front of Dan and stood face to face with the Indian. "I'm Dr. Sinclair," she said, holding out her hand.

He studied her with a stern face, then began to smile. "You Medicine Woman?"

"I'm Medicine Woman." She continued to hold out her hand.

He stared down at her hand as if he was uncertain what was expected. Then, smiling more freely, extended his own and shook hers seriously. "I am Bear Claw, son of Black Hawk. He wishes to repay you for your help."

"Oh, no. That isn't necessary."

"Annie," Ginny started, "you're a doctor. Doctors get paid. We need living quarters, remember?"

"Black Hawk's life is payment enough," she repeated.

The tall Indian nodded. "Our people are in your debt. When you have need of payment, you ask. It will be given."

"Thank you, Bear Claw," she said. She stopped and thought a moment, then added, "Perhaps there is one thing you can do. Protect Mr. Miller." She nodded at Dan.

Bear Claw eyed him curiously and nodded.

"And when I get my office open, I will be pleased to treat anyone who needs my help," Annie said.

"Inviting the Indians into town isn't wise," the sheriff commented quietly.

"We'll discuss this later," Dan intervened. "Annie doesn't yet understand the potential problems their coming here would cause."

Annalise turned toward Dan, the moment of their passion still racing beneath her skin.

"I thought I made it clear, Dan. I'm a doctor and I made an oath to treat the sick. There was nothing in that oath that mentioned the color of their skins or their nationality."

Annalise straightened her shoulders and turned back to Black Hawk, laying her hand on his forehead. Cool. His eyes were open. He'd heard the exchange, but she couldn't be certain how much he understood.

"Black Hawk man of honor. Your man will be safe."

Annalise wanted to correct the chief, but she only nodded. "Thank you." She reached into her bag and pulled out a packet of powders. "Take these and apply them to your wound every day. I'd like to see you again in two weeks."

"Two weeks?" Bear Claw questioned.

"Fourteen suns," the sheriff said, holding up seven fingers twice.

Bear Claw nodded. "We go now. Be well, Medicine Woman."

16

—❦—

"That was close." The sheriff walked over to look out the window, eagerly watching as the chief was placed on a travois pulled behind a huge black horse. Bear Claw mounted the horse and the other Indians fell in beside, as the group moved down the frozen road toward the distant mountains.

"What do you mean, close?" Ginny asked. "Annie's a good doctor."

Will looked sheepish. "I wasn't referring to her skills. I didn't expect them to be so agreeable about leaving *her* behind."

Annalise opened the door and stepped into the street. "I'm a doctor. They know where I am if I'm needed."

Dan followed. "That's what we're worried about."

"Dr. Sinclair, please take this seriously. Women like you are scarce, and men will do almost anything to stake their claim on you. I don't even want to think about what these Indians could do to you."

"But I'm a medicine woman, they said."

"And tomorrow Black Hawk could decide that a medicine woman would make a good wife for the chief, or worse—a slave. Keeping order around here is a big enough job; now I have to worry about a possible Sioux attack on Laramie."

Dan nodded. "That worries me too, Spencer. I'm riding out this morning to look over the site for the railroad spur. I want to see the problem with the site first hand. Maybe I can talk with Black Hawk about the Indians' troubles."

"Maybe, but with a bullet hole in his leg, I doubt he'll be much interested in listening. There's been too much talk that went nowhere."

"Still, it wouldn't hurt to try. While I'm gone, I hope you'll keep an eye on Annie and the others. I've given the banker a deposit on the old trading post out by the river. Will you go out there with her?"

Annie's voice returned with a vengeance. "*You* paid the deposit?"

"Yes, Annie, I did. It was only a small deposit, and the only reason Harper took it was to make it legal for Spencer to evict the workers who'd taken it over."

"I thought I made it clear. I'll pay my own way."

Dan let out a deep sigh. "Fine. I just thought Red would be more comfortable in a building with a fireplace. And unless you've played poker with someone else, the way I figure it, the money you'd use was probably mine to start with."

Dan turned and stepped off the sidewalk into the street. The last she saw of him was his back disappearing into the livery stable. He hadn't even said good-bye.

"Is it safe for him to ride out?" she asked.

Will Spencer shook his head. "If you'd asked me last night, I'd have said no. But you asked Black Hawk to watch after him. That was a smart move on your part. The Indian's word is good."

By the next day, Josie had picked the lock so that Annalise could see their new quarters. Annie enthusiastically approved of the post, and agreed to move Red, Ginny, and Josie in immediately. The sheriff evacuated the men who'd been living there and arranged for Laramie's new doctor to have credit at the general store.

"About that lock, Josie," Ginny said, "how'd you learn to open it?"

Josie pursed her lips. "I don't think you want to know, Ginny. Let's just say I done a lot of things before—before you and Annie."

"We all did," Ginny admitted.

"All right, let's get busy," Annie interrupted, pretending she hadn't heard the conversation. "Make a list of everything we must have, Ginny. *Must,* not want. We'll have to make do until we find some paying customers. Then we'll get started on making this place livable."

"Can we have some biscuits?" Josie asked. "I'll trade my fancy dress for some flour."

"You will not," Ginny said. "You'll be wearing it to church on Sunday and to school as well."

"I ain't seen no church. I ain't seen no school, either," Josie said, her mouth forming into a wide grin.

The railroad crew moved the two cars left on the trestle into Laramie. The investors who'd occupied the Casement Pullman had been forced to stay in one of the cars being used by the local railroad supervisor. Now they had their quarters back, but they were stuck in Laramie until the bridge was repaired.

Annalise and Ginny spent their time settling into their new home, with Red supervising the work of her growing band of volunteers. They'd thawed out frozen earth, mixed it with straw from their packing crates, and poked it into the cracks between the logs. Annie spent money she shouldn't have buying whitewash for the walls. Practicing medicine in a place that was dark and dirty-looking was more than she could accept. Now she and one of Dan's men were brushing the whitewash on the walls of the storeroom she'd turned into her clinic.

She'd expected that Dan's absence would free her mind of him. It didn't. She worried about him. She dreamed about him—such erotic dreams that she'd wake trembling and breathless. None of her powders had a calming effect. She drained herself physically, hoping that she'd become so exhausted that she'd sleep.

She didn't.

The third day, when Sheriff Spencer turned up bringing coffee, Annie called for a break. "Thanks for coming by, Will, but you don't really need to check on us. We're fine. Honest."

"I know. But it's nice having someone to talk to who isn't mad at me about something."

"Who's mad at you?"

"Those two investors brought in by Casement, the chief of construction, are at the top of the list. Having too much money is as bad as having too little. They're paying the men to work around the clock to get the bridge repaired."

"Guess they must be in a hurry to leave," Ginny said.

"I think the one who donated his dressing gown to Red is, but I haven't seen the other one in a day or so."

"He's supposed to be under the weather."

Annalise looked up. "Tell him to come and see me."

"I already did," Will said sheepishly. "He . . . refused."

A knot clenched in the pit of Annalise's stomach.

"So, he's turning me down. Because I'm a woman, I suppose. Well, I'm not going to worry about him. If he gets sick enough he'll come, if he doesn't die first."

The doctor's uncharacteristic bitterness caught Will's attention. "You all right?" he asked.

"I think Annie's worried about Dan," Josie said quickly. "He shoulda been back by now, shouldn't he?"

Annalise started to shut off Josie's observation by telling her to practice her penmanship. Then she swallowed her orders. Josie wasn't saying anything Annalise hadn't thought. "How far is it to the place where Dan's going to build the spur, Will? Did he say?"

"Said he was looking over the land between here and Cold Springs. It's a day's ride there and a day back."

"But he's been gone three days," Annie whispered, making her way back toward the window.

"Maybe you ought to take some men and go look for him," Red said.

"All the available men are either working on repairing the bridge or searching for the missing man who went down with Dan's supplies. If Dan doesn't turn up by morning, I'll ride out myself."

It had started to snow heavily again. "There's a storm coming in," Annalise said softly. "He could get lost."

"Don't worry," Ginny said. "Dan's a man who can look after himself. He'll be back."

"He'd better. If he doesn't, I mean to give him a piece of my mind."

Josie giggled and picked up the lock she'd been playing with. "I don't think that's the part of you he's hankering for."

"Josie!" Annie snapped.

"I mean, I think a map would be more help."

At the base of the mountain, Dan Miller couldn't see two feet in front of his face. The only thing he could do was let the horse go and trust that he'd be able to find his way back to Laramie through the blinding snow.

The first day had been no problem. All he had to do was follow the tracks left by Black Hawk and his escorts. The snow had been deep, but soft enough so that his horse could move through it. He'd ridden into Black Hawk's camp as if he'd been invited. Bear Claw had received Dan cautiously, making him wait until he'd informed Black Hawk of the outsider's presence.

"Chief say come." Black Hawk escorted Dan to the chief's tent.

Inside, a fire burned, illuminating the darkness and providing a surprising amount of heat.

"Come closer, man of Medicine Woman."

Dan moved into the center of the tent.

"How are you, sir?"

"I am old and the Spirits test me. Why you come to our camp?"

What should he say? Dan had rehearsed his speech since he'd left Laramie. But until he'd entered the valley, he hadn't realized the enormity of his task. The Indian camp was exactly where the spur needed to be built.

"I will speak the truth," Dan said. "I hope you will hear me."

"Speak."

"I was sent here to build a railroad through this valley to Cold Springs."

"No!"

"The people I work for own this land, Black Hawk, and they have the support of the Army to move you to a reservation."

There was a long silence. "What does Medicine Woman's man say?"

"I believe that you and your people are here, and my people don't know what this valley means to your survival."

The chief nodded in agreement.

"So you will tell them."

"I will tell them, but . . . the truth is, they won't accept that. You will fight, but the soldiers from the fort will move you unless we can find another way."

"There is no other way. We will not fight you, Dan Miller, but we will kill those who come to take us away."

"And many will die."

The chief's answer was weak. "Yes, but we do not go," he insisted softly.

"Will you talk again if I can find a way?"

There was a long silence before the answer came.

"I will listen."

As if he had been summoned, Bear Claw appeared and led Dan to his horse. He handed Dan a skin from which the smell of food wafted, and a bearskin blanket that Dan draped over his shoulders. He mounted his horse, tired and reluctant to go. He'd hoped to be asked to stay for the night, instead, he was escorted to the entrance of the valley with a stern warning: "Our people spend winter here. Plenty water. Good shelter. Food. No iron horse here. Man of Medicine Woman not come back."

"Suppose Medicine Woman refuses to treat your sick?"

Bear Claw winced, but willed his facial expression back to a stoic calm. "Medicine Woman gave word."

"And I give my word that I won't do anything to hurt your people. All I ask is that you listen."

It was clear that Bear Claw didn't trust Dan, but finally, he nodded. That small admission of acceptance didn't come easily, and it didn't stop him from gesturing toward the path that left the valley.

As Dan rode down the trail, he heard the Indian remark, "Medicine Woman's man could look beyond mountain to the west. Land flat there, too."

A gust of snow hit Dan from the side, almost dislodging him from his horse. When he'd left New York, Dan hadn't expected his job to be easy, but he hadn't expected to find such a harsh environment in which to work. He wanted to investigate the other side, but the snow was coming down at such a fast rate he feared that he'd get lost. Best he find shelter.

Some time later, he managed to find an overhang that protected him from the wind. Grateful for his bedroll and the food Bear Claw had given him, he made camp. His horse was allowed to forage, knocking the snow from the vegetation and grazing on the frozen limbs uncovered. The ledge was big enough to offer the animal shelter from the weather if he chose.

Dan ate from the Indian stew, then covered himself with the bearskin and slept. The next morning he set out to discover other possible routes that might not disturb the Sioux. Without maps of the surrounding area, he was forced to rely on Bear Claw's suggestion. If he were being deliberately led astray, he'd have wasted valuable time. Finally, from atop a plateau, he viewed the side of the mountain to the left of the valley. Cold Springs lay just beyond the small range. If the plateau on which he was standing could be removed, the train could be routed along the narrow flat bed that rimmed the elevation.

If the plateau could be blown up.

If that land could be bought.

That night, the temperature grew even colder. Dan burrowed a hole in a snowbank, shored up the ceiling with his saddle and two tree limbs, and rolled himself up in his bedroll. Finding grass beneath this much snow was unlikely. He could only hope that the horse could survive the cold. At least the wind had died down and the snow had stopped.

He hoped Annie was having better luck with her work than he was with his.

Annie. Dr. Annalise Sinclair. Who would have thought that Ginny was the maid and the feisty woman accompanying her was a doctor? Thinking about Annie was infinitely more appealing than trying to figure out what to do about his railroad. This bothered him. No matter how appealing Annie was, he didn't have time for a woman, certainly not one who already had a future planned that didn't allow for a man. He hadn't thought that would bother him, but it did.

Annie bothered him. He'd run away from marriage.

He'd even run from her, though he hadn't known it. The idea of an arranged marriage to merge families and fortunes was abhorrent. Yet, halfway across the country he'd found himself thinking about just that.

Marriage to Annie. He let his mind wander to the Indians and the trouble that lay ahead. He'd told Black Hawk he'd try to come up with a solution, but what? Nothing in his training had qualified him to deal with Indians. Even if he managed to get the other piece of land and replace his supplies, he still didn't have the manpower to build the spur.

But one thing he'd learned from Annie was not to give up. Annie inspired him. Her spirit and determination were like a beacon, drawing everyone to her, sharing her passion and strength. If a woman could brave the odds and face the dangers of starting a new life away from everything she knew, so could he. Maybe success translated to something more than wealth. His father would disagree with him, for he measured everything in terms of money. His mother measured it by love. Dan saw no reason why a man couldn't have both.

He touched the bead in his pocket. He didn't know why he still carried it. The bead was part of a fantasy, and it was time he put fantasies away. His thoughts spilled over into sleep and dreams of a woman who appeared first as a bird, a beautiful white creature with dark eyes and green-tipped wings. She teased him by flying close, then dipping her small body into the wind and floating gracefully away. For a long time he watched her, envious of her freedom.

As he watched, his heart soared with the bird. Suddenly, she changed, her body turning from white to black. Her wing tips became crimson in a sky filled with fiery explosions. Her flight became more erratic. Then she seemed to falter, and she fell to the ground, her wings crumpled in the snow. The bird's body dissolved, turning into human form.

"Annie," he cried out, running toward her and gathering her into his arms. Her wings were frozen across her body, holding the cold against her. "Annie," he whispered.

"No. I can do it. Let me go, Dan. I can fly."

"You can't fly, Annie. Please, let me help you. You once said you trusted me, Annie. Trust me now." He laid her down, covering her body with his own.

Soon a warmth began to spread over him, transferring itself to Annie. As the heat left his body, seeping into hers, she began to stir, freeing her wings, draping them around both of them. With his hands he rubbed her face, her back, her breasts. Slowly he felt little quivers of response.

"Are you getting warm?" he asked.

"Yes," she said, drawing her wings tighter, holding him closer. "But you're growing cold."

"Fly away now, Annie, and let me sleep." As he lowered his lips to meet hers, he began to fade. In the dream, he wasn't cold any longer. He simply felt good. He would soon be back in Laramie, with Annie. She might not think she needed him, but he needed her, and it was time she knew it. He'd tell her—soon.

But for now, he'd sleep.

As the snow fell, the Indian searched. The white man had followed his suggestion and ridden beyond the mountain. He'd watched him go and struggle through the first day. But he hadn't turned back. And Black Hawk had promised the medicine woman that he would protect her man. Bear Claw must find him and take him home.

He saw no movement. No campfire. No sound. Only because he knew the area was he finally able to find the white man's horse. The man, wrapped in the bearskin, was covered with snow and so cold that he was almost frozen to death.

Bear Claw tied Dan's horse to his own, then assembled a crude travois, where he laid Dan's wrapped body inside.

Forcing Dan's horse into submission, they started back toward Laramie.

He didn't know whether they would make it. It might already be too late. The man's life would be in the hands of the Great Spirit and the medicine woman.

"Do you think Dan's dead?" Ginny asked Red quietly, knowing that the same question was lurking in the back of all their minds.

Under the guise of shifting his broken leg, Red moved nearer to Ginny's pallet in front of the fireplace, put his arm around her, and drew her closer. He'd promised he wouldn't touch her, wouldn't want her, until he knew about his leg and settled his conscience. But that hadn't worked. She was positive his leg would heal properly, and she refused to allow him to push her away. "I hope not, lass. I'd hate to think something happened to Dan because of me."

Ginny raised up. "Because of you? What kind of foolishness are you talking? First you won't marry me because you have family counting on you back in Ireland. Then you might not be able to make a living because of your leg. Now you're responsible for Dan's troubles? Well, you can just forget all that. I'm thinking this baby isn't going to wait too much longer. I don't know why you'd want me. I look like a duck and I'm so fat I can hardly move, but we're getting married."

"You're beautiful, Ginny."

"Then why don't you want to—you know."

"Why don't I want to lie with you? Ah, Ginny, lass. I want you so much I'm hurting with the want of you."

"You are?" She raised up on her elbows and looked down at him in the darkness. "Truly?"

Red groaned. He reached out and took her hand, placing it on his swollen organ. "Does this tell you?"

"Oh, my. Oh, Red. I don't know a lot about these

things, but I was told that when a man got like this he was in awful pain if it wasn't taken care of."

"That's true enough, darling. And with me broken leg, it's been powerful hard to take care of it without you knowing."

"It's all right if I know, Red. I'm going to marry you as soon as Dan gets back, and I don't want to hear anymore excuses. I'll just lie back and let you—take care of it."

"You will not. It's too near your time. I'll not take a chance on harming the babe."

"But what about your pain?"

"Well," Red said softly, "there is another way."

"How? Show me," she said.

He did. And then he showed her another thing she'd never known—how women felt pleasure in a different way.

Later, his hand on one full breast, Red let out a satisfied sigh. "I'm thinking that Dan had better hurry back," he said and laid his hand on her stomach. The baby kicked and he chuckled. "If I can't work, I'll hire you out as a cook and take care of the boy myself."

Ginny snuggled closer. "What makes you think it's a boy?"

"Me ma had the sight. She gave it to me. I can see him plain as the clover in spring. He has a shock of red hair, just like his da, and he's powerful strong."

Ginny smiled. Red would be this babe's father and he'd be lucky for it, just as she was. "Now tell me why you think you had anything to do with Dan's troubles?"

"I'll tell you, but I have to tell Dan first. Just know that if I hadn't been somewhere I ought not to have been, it wouldn't have happened. If I'd been honest with Dan from the start, he might not have lost his supplies."

Ginny looked at the man she was going to marry. "Red, I don't know what you think you did, but I know you would never have hurt Dan, and he knows that, too."

"Ah, Ginny, my love. I hope you will still feel that way when you know the truth," he said.

17

—⚭—

Dan. Annalise came suddenly awake, a shiver of dread cutting through her. She rose from the pallet in the clinic where she'd been sleeping and went to the window. Beyond the glass there was only snow. She couldn't see any sign of the dark-eyed man who had tormented her for the last weeks. But he was out there somewhere. She could feel him.

And something was wrong.

Annie started to pace, taking care not to wake Ginny and Red, whose pallets were now permanently moved side by side by the fireplace in the big room. More than an hour passed. Then an urgent pounding shattered the silence. Someone was at the door. She hurried to answer it. Ginny sat up.

"Josie, you stay put. Don't unlock that door, Annie," Red said quietly.

"I have to. Someone may need help," Annalise said as she opened the door. "It's Bear Claw—and *Dan.*" She took one look at the comatose man and gasped. "Follow me," she said, hurrying into the newly set-up clinic. "What happened?"

"Too cold," Bear Claw said. "Snow make cold. He sleep."

Her heart felt as if it were stopping. "You mean he was covered with snow?"

The Indian, also frosted with snow, nodded as he laid Dan on the table.

Annie touched his stiff body and gasped. He was like ice. She had to warm him up or he would die. He might die anyway. "Ginny, build up the fire. Josie, put all the kettles and pots in the coals to heat."

"You want me to fill them with water?"

"Yes. We'll wrap them in bed covers and use them as heating bricks. Josie, bring me our blankets. Bear Claw, go warm yourself."

In seconds everyone was up and moving, except for Red, who took charge of the fire, poker and bellows in hand.

Dan's clothes were frozen. They had to go. Annie's fingers refused to cooperate. Suddenly Bear Claw was beside her, cracking away the ice and unfastening the buttons. Annie stepped back, giving him room, then thought about her supplies. She could treat a wound, set a broken leg, deal with fever and a fainting heart, but there were no medicines to revive a half-frozen man.

Think, Annie. You wanted to be needed. Now you are. Think! What happened when a body started to freeze? The internal organs slowed down. The major organ that had to continue functioning for Dan to live was his heart. From her medical supplies, she selected a Chinese root that was said to act as a stimulant. "Ginny, take these and boil them in a small amount of water."

Bear Claw grunted and signaled to Annie that he'd loosened all Dan's clothing. "Thank you," she said. "Now, go back to the fire."

"See to horses first," the Indian said, and disappeared into the cold night once more.

Annie stood over Dan. He moaned, propelling her into

action. She'd disrobed men, not often but she'd done it. But taking off Dan's clothes was different. She hesitated, then chastised herself for that hesitation. Moments later she had removed every stitch of his clothing, even his woolen underwear, mentally reviewing her medical list of observations, the same list she'd used to eliminate husband prospects at the ball. This time there were no faults. Dan Miller was absolutely perfect.

Quickly she covered him with blankets, then took one hand in hers. She knew that frostbite of the fingers and toes was common. Slowly she began to rub. He lay, unmoving, and she was afraid.

"Is he going to die, Annie?" Josie's voice was barely audible.

"Not if I can help it. You take his other hand and rub it gently. How are the kettles coming? Are they hot yet?"

"Almost," Red answered, his poker turning them so that all sides were equally exposed to the hot coals. "The small pots are probably warm enough. Ginny, bring the muslin sheets."

Soon Dan was surrounded by warm iron cooking pots and kettles. Annie plunged a cloth into the hot water, and ignoring the pain, squeezed it out. Fanning it slightly to cool it, she began bathing Dan's face and lips. He moaned again, opening his mouth. "Good. Bring the broth, Josie."

For the next hour, she dripped the warm broth into Dan's mouth while Josie rubbed Dan's fingers and toes and Ginny kept alternating the hot water pots. At one point Annie looked up and saw Red leaning against the end of the bed, his face furrowed with worry.

Finally, Dan's body began to warm, a faint color tinged his cheeks and, through her stethoscope she could hear a steady heartbeat. She stood up and looked around. "We've done all we can do, for now. Are you all right, Ginny?"

Ginny grimaced and nodded. "I'm fine, Annie, just a little . . . tired."

"Red? You ought not to be standing on that leg."

"It's all right, Annie. Tomorrow, I'm thinking I'll see to making me some crutches. I'm not good for much, but if I can move about I can help do something."

"Annie, I can rub his feet some more," Josie said.

"No, go to bed now. It's almost morning. I will need you tomorrow. All of you, take your blankets. Dan won't need so many now."

Reluctantly the three assistants went back to their places on the floor. From the shadows, Bear Claw came forward and draped his own bearskin over Dan's body. "I leave this to protect the white man of Medicine Woman. It is from the bear I killed. The bear gave me his claw and my name. I give his spirit to Dan Miller."

Annie watched as the Indian tenderly covered Dan's body. "Thank you, dear friend," she said, and startled Bear Claw by hugging him. "You sleep by our fire tonight."

Bear Claw nodded and left her alone with the man she loved. She pulled her stool close and laid her head on his chest. "You can't die." She shivered and looked away. Seeing that still, unmoving face was unbearable. She didn't know what else to do medically. She had to wait it out, and she didn't know if her heart could take it.

Later that night, Dan's body began to twist. Severe muscle tremors racked the unconscious man. Annie could only guess at the severe pain that came with the unthawing process. But she knew that if Dan rolled off the bed he could break a bone, and she couldn't let that happen. Finally she simply slid beneath the bearskin and lay on top of him, holding him still with her own body.

With Dan beneath her and the bearskin over her, Annie felt heat steal over her. This was what she'd trained for, why she'd come to this wild, untamed country. Here was where she was needed, and here was the man who needed her. Soon her eyelids grew heavy. She laid her face against Dan's chest and slept.

———

Gradually Dan came back to consciousness. The storm must have stopped, for he was warm. He could feel a weight across him, pleasant but solid. He could hear the sound of breathing and caught the scent of an illusive yet familiar odor.

Finally, he struggled to force open his eyes, the weight of his eyelids protesting the movement. A pale gray light lit the darkness, but he didn't know where he was. He closed his eyes, then opened them again. He was lying on something, a table or a cot, so he wasn't in the mountains. Yet he was covered by the bearskin that had been given to him by Black Hawk's son. No, he decided, this skin was much bigger, much heavier. Then it moved.

"Dan?"

He must still be dreaming. He'd been caught in the storm and he was hallucinating about Annie, that she was here, touching him.

"Oh, Dan, you're awake. I was so scared."

If this was a dream, it was like no dream he'd ever had. It came to him slowly that Annie was really there. Her legs straddled his bare body, her breasts were thrust against his chest. "If this is heaven," he said, "I like it, but how come I'm naked and you're wearing clothes?"

Annie raised up, took his face in both her hands, and planted eager kisses across it. "Can you move?"

"I hope so," he murmured. "I surely hope so. I wouldn't want to lose this moment." He tried to lift his arms, tried and was hit by a thousand prickles of fiery pain. "Damn! What happened to me?"

"You nearly froze to death," she said. "Bear Claw found you and brought you home."

Snow, cold, storm. He remembered. "My horse?"

"He brought him in, too. Try to move your legs."

He did, with the same results—ripples of pain shot through him with every muscular contraction. "Annie, am I paralyzed?"

"No. But I suspect you may have frostbite." She slid to his side. "Let me look at you."

"No! Don't go," he said, and forced one arm around her, drawing her close.

"At least we know you can use your arm," she said, allowing him to hold her. "Do you have feeling in your fingers?"

"I don't know. Let's see." He grunted, as he moved his other arm across his chest, forcing himself to turn slightly so that he could touch her. "I'm not sure. Let me try again."

This time his fingers moved lower, sliding between the buttons on her bodice to the chemise beneath. Then he was holding her breast. "I think they're working fine," he said. "But I'd better keep moving them to be sure."

"Stop that, Dan, this is serious. You could be suffering from frostbite."

"You mean my fingers might die and fall off?"

"I've seen it happen."

"Then let them die happy."

She gave up struggling and let him touch her, reasoning that any movement was good for his recovery. "Seriously, how do you feel?"

He stopped his movement, considered his answer, then said seriously. "It hurts to move, and I feel very tired, but I'm all right."

"What happened to you?"

"A storm, so bad that I couldn't see. I made camp in a snowbank, but I couldn't stay warm. Finally, I guess I went to sleep, for I dreamed of a white bird. The bird turned into you and she fell in the snow. Then I think I was lost again, wandering in the darkness. And there was an animal. A bear, I think. It came toward me but I knew it meant me no harm. It lay down and put its arms around me, and I began to feel warm."

"That must have been when Bear Claw covered you with this skin."

"Maybe, but it was more than that, I think. I actually

felt my heart start to beat faster and the blood began to move through my body. It's as if I came back to life."

Annie laid her arm across his bare chest, feeling his heartbeat. Bear Claw had given Dan the bear's spirit. She'd heard about those Indian legends, but she'd hadn't believed in the power of spirits. For now, it didn't matter how it happened. Dan was alive. "Maybe you did come back to life. But you must sleep now."

"No, I've been resting. I've been asleep but now I'm awake and I want . . . no, need to talk about what I learned."

"All right, for a few minutes. What did you learn?"

"Black Hawk and his son saved my life. I won't move the tribe."

"But what about the cattle spur you came to build?"

"Annie, I found another route for the spur. If I can figure out a way to get the land, we'll lay our track there."

"Then we'll buy the land."

"Oh, Annie. I can't even replace the lost supplies. Where am I going to get money to buy land?"

"There has to be a way. We haven't come this far to fail. We'll figure it out."

"We? I like the sound of that." Dan gave a dry laugh. "You know, if I'd followed my father's wishes, I wouldn't have a problem."

"How's that?"

"I told you, he wanted me to find a rich wife. He actually threw a New Year's Eve party he couldn't pay for so that I could check out the eligible women. Wouldn't have worked, you weren't there."

Annie's heart skipped a beat. "Dan, at the party, did you see anyone you liked?"

He hesitated. "Actually, I thought I did. There was a woman, a woman who wore a masque of egret feathers and silver beads."

Annie hid a secret smile. "And you liked her, this woman in the feather masque?"

"I did. It was the strangest thing. Somehow we connected. Then she was gone. Vanished completely. I looked for her, but I could never find her."

"If you'd found her and she had no money, would you still have wanted her?"

A shaft of sunlight pierced a crack in the logs and fell across Annie's face, banding her dark eyes with light. Dan felt an instant jolt.

Those eyes. Since the first time he'd noticed Annie, those eyes had spoken to him. In pride. In anger. In confidence. Only now, as they lay close, each breathing the air the other exhaled, did he know where he'd seen them before.

Annie was his mystery woman in the mask.

"It was you," he said. "That night at the ball. It was you. I found a silver bead from your mask. I've carried it in my pocket ever since. You were my mystery snowbird. That's why I dreamed about the bird."

"Yes."

"But you ran away. Why?"

"I don't know. I guess I was afraid. I'd never been so close to a man before. I never knew how it could make me feel. And I couldn't take a chance on anything coming between me and my dream."

"Then you knew who I was from the beginning, and you never said anything?" He felt a twinge of anger, followed by confusion.

"Yes. I knew who you were, but if you'd known who I was, you would have told my father, and he would have come for me before I ever left New York. I couldn't let Ginny be hurt. No, I'm blaming Ginny when it was really me who wanted to leave. Not one medical office in New York would give me a chance. I had to go where I could be a doctor. My father would have stopped me. I couldn't let him find me."

She had been running from a man, but not a lover or a

husband, and not for the reasons he'd thought. "You're right. I probably would have contacted your father. But that was before I knew the real Annie." He turned his head, ignoring the storm of protest that movement set off. Annie the doctor had just saved his life. But it was Annie the woman he'd dreamed about. Annie the woman he was holding in his arms, that he had fallen in love with.

"But now he knows where you are."

"Yes, and as soon as the bridge is repaired, I expect him to come out here. I love him, but he'll never believe that I don't need a husband."

"Tell him to ask me. I'll say you're the most competent woman I ever knew. If I wanted a mountain moved, or a life saved, you're the one I'd ask to do it."

"I can't think I'd be much good on a mountain, but I hope I'm a good enough doctor to treat the sick. I'm glad you appreciate my skills."

"Oh, I appreciate your skills, even the 'special' ones like vamping and gambling. You're a spectacular doctor and a truly unique woman, Annie, and you don't need a man to make you either."

"Thank you," she said softly, wondering why his validation didn't give her the pleasure she'd expected. "I'm glad someone appreciates me. I wasn't certain that would ever happen."

"You really don't know how special you are, do you, Annie?"

How to answer that? "I . . . guess I don't," she said. "I mean, my brother always said I was born to be a doctor. My mother always told me I'd never find a man if I didn't learn how to please one. My father loves me, but he's convinced that no self-respecting man would marry a doctor. So, I guess I never thought I was special at all."

"Annalise Sinclair, the first night I saw you, I thought you were the most fascinating woman I'd ever met. Then when I met Annie, I found a strong, courageous woman who was determined to follow her dream. Now I know what that dream was, and that you're both the same woman. I think I may be in love with both of you."

"No, Daniel," she said, sliding from the bed. "That can't be. I don't want you to love me. I'm a doctor, not a wife. I'll never take a husband." She started backing away, turned, and before he could stop her, left the room.

And Dan's body was too weak to let him get up and go after her. Maybe, he thought, that was just as well. He couldn't take a wife, even if he wanted to. He had no money and no open land, a crew of eight, one of whom had a broken leg, and he still had a railroad to build.

18

---❦---

Inside the living quarters, Ginny was already awake. "How's Dan?"

"He's weak," Annie said, "but he's going to make it. I can't be certain about the frostbite yet. We'll have to give that time."

"According to Bear Claw, Medicine Woman's man is 'good' now," Red said, struggling to his feet. Using a small stool to balance himself, he hopped to the table. "I went through Dan's things and found him some dry clothes."

"You take them in to him, Ginny," Annie said, crossing her arms across her chest and looking around. "Where is Bear Claw?"

"Don't know. He was here by the fire one minute and the next, he was gone. So was Josie."

Annie didn't like the sound of that. Bear Claw might not take to Josie's little "talents." She let out a deep sigh that seemed to catch in her throat. "I need to get out for a while. I'd better go look for her."

"Annie. Annie!" Ginny stopped her by taking her friend by the arms and holding her. "What's wrong?"

"Wrong? Nothing. I've just saved my third patient. That's what I came out here to do, isn't it? Well, I'm a success. I have an office. I have patients who need me. Why should there be anything wrong?"

With that said, she picked up her shawl and left the old trading post, leaving an astonished Ginny and Red behind.

"Well, seems our Annie is in something of a snit," Red observed. "If that's success, maybe we don't want any."

Ginny smiled knowingly. "That's success all right, but not the kind she expected. Our Annie is in love and for now, it's eating her alive. Maybe I'd better check on Dan. I'm not sure his condition could handle this kind of pain."

Ginny picked up Dan's clothes and walked to the surgery door. She knocked, then went in.

"You don't have to marry me, Annie," Dan said. "But it doesn't change the way I feel."

"That's good," Ginny answered with a giggle. "For I'm going to marry Red. And one husband is enough."

By the time Annie stopped walking she was almost out of sight of Laramie. She'd seen no sign of Josie. In fact, she hadn't even looked for her. Ice crunched beneath her feet and she felt the cold seeping through her clothes.

They were deep into February—Uglyruary, her father had always called the month. *Father.* She wondered if he were on the way out here. What would he say about her crude facilities?

What would he say about Dan?

Even she didn't know what to do about Dan. In medical school they'd never taught about feelings, about how a body responds to emotional needs. But she understood now that certain men and women respond to each other. Their bodies ask physically and reach out for each other. Did that only happen when two people fell in love? She didn't want to think about that—or about what being in love would do to their futures.

She'd come out west prepared to devote her life to being a doctor. Dan was here to build a railroad. She was already on her way, but Dan's path was more dangerous. She knew he'd do what he set out to do, but she wondered if this plan was making the best use of his talents. Dan Miller was a man who inspired confidence with his mind and his words. Perhaps he belonged in Washington, where he could use both to his advantage. If so, his feelings for her could interfere with his future, for she knew now that she was where she belonged. Where Dan belonged wasn't certain yet.

Suddenly she heard the sound of running feet. "Annie! Annie, come quick!"

It was Josie, standing in the road, leaning over to catch her breath.

"What's wrong? Is it Dan?"

"No. Annie, it's Ginny. She's having the baby—now!"

"Oh, no!" Annie started to run. It was too early. According to Ginny's own words she'd been six months gone on the first day of the new year. That made her less than eight months now—unless she'd calculated wrong. Women did that sometimes. If she were wrong by a few weeks, the baby would have a better chance.

Dear God, had she brought this on by allowing Ginny to overexert herself? She'd suffered the physical hardship of crude facilities on the train without complaint. Then there was the train wreck and preparing their living quarters. She'd cared for Red and then, last night, she was up half the night filling and carrying heavy pots when she should have been resting.

And Annie had thought she was helping Ginny.

"What happened?" she asked Josie, who was running beside her.

"She was helping Dan get dressed when I got back. He walked into the keeping room and then she fed him breakfast. Seemed all right then. Until she leaned over to get the kettle of hot water. She gave a little moan and got a funny look on her face. Red went crazy. He ran over to her like his leg wasn't broken and caught Ginny before she fell. Dan got Ginny into your hospital room and onto the bed. When I left she was moaning and crying and Red was hopping around on one leg and cursing like a sailor."

"And Dan?" Annie asked, "did he seem to have any trouble walking?"

"He's a little stiff. I couldn't see his toes, but I didn't see nothing wrong with his fingers."

"Good, I may need his help."

"I can help, Annie. I helped deliver my mama's baby."

Annie stopped running and looked at Josie. "You helped deliver a child?"

"Mama told me what to do . . . but it died. My mama died, too. Annie, Ginny isn't going to die, is she?"

Annie hugged Josie. "She is not. Your mother didn't have a doctor, Josie. Ginny does. And she has you, too. I'm sure I'll need your help, too."

Josie swallowed back her tears and nodded. "You just tell me what to do."

They started running once more. "One thing," Annie said, her lungs bursting with effort, "you're going to have to keep Red occupied. Men just get in the way at a time like this."

By the time they'd reached the trading post, Annie had mapped out her plan. In her bag of Chinese herbs, there was one packet of paper labeled *Women*. She didn't know what the leaves and roots were, only that they were used to stop early labor. She'd start by making a tea of that.

Bursting through the door, she fired orders. "Red, build up the fire. We need boiling water. Dan—where's Dan?"

"You were gone, so he went to find a woman to help."

Annie groaned. He was bringing help. Didn't he think

she could do a simple thing like deliver a baby? Then she chastised herself. She was gone, and this wasn't simple. Suppose Josie hadn't found her. Ginny needed help and Dan was trying to take care of her, just as he'd cared for them all along. At least he was able to move well enough to go.

"How'd you find me?"

"I didn't. Bear Claw saw your tracks."

"Where is he now?"

"Gone back. Said his father needed to know about Dan. Said Dan was his father's friend."

Friend? How'd Dan manage that?

One look at Ginny told her she was too late with her plans to stop labor. She caught her friend's hand and squeezed it. "Don't worry, Ginny. I'll help you."

Pain racked Ginny's body. She moaned and drew her knees up to her stomach. "My baby, Annie. It's too early. It hurts so bad. I didn't know it would hurt so bad."

"When did it start, the pains?"

"I've felt them, only a little, for a couple of days. I just thought it was because we were working so hard. Then last night, right before Bear Claw brought Dan, they got stronger."

"Why didn't you say something?"

"Annie, you had enough to deal with. Besides, I just thought it was my back hurting. Does this mean something is wrong with the baby?"

Annie held Ginny's wrist. Her pulse was strong but irregular. "I think this baby is just trying to help Red," she said, placing her hand on Ginny's stomach. It was hard, so tight that she couldn't feel the baby.

Ginny blanched. "Help Red? How?"

Ginny was already pushing. "By coming early so you'll get your girlish figure back in time for a wedding."

"Red didn't care about my figure," Ginny said. "But he said we couldn't . . ." She gasped. ". . . you know, Annie. Until the baby came."

"You didn't?"

"No, of course not. But only because Red wouldn't. Oh, Annie. I didn't want . . ." she breathed hard and caught the sides of the bed ". . . this baby to begin with. But I . . ." She let out a long breath and relaxed her knees. ". . . I don't want him to die."

"He's not going to die, Ginny. Josie, you and Red set up those boiling pots again. We'll have to make a warm place for the baby. When you're done with that, give Red another sheet and let him tear it into large squares."

"What for?" Red asked, his voice tight with worry.

"For diapers and blankets."

"Oh, Annie," Ginny said, her forehead wet with perspiration. "I never prepared anything. I thought I'd have plenty of time."

Annie covered Ginny's body with a sheet and pushed up her skirts. "I'm sorry, Ginny, but I'm going to have to examine you to check the position of the baby. It may hurt. Just close your eyes."

Annie took a pan and filled it with water from the kettle in the fireplace. She added a cap of carbolic solution and rinsed her hands, drying them on one of the unused cloths left from the night before. At the rate she was going, she'd have to buy new supplies or hire a washwoman.

Turning back to the bed, she took a deep breath and slipped her hand beneath the sheet and inside Ginny's body. Warm blood, too much blood, lubricated her search, allowing her to touch the child. She encountered a smooth surface, not the head she was expecting, not even feet.

Ginny groaned and clutched the sides of the bed.

"Try not to move for a moment, Ginny." Annie moved her fingers back and forth. What was she feeling? Finally, she encountered something different. Then it came to her. It was the baby's spine. He was lying like a U, his back pressed against the path of his exit.

Ginny screamed and strained, pushing Annie's hand out of her body with her contraction.

Annie cursed her decision to become a doctor. *Why did you think you could do this?* This baby wasn't going to be born, and Ginny was tearing her body apart trying to deliver him. If she didn't do something, they would both die.

"What's wrong, Annie?"

It was Red, outside the surgery, leaning against the wall beside the door. She knew his splints were sturdy, but moving about had to be painful. "The baby is turned wrong, Red. And I can't move him. I'm going to have to operate to take the child."

"Can you do that, Annie?" he asked.

Annie stepped outside the door and spoke in a low voice. "I don't know, Red, but they'll both die if I don't. Have you heard from Dan? I'm going to need some help, and," she lowered her voice to a whisper, "I don't want it to be Josie."

"I'll help." It was Dan—alone.

"Where's the woman you went after?" Annie said, a steady joy filling her. She took a quick look at him, filling her eyes with his calming presence. If she needed help, Dan was here.

"She's home with her sick child. But someone else is coming."

"Who?"

"Her name is Agnes, one of the new women who came in on the train. She's opened up a wash tent like the one in Boggy Gut. Sheriff Spencer has gone to get her."

Another washwoman, Annie thought, remembering Pearl and Dan's tender ministrations. "Are you really all right, Dan?" she asked.

"I'm weak, and I feel like my arms and legs have been asleep, but they're waking up now. What do you want me to do?"

"Help me take off my coat and get rid of yours. We have to work together, free of restraint."

Dan grinned wanly. "That's something we can certainly

do." He glanced down at the blood on Annie's fingers and frowned. "How bad is it?"

"I don't know yet."

"Well, she's got the best doctor in the West," he said, and gave her a confident smile.

"I hope you're right, Dan. But I'm scared."

Dan pulled off his jacket and walked behind Annie, catching the collar of her jacket in his hands. For just a moment he paused with his hands beneath her chin. "Don't be, Annie. You can do this."

Ginny moaned, pulling Annie back to the situation at hand. She slid into her white surgeon's coat and headed to Ginny's side. "More hot water, Josie," Annie said, washing her hands again, and slinging them until they no longer dripped.

"Empty that water, Josie, and bring more." As Josie complied, Annie laid out her surgical supplies, then dropped them into the boiling water Josie poured into the pan. "Bring some of those squares, Josie. Dan, lay this metal rod in the fire but don't let the end touch the coals. I want it hot but not soiled."

Ginny looked at Annie and smiled. "Don't worry, Annie," she said. "I'm not."

"That's good," Annie replied as she pulled on her white medical coat, "because Red's worrying enough for both of us. Now, I'm going to put something over your nose. I want you to breathe deeply. It will make you sleep while I—I deliver your baby."

"Sleep?"

"Yes. You won't feel a thing."

"Will I wake up?"

"Of course you will."

"Then I'm ready. No, wait. Red?"

"I'm here." And he was, standing in the shadows by the door. He was holding Ginny's broom to support his weight.

"I just want you to know that I love you, Red, and when

this is over, I'm going to marry you—no matter what kind of secret you have."

"Yes, you are, lass," Red said, making his way to the bed. He kissed Ginny lightly. "If you still want me."

"I do. Now you go back to the fire and start thinking about names for our son," Ginny directed. "I don't want you to hurt your leg so that you can't help Dan build his cattle spur."

Annie looked at Dan, but neither questioned Ginny about any *secret*. And Red followed Ginny's instructions, disappearing into the other room.

"Go with him, Josie," Annie said. "Make a pallet by the fire, as close as you can get it. And when I tell you, arrange the water pots around it and cover it with blankets, just like we did last night for Dan. When the baby is born, we'll put him inside and cover him with another warm blanket."

"Yes, ma'am."

"And stay there until I call you."

"Yes, ma'am."

Another spasm of pain hit Ginny. As soon as the contraction passed, Annie poured some liquid on a folded cloth and handed it to Dan. "Hold this over her nose."

Dan stood at Ginny's head and followed Annie's instructions.

Annie draped a sheet over Ginny's lower body to shield her from view.

"She's already asleep, Dan. I don't want her to sleep too deeply, because the baby gets the sleeping medicine, too. You can remove the cloth, but I'm going to leave this bottle on the table. If she begins to stir, you may have to add more."

"Is she going to be all right, Annie?" It was Red, standing awkwardly across the table.

"I don't know, Red."

"Can I sit here, beside her?" he asked.

"Bring a stool, Dan," Annie directed. "You can stay as

long as you don't interfere, Red." Then she caught sight of his worried expression and realized how sharp her reply had been. "Why don't you hold her hand and talk to her. I don't know how much a patient hears when they're asleep, but it might give her courage."

Gratefully, he sat on the stool Dan dragged up and held Ginny's hand. He didn't watch Annie, only Ginny, whispering to her and touching her face.

Annie washed Ginny's belly with a cloth dipped in the boiled carbolic water. "Are you all right with this, Dan?"

"Don't know," he replied honestly. "I've never been a nurse before. But I'll do the best I can."

She studied him for a second, allowing his stoic expression of confidence to feed her own. "Pull the stool around there and you can sit," she said. "There's going to be a lot of blood."

Annie knew what she was doing was risky. She'd seen it done only twice, and only by Dr. Lindsey at the university. He had managed to save both women, but only one of the babies survived. At least, out here, she was less likely to be censured for performing a radical procedure.

Finally, she retrieved her metal rod, placing it and some of the coals into an iron pot which she set on the table with her instruments.

At last Annie picked up her scalpel and began to cut, pinching off the tiny vessels with her fingertips. The larger ones she touched with the tip of the metal rod she'd heated. A sear, the smell of flesh, and the bleeding stopped. Another cut and she'd exposed Ginny's uterus. She had to act quickly now.

"How's her breathing, Dan?"

Dan leaned over Ginny and placed his neck in front of her mouth and nose. "Come on, Ginny, breathe for me. Yes, that's it. Okay, Annie, she's breathing."

Swiftly, Annie slit the outer wall of her uterus and slid her fingers inside. "Damn!" The baby's body shifted slightly and blocked her incision. She began to pull, more vigorously than she would have liked, but the baby's head had to come out before it smothered. Now perspiration was pouring down her face.

"Wipe my face, Dan. I can't see."

Dan didn't ask questions, nor did he hesitate.

"Get the water pots ready, Red."

Sliding one hand forward, she caught the baby's shoulders and pushed them down at the same time she worked its knees forward. The body twisted. A spasm rippled Ginny's body and the baby's head popped out. In seconds, Annie had the discolored baby lying on the sheet and was wiping fluid from its nose and mouth. The baby was tiny, but she was breathing. "Red, you have a little girl."

"A girl, Ginny," he said. "We got us a fine colleen to start our family."

Annie hoped she was fine. She hadn't taken a breath yet. She called Josie into the room. "Josie, bring me a large section of cloth." When it appeared beside her, Annie laid the baby inside it and handed the baby to Josie. "Dry her off and massage her. Move her around. Make her mad enough to yell."

Annie checked Ginny. No more anesthesia was needed here. Now she had to move quickly, lest Ginny go into shock. She threaded a needle and stitched up the uterus, then, after refreshing the seared areas, she closed the outer wall of her belly. Once done, Annie ripped the bloody clothing off Ginny's body and pulled the soiled sheets from beneath her. Then she washed her own hands once more.

Annie could hear Josie and Red talking to the infant, but she hadn't heard her cry. "Josie, how about the baby? Is she breathing?"

"She's trying," Josie said, panic evident in her voice. "Oh, Annie, don't let her die!"

"Bring her to me. Dan, will you get some blankets to cover Ginny. We have to warm her up, too."

Josie handed Annie the child. Her skin was covered

with a filmy white substance. No pink showed through. If she didn't do something, this little girl could die. Finally, in desperation, she took her by the heels and slapped her bottom.

"You're the first baby I've delivered and you're going to live." She slapped her again. "Do you hear me? Cry!"

From sheer anger, or frustration, the baby whimpered. Halfheartedly at first, then with more exuberance, finally letting out a healthy yell of displeasure. Annie began to laugh. She might be early and she might be small, but she was a fighter.

Annie walked back into the keeping room and sank down on the bench at the table, tears of joy streaming down her face. She'd wanted to be needed. Out here she'd saved four lives: Red's, Black Hawk's, Dan's, and Ginny's. But this new life she'd helped bring into the world was special. She was a kind of symbol, a validation of her dream of being Dr. Annalise Sinclair, physician.

At that moment, a mountain of a gray-haired woman entered the post. "You don't remember me, but I'm Agnes. Give that child to me. You may know about doctoring, but I've raised ten young'uns."

"Yes, ma'am," Annie agreed.

Josie laughed at anyone's giving Annie orders. But Red looked worried. "What about Ginny?" he asked.

Wearily, Annie rose and made her way back to Ginny's side. She was still sleeping and her color wasn't good, but her pulse was steady. "I won't lie to you, Red," she said. "If she didn't lose too much blood and if the surgery doesn't fester, she'll make it. We'll know soon. I've done all I can for now."

"Agnes? Josie?" Dan asked, "Can you look after Ginny for a while? Annie spent most of the night caring for me, now this. She needs to get some rest. She's exhausted."

Agnes answered. "Yep, reckon I can. Them men can just go dirty another day or two. Can we move the mama in here by the fire?"

Agnes, Dan, and Annie picked up the sleeping Ginny and laid her on the pallet they'd arranged for the baby. With the hot water pots around, they'd both stay warm.

Annie left instructions to care for Ginny, and a vial of laudanum to be administered if she should wake in pain.

"You just gather up all them soiled sheets and rags," Agnes was telling Josie, "and me and you will take 'em down to the wash tent later. I put more wood on the fire so the water will still be hot."

"Wash tent?" Josie said, horrified. "I ain't too partial to wash tents."

"I have an idea." Dan conferred quietly with Agnes, then said, "Come on, Annie, let's take a walk."

"All right," she said, puzzled at his suggestion of a walk when he'd just said she needed to rest. "Where are we going?"

"To the only unoccupied place in Laramie."

She was too tired to ask where, noting only that, "There's no hotel. Where do you expect to find privacy?"

He smiled, slid his arm around her waist, and kept her tired legs moving. Once they reached town, he moved her behind the general store.

"Are we hiding?" she asked.

"We are. Our destination is warm and private and clean. I think you'll approve. At least you did the last time we used one."

And then she saw it, a tent. The sign over the door said *Agnes's Wash Tent*. Beneath that sign was a second, pinned on the entrance. *"CLOSED till I say different."* Annie gave Dan an uneasy smile. "I'm afraid that if I get in a tub of warm water I'll go straight to sleep."

"Good. You need the rest."

He lifted the tent flap and, with his hand on Annie's back, guided her inside. "Your private quarters, Dr. Sinclair."

"Not Doctor Sinclair, Dan. Just Annie. From now on, I'm just Dr. Annie."

Inside, the wash fires still glowed, warming the frigid

air. One corner had been cordoned off with muslin, making private sleeping quarters for Agnes. Dan smiled and gathered up a stack of blankets. "Agnes gave me instructions that I'm to make certain you go to bed after your bath."

Too tired to do more than smile, she followed Dan. What she needed more than sleep was Dan's presence. And he seemed to be so certain she needed rest that he was about to tuck her in and leave. But she didn't want to be alone. She needed something. She needed Dan.

Deliberately, Annie removed her clothes, dropping them as she walked. When Dan had finished covering Agnes's linens with clean ones, he rose, caught sight of Annie's nude body, and swore.

"What are you doing?" he asked.

"Freezing," she answered, and lay down. "I warmed you when you were cold. Now it's your turn. Take off your clothes, Dan Miller."

Slowly, confused, he removed his boots and his shirt, and then he hesitated. "Are you sure, Annie?"

"I'm sure that I'll turn into a chunk of ice if you don't hurry. We don't have Bear Claw's skin here. You'll have to make do."

"All right," he said, "but only until you fall asleep." He stripped off his trousers, then, still wearing his wool underwear, knelt down.

"Everything," Annie said. "I'm not sleeping next to those scratchy things."

One look at Annie's rosy nipples and Dan decided she didn't have to. Once Dan put his arms around her, Annie wasn't sleepy anymore.

"Tell me what you want from me, Annie. I'm confused."

"Do we have to talk about it, Dan? Can't we just feel?"

"All right. Tell me what you feel." he said.

She put her hand on his chest. "I feel your body asking for me, Dan."

"You feel my heart beating, Annie. That's desire, yes.

But this too, is desire." He took her hand and placed it on that part of him now swollen with need. "That's the physical evidence of a man's desire, but this," he returned her hand to his chest, "this is much more."

Annie trembled. Every part of her seemed to be moving in different directions. "Dan, I don't want to talk. Can't we just be with each other without talking?"

"You know I want to make love to you, Annie. There is rarely a time when I don't want you. But there has to be more than that between us. I want to hear you say you care."

"I think it's easier for you, Dan. It is very different for a woman. I don't know how to say what I don't understand."

Dan put his hand on her breast, feeling the nipple harden instantly. "A woman's body feels desire too. See, this is one of the ways it shows its need."

Annie groaned.

Dan raised up and took her nipple in his mouth as his fingers moved lower, trailing across her stomach, reaching through the thatch of hair that nestled between her legs and finally into the pool of moisture waiting for him.

She was wet and warm, and she gasped as his fingers moved inside. "Dan, I . . ."

"Hush, Annie. I know. A man can always find his satisfaction. But a woman is different. I believe she has to feel something special for the man, and this is the other way her body shows her need. When a man and woman make love and it's right, it's the most powerful feeling on earth. Now, tell me what you're feeling, Annie."

"I can't."

Dan sighed. She wasn't ready yet to say the words. "Then show me."

Annie rolled over catching his male part between her legs, lathering it with her slick wetness.

"I lay across you like this last night, Dan. You were wearing no clothes and . . . I liked it."

"I liked it, too," he said in a low, tight voice.

"But you were unconscious."

"My mind was asleep, but my body wasn't. It knew you were there, and it waited for the strength to show you how it felt."

"Has your strength returned?" Annie asked, breathlessly.

"Oh, yes. I think it has."

"I think I ought to be sure. As your doctor, I mean."

"You're the doctor. You studied anatomy. All you have to do is put the body parts where they were designed to go. But you'd better hurry, darling."

"Suppose someone comes," she said, lifting her body.

"I'm counting on it," Dan gasped, caught her body in his hands, and lifted.

Annie lowered herself slowly, taking all of him inside her, one exquisite inch at a time. "Nobody ever taught us this in anatomy," she whispered, planting her knees on either side of Dan's thighs.

"I'm glad," Dan said.

"Oh, I don't know, this would have made studying a lot more fun."

Dan began to moan. "Annie, I'm not going to be able to hold back. I'm sorry. I'll make it up to you." And then he caught her once more, holding her as he bucked beneath her.

Annie flung her head back and moaned. "You wanted to know what I'm feeling, Dan. I'm feeling as though I'm about to explode. It's like I have a coiling spring of heat getting tighter and tighter. Oh, Dan." She felt the hot gush of Dan's release just as she surrendered to her own.

Finally, the last ripple died away and she fell against him. "Oh, Dan, I must be a wicked woman. It felt so good—so *right*."

Later, sated and entwined, Dan held her. He realized that Annie would never admit to more than desire. She refused to say she loved him, choosing instead to call herself a wicked woman so that she could separate the sensual from the spiritual. For now, he'd let her believe she could.

She was a woman, his woman, and sooner or later, she'd understand.

He just wished he did. Every time he made up his mind to concentrate on his mission and separate himself from Annie, they ended up making love. He was no better at keeping his distance than Annie. But there was a big difference. Annie, as a doctor, should be the first to know they were playing with fire and heading straight for disaster on this course. She'd better marry him soon.

Marry him? Wrong! He'd lost his supplies and had no money to replace them. Now he had an Indian tribe right in the middle of the site for the cattle spur. Marrying Annie would only create more problems. If he had to admit failure and return to New York, Annie wouldn't go. He couldn't ask her to. If he stayed, what kind of future could he build for himself out here? He moved restlessly.

"What's wrong, Dan? Is your body asking again?"

She pulled down the sheet and lifted her breast, then grinned. "See, I'm learning to recognize the signs. Are you hard, too?"

Between the time she pulled his head to her breasts and caught his manhood in her hand, she didn't have to ask. She knew.

"This time, you come to me, Dan."

Any thought of refusal vanished when she nudged her way beneath him. Dan couldn't refuse her, but this had to be the last time. He'd make love to her, slowly showing her with his body what he felt in his heart. It might have to last forever.

Later, when she was asleep, Dan slipped out of her arms, dressed, and left the tent. He had some thinking to do and some decisions to make.

19

Ginny came slowly awake. She could hardly move, but she was alive. What about the baby?

"Annie?" she whispered. "Red?"

"Yes, darling," Red instantly replied. "I'm here. We're here."

"We?"

"I'm holding our little girl, a fair colleen she is, just like her ma."

"A girl? And she's all right?"

"Well, she's a wee one, but she's a fighter."

"Can I see her?"

"Just for a minute." A very large, gray-haired woman moved into view, leaning over Ginny and holding a tiny bundle of cloth. "Here you are, dumplin'. Your mama is gonna give you some dinner, then Agnes is gonna rock you to sleep."

Ginny took the baby, holding her in the crook of her arm and gazing down at a perfect little face. "Oh . . ." she said softly.

"All right, Papa," Agnes said, "help Mama uncover the dinner plate. Josie, let's me and you go down to the general store and get us some food. We got hungry folks to feed out here."

"But I don't wanna go," Josie protested. "I want to stay with the baby."

"Don't matter what you want, child. They's times when a man and his wife need privacy."

"But they ain't married," Josie argued.

"We're gonna be," Red said. "Now get."

He slid down to the floor, moved the water jugs away and lay down beside Ginny, supporting himself on one elbow.

The baby began to fuss, nuzzling the blanket with a little mewing sound.

"She's hungry, Ginny," he said, reaching out to pull down the blanket in which Ginny was wrapped.

Ginny blushed and turned away. "Red . . . I . . ."

"It's all right, darling. I'm going to watch you do this for the rest of our lives. We're going to have lots of babes, and you're going to feed them in front of me without feeling ashamed. Can you turn toward me, just a bit?"

Ginny tried, caught her lip in her mouth to stifle the pain, and stopped. "I'll help you," Red said. He reached around Ginny with his free arm, catching the lower portion of her body, and lifted it. This time Ginny did groan.

"Annie left medicine for the pain," he said. "I'll get it."

"No, don't go. Not yet." She let the baby down to the pallet between them and pulled back the covers to see her daughter. The child opened her rosebud mouth, her small tongue licking in and out as she tried to find something to fasten on. It was as if the child knew more than Ginny.

Red reached out and lifted Ginny's breast, now full of milk. "Lift her up darling. She'll grab hold."

And she did. Ginny felt the tug of the baby's mouth and smiled. She looked down at one tiny hand, reaching out to grasp Red's finger as it lay on Ginny's breast. "Oh, Red, she's beautiful."

"You're both beautiful, Ginny. My two girls. What are we going to call her?"

"That's easy. She's Anna. Anna . . ."

"Caitlan," he finished, "for my youngest sister. Anna Caitlan, that's a fine name."

"Anna Caitlan what?" Ginny asked. "Red, I don't even know your last name."

This time it was Red's turn to blush. "I hate to hang my moniker on you, Ginny, but me name's Redfield O'Reilly. My mama had great expectations."

"And you've surely fulfilled all of them, Redfield," Ginny said. "Mr. and Mrs. Redfield O'Reilly and their daughter, Caity. Oh, Red, are you sure you want to marry me?"

"Oh, yes, Ginny. I've never been more sure of anything in me life."

Caity gave a final satisfied suckle, let go of Red's finger, and went sound asleep, leaving Red's hand resting on Ginny's breast.

"Red," Ginny said shyly, lifting Caity. "Please move closer. I think I've just become an engaged woman. Doesn't a kiss usually accompany a proposal?"

It did. And neither Ginny nor Caity seemed to worry about Red's most obvious announcement of anticipated future pleasure. Ginny only smiled and asked, "How long do we have to wait?"

"I don't even know if we have a preacher in town," Red said in a tight voice.

"I wasn't talking about a preacher," Ginny said, and kissed Red with more passion than was wise.

"That's good," Red said. "But you'd better not do that again or we'll have some explaining to do to Dr. Annie."

Ginny turned on her back and pulled up the blanket. "Annie will understand. But you're right, Red. I think I need to sleep some. I have to get better—quick. A few days and a dose of that pain medicine and . . ."

But Ginny was already asleep. Red hoped that her recovery would be that simple. He reached out and cuddled the baby to him, returning his hand once more to Ginny's breast. A few days might be just about all he could wait.

On Fifth Avenue, the snow melted only to be replaced with another fresh fall. On Wall Street the five stockholders of the Cold Springs Spur, now known officially as Teddy's Rogues, managed to traverse a mire of melting snow and frozen ruts to reach the Finance Club for Roylston Sinclair's emergency meeting.

Stomping the snow from their boots and brushing it from their top hats, they gathered in one of the private rooms for a hot toddy and the report. "All right, Sinclair," Teddy said, "why have you sent for us?"

"To tell you that I've solved your problem. I've found another investor who has enough capital to replace our lost supplies and hire more crew members."

Teddy eyed him suspiciously. "Who?"

"His name's Mason Clanton. From Chicago."

"How'd you find him?" Louis Riddenhouse asked.

"I didn't. He found me." Roylston cleared his throat. "I hadn't formally announced it, but my daughter, Annalise, has been—missing."

The men seemed shocked. "But you said she was home from school," Teddy said. "Why didn't you tell us?"

"I—I thought I knew where she was. I was wrong. Rather than cause every bounty hunter in the country to go after her, I hired the Pinkerton Agency. They traced her to Brooklyn. But we couldn't find any record of her after that."

"These modern women," Riddenhouse said. "What'd she do, run off with the butler?"

"No, nothing like that. Most of you didn't know, but my daughter graduated from medical school. She's a doctor and she came home determined to open her own clinic.

I'm afraid I wasn't supportive, so instead of going to our summer cottage as she'd said she was going, she disappeared, determined to find a place where she was needed. I felt bad about the way I'd treated her and went after her. That's when I found out she never arrived."

"Can't blame you for not wanting her to be a doctor," Albert Bolt said, "but what does this have to do with a new partner?"

"She went out west, took her maid with her. I didn't know where she was. Eventually I offered a reward for information about my daughter," Roylston explained. "It was Mason Clanton who found her and claimed the money."

The men still looked puzzled. "How'd he find her?"

"Clanton does business with the cattle ranchers in Laramie. He learned about a woman doctor settling there, and he'd seen my ad in the newspaper. When he contacted me, he came up with a proposition that I thought you'd want to hear."

"Then tell us, Sinclair," Albert Bolt said. "Get on with it."

"Clanton is in the meat-packing business. He wants to buy into the Cold Springs Spur to get first pick on the cattle being shipped to market. He offered to return my reward money and kick in more of his own for a piece of the line." What Sinclair didn't tell them was that he'd demanded a guaranteed profit. He'd figure out how to deal with that later.

"So, you get your daughter back, and we get enough money to replace the lost supplies," Riddenhouse said, his expression brightening with understanding.

"But this Clanton," Teddy said, "what do you know about him?"

Sinclair swirled the last of his toddy around his glass, then swallowed it down. "Nothing. And I don't care. He's one man with one vote. There are five of us; we can outvote him at any time."

"Sounds peculiar to me," Teddy said. "Where is Annalise?"

"She's in Laramie."

Teddy looked surprised for a moment then smiled. "What a coincidence. That's where Daniel is."

Riddenhouse cut a sharp eye to Sinclair, who ignored the comment and said, "So now with Sinclair's money and Clanton's, we can buy new supplies. You're right, we have no choice."

"I thought you'd see it that way," Sinclair said. "I've already told him that we'd accept."

"Wait a minute," Teddy argued. "Mason Clanton. That name sounds vaguely familiar. Maybe we ought to think about this."

"I agree with Sinclair," Albert Bolt said. "We need a miracle and we've just been handed one. I say we take it."

Robert Townsend, who rarely had an opinion, surprised the others by offering one. "As far as I'm concerned, there's nothing in our agreement that says we can't have six partners instead of five. As it stands now, we have shares in nothing. Roylston has the money we need. I say we use his and we add this Clanton's to the pot."

With little further discussion the others agreed. Ignoring Teddy's concern about Clanton, they voted to take in another partner. They finished their drinks and went jovially into dinner. The Cold Springs Spur was moving again, and they didn't care whether the new man was acceptable or not. He was in Chicago and they were here. He was only one man, and that meant he had no real voice.

Teddy Miller didn't argue anymore. The deal was done. He'd do some checking, just to make himself feel better, but for now, Roylston Sinclair's daughter and Teddy Miller's son were in the same place. The partners' coffers might be temporarily empty, but they wouldn't remain that way. Teddy's spirits were high.

After dinner, Teddy joined Sinclair for cigars and brandy.

"What are you gonna do about that daughter of yours, Roylston?" he asked, playing the skeptic. "I'd kinda thought she'd be a good match for my Daniel. But I don't know about this doctoring business."

Sinclair shook his head. "Neither do I. She has some foolish idea about healing the sick. Started with her mother's illness. Then my son Steven died. I thought she'd find out for herself that people won't accept women doctors."

"It will take a strong man to take her in hand," Teddy mused, sipping his brandy. "But I expect Daniel could do it. *Miller and Sinclair*," he mused.

"*Sinclair and Miller*," Roylston corrected.

"What are the odds that they'd end up in the same place?" Teddy closed his eyes in thought.

Roylston let him think. Miller didn't know it, but this marriage had been his plan from the beginning and, like Teddy, he'd made an art out of knowing his competition. Whatever his financial condition was at the moment, Teddy knew how to make money. And he knew how to make it grow. This new situation could be a stroke of luck.

He wasn't surprised when Teddy said, "Tell you what, Roylston, just to make things interesting, let's you and I make a little wager. Headstrong or not, I'll bet you that Daniel can have a ring on her finger before she knows he's done it."

Teddy Miller would bet on his own funeral, Roylston decided. But he did want to see Annalise settled. Of all the people available, Daniel Miller was the best choice. He'd tried everything else to make Annalise change her mind about taking a husband. Maybe fate held an upper hand. "Why not? Name the terms."

Teddy frowned. "Okay, I'll bet you ten thousand dollars that by the time the Union Pacific and the Central Pacific meet, my Daniel will have a ring on your Annalise's finger."

Ten thousand dollars was a little steep, but it would be worth it if Daniel were successful. If not, he'd enjoy winning another bet from Sinclair. Roylston nodded and held out his hand. "Done!"

Teddy broke into a huge grin. "I've been thinking about ordering one of those private cars Pullman is making. Your ten thousand dollars will be my down payment."

"Go ahead and order it," Roylston agreed. "Either way, we'll use it to attend the wedding." In New York's Wall Street, recovery came quickly.

In Laramie, Ginny's recovery also came quickly. She was awake and nursing Caity when Dan entered the former trading post. Red was sitting nearby, beaming from ear to ear.

"Dan, you don't look very rested," Ginny said with a knowing smile. "How's Annie?"

"She's asleep. How are you?" he asked.

"Sore and weak, but happy. Did you see our baby?"

"I did. I was right there when Annie delivered her. What are you going to call her?"

"We've named her Anna Caitlan, for Annie and Red's sister. We're going to call her Caity."

"Agnes's agreed to stay with you until you're up and going," Dan said. "Where is she?"

"She and Josie are bringing in more firewood," Red said. "I told them that some of the crew would be by later, but Josie can't be still, and they're driving Caity crazy looking after her. Are you okay?"

"I'm okay. You're okay. Ginny's okay. The baby's okay. We're all okay," Dan snapped.

Red frowned. "Whoa, boss man. What's wrong?"

"Nothing. I've just come to get my things. I'm going to move in with the crew for a while—if I still have one."

"What's wrong with staying here, Dan?" Ginny asked. "We have the upstairs."

"It's not that. I just don't think it's a good idea for us to be here like this. I mean two single women and two men. It could get very—awkward."

"One of them isn't going to be single for long," Red said with a broad smile. "Ginny and I are getting married, unless you have a problem with that."

Dan shook his head. "If you and Ginny want to get married, I think that's a fine idea. Too bad the other single woman living here isn't as smart as Ginny. I guess the only way she'll see reason is by following Ginny's lead."

"You mean have a baby?" Ginny said. "Our Annie?"

"I mean exactly that. But she's a doctor, isn't she? She probably knows ways to keep that from happening."

Ginny looked at Dan and asked softly, "Does she need to?"

A faraway look was Dan's only answer.

"Uh-oh!" Red said. "I don't know what happened in the two hours you were gone, but you look like you've been run over by one of them new railroad push-cars. Help me up and we'll go into Annie's office and talk. Maybe I can help."

Dan shook his head. "You can't help me with this, Red."

"Maybe not, but you put me off once before. This time we're going to talk." He pushed himself up. "You gonna give me a hand, boss man?"

Dan nodded and allowed Red to slide his arm around his neck and across his shoulder. Throwing his weight on his employer, he hobbled into the surgery and over to Annie's stool. "You first, Dan. What's wrong?"

"Too many things."

"Make a list and start at the top."

Dan dropped his chin in thought, then said, "List? That's good. That's what I usually do, but this time, the list is killing me."

"So, what's first?"

"First would be building the railroad, Red. I'm not going to be able to build it where we'd planned. I've found another site, but we don't own the land and we have no money to buy it. Even if I had land and money, I don't have enough men."

"Yeah, and with this leg, I'm not much help."

"Red, one man isn't going to make a difference. Besides, the leg won't always be broken."

"But when I tell you the rest of it, I'm guessing you'd tell me to hit the road, even if my leg was healed."

"Rest of what? What's on your list, Red?"

"Okay, this is the top," Red said, grimaced and went on. "Dan, I didn't just pick out the train you were on by accident. I wasn't even going out west. I was sent to the pub to find a way to get myself hired on your crew. But I got there too late. I followed you on the train."

Dan frowned. "I don't understand. Who sent you? My father?"

"No. I was hired by a fellow representing a meat packer in Chicago named William Russell."

This time Dan really looked blank. "Why? I don't even know any William Russell. What'd he want you to do?"

"I was supposed to be a snitch, let them know what you were doing and . . . to make it as hard on you as possible."

"Somebody hired you to interfere with the construction of the Cold Springs Spur?"

"That's about it. But I couldn't do it. I was going to back out, then I found out that I wasn't the only one he'd sent. I thought I'd better keep quiet until I figured out what was going on." Red swallowed hard and stared for a moment at the floor.

"I'm listening," Dan said.

"The train wreck was what threw me. I think Russell's man caused it. I met him, back in Chicago, a man in a beaver hat and a jacket with a fur collar. I thought I saw him at Boggy Gut. I've been looking for him ever since. I was going to tell you that night, Dan, but you wouldn't let me."

"I know. I should have listened. Have you seen the man since?"

"No. But when the bridge collapsed, I . . . I was worried. I went through the train, searching."

"And you got caught between the cars and your leg was broken. Damn! I'm sorry Red."

"I'm sorry, too. If I'd warned you, you might not have lost the supplies. I should have told you straight off. Then I should have made you listen that night, but there were too many people around and I didn't know who to trust. I figure he went down with the car, but the sheriff hasn't found anybody."

"The dynamite might not have been in the car, Red. It could have been under the bridge. You said you saw him in Boggy Gut, then he disappeared. You know the railroads have hand cars they use to check out the track. He might have come ahead. Until we get it checked out, we won't know how it happened. But he didn't have to be on the train to set it off." Dan furrowed his brow. "My guess is, if he's still around, he'll find you. Russell, whoever he is, won't want to leave any loose ends, and you're definitely a threat."

"You don't think he'd hurt Ginny, do you?"

"Not unless she knows something."

"I haven't told her about the dynamite, but she knows I lied about knowing how to cook. I'm sorry, Dan. As soon as she and Caity are well enough to travel, we'll be finding someplace else to live. I hope you know I would never have have taken the meat packer's money if it hadn't been for my family back in Ireland. I hadn't been able to find any work, and I'd promised to send money home to pay my sister's doctor bills."

"This is beginning to fit together, Red," Dan said, ignoring his employee's offer to move. "Rosco said that the tree holding up the logs had been cut, and the man who was supposed to keep the river clear disappeared. That must have been your contact. But why?"

"Mr. Meat Packer doesn't want you to build a cattle spur to ship his cattle to Chicago," Red said, "but for the life of me, I can't see why."

"Neither do I, but I'll bet I know someone who will. I

think I'll go down to the depot and send a telegram to my father. He knows a lot of rogues, and not all of them have Wall Street addresses."

"Dan, wait! What about the rest of your list?"

"Oh, my list only has one other item on it—Annie. I'm going to marry her when I can figure out a way to convince her. Between now and then, it isn't safe for me to be close to her."

"Then you're not going to replace me?" Red asked.

"Not on your life. I need you, Red. I can't pay you yet, but I'll figure out how to make it worth your while."

Red heard Caity cry and said softly, "Dan, you've already done that. Now it's time I did the same for you."

"Then help me stay away from Annie. I can't seem to do that myself."

Dan spent the day asking questions. First he asked for a loan at the bank and was turned down. Next he went to the Casement Construction Company office to consult with Pete Ross, the foreman.

"What can I do for you, Miller?" Ross asked.

"You know I'm here to build a cattle spur to Cold Springs?"

Ross nodded.

"You also know that Black Hawk and the Sioux are wintered right in the middle of our proposed route. Moving the tribe could start an Indian war that might stop construction on the Union Pacific as well as on my spur."

"Believe me, we've thought about that," Ross agreed.

"I understand the railroad owns the strip of land along the mountain outside the valley. I want it."

"So far as I know, it still belongs to us. What you got on your mind?"

"You think Durant would sell?"

"Maybe. But have you seen that strip? There's a low mountain right in the middle that will have to be moved."

"I've seen it."

"Well," Ross said, "it could work. We've built through a lot worse, but once Durant finds out you're interested, he'll raise the price. He's never been a man to do something without a little money changing hands."

"A bribe?"

"Well, I didn't say it, but if you offered."

Dan groaned silently. His father had tried to warn him about Durant. Everything came down to money, and that was the one thing he didn't have. "I'll get back to you on that, Ross," he said. "Thanks for your help."

Pulling the collar of his jacket tighter, Dan leaned into the wind. The telegraph office was his next stop. As he passed the jail, Will Spencer opened the door and called out, "Hold up, Dan, a telegram came for you while you were gone. I was about to bring it up to you."

"You delivering messages now?"

"Thought you ought to know about this as soon as possible. Representatives from the Bureau of Indian Affairs in Washington are on the way. Seems that moving Black Hawk and his people north to the reservation has been their plan all along."

"No," Dan said. Black Hawk and Bear Claw had just saved his life. He wouldn't be responsible for uprooting them, even if it would solve his problem. There had to be another way. "Having them moved would solve my problem, at least temporarily," Dan admitted, "but why does the Indian bureau care where they camp?" Dan asked.

"Somebody contacted the officials in Washington and said the Sioux are interfering with progress, Dan. They're in the way of the ranchers, the settlers—and your own railroad construction. I wondered if it was you."

"No. I don't know anything about it. What do you think about moving them?"

Will planted his feet on his desk and leaned back into his wooden chair. "Between me and you? They were here

first. Been relocated myself, so to speak. I didn't like it
much."

"You lost your home?" Dan asked.

"Yeah. Yankees burned it to the ground. Belongs to a—
somebody else now."

"Sorry. Everybody loses in a war."

"Yeah, well, it was time for me to move on. Came out
here. Thought about raising a few cattle myself, me and
my brother. So, I'm in favor of the cattle spur."

Dan opened his telegram. "You read this?"

"No, didn't have to. The operator read it. Had to. He
took it down. He thought I needed to know what else was
coming."

"Oh, and what would that be?"

"You'd better read it yourself."

Dan unfolded the paper.

GOOD NEWS. TOOK IN PARTNER WITH
MONEY. REPLACEMENT SUPPLIES
HEADED YOUR WAY. GET TO IT, BOY.
TEDDY MILLER.

A second paper clung to the first, also from Teddy.

SON, LOOK UP ROYLSTON SINCLAIR'S GIRL. SHE'S
SOME KIND OF DOCTOR OUT THERE. SEE IF YOU CAN
CORRAL HER. I'VE GOT A FAIR-SIZED BET RIDING ON
YOU GETTING A RING ON HER FINGER. WE COULD USE
THE MONEY. I MAY JUST COME OUT AND SEE THE
PROGRESS FOR MYSELF. TEDDY MILLER

Dan swore. "Guess you got to the second one," Will observed, trying to hold back a grin. "You didn't tell me you
and Annie were getting married."

"According to Annie, we're not."

"Oh? I got the word that Dr. Annie was Dan Miller's

woman." He grinned. "Another little thing you forgot to mention. You're Teddy Miller's son."

"You know my father?"

"Not personally. But everybody out here's heard of him. He grubstaked a few of the prospectors who came through."

"Any of them discover any gold?"

Will shook his head. "Guess Teddy don't know you and the doc are already—acquainted."

"No, and I'd like to keep it that way."

Will nodded. Dan was pleased about the supplies, but he felt like a fool. After telling Annie that both her father and his were flat broke, she'd think he was lying about everything, including wanting to marry her. How had Teddy pulled it off? Annie had said her father would be along to get her. Dan hadn't expected his.

Annie had suddenly decided that marriage was out of the question, but that living in sin was acceptable. If she found out about their fathers' little bet, she'd never believe that he hadn't known about it from the beginning.

"Good luck to you," Will said. "You'll need it."

When he got back to the wash tent, Annie was gone. He found her, Josie, and several men standing outside the clinic. They were looking up at a sign over a newly cut door to her office. The sign read:

DR. ANNIE
PHYSICIAN

Annie was looking up at the crude board, her eyes wet with moisture. Dan understood how she felt. Her dream had finally become real. She had everything she wanted. And he already knew that her wants didn't include marriage.

Seconds later his eyes wandered down to the second

sign, crudely painted and nailed to one of the posts holding up the roof over the porch.

GINNY AND AGNES'S KITCHEN
Good food—Cheap prices

"Well, it looks like they've been busy since I've been gone," he said, and walked over to stand beside Annie. "Seems like my situation is about to improve as well. My supplies ought to be here in a few days—as soon as they get the bridge repaired."

"See," Annie said, "I knew they weren't really broke."

Dan didn't argue, saying instead, "I guess it's a good thing those investors were on the train. They're paying the crews overtime to get the bridge repaired."

"I know my father. He got my telegram. He knows where I am and he knows about the bridge. Once it's open, he'll be on the first train out here," Annie said.

Dan heard the regret in her voice. "I'm sorry, Annie."

"I'm not. He'll see that I've done it, found a place where I'm needed. He just won't understand the conditions out here. I guess I need some of your diplomacy, Dan. You need to start practicing your skills."

"You're right. Your father won't be the only one I'll have to deal with. A contingent of men from the Bureau of Indian Affairs are on the way. They plan to tell Black Hawk that he's being moved to a reservation."

"Oh, Dan. Will he go?"

"No. He isn't going. He belongs here. We don't. I think I've found another site for the spur. If I can come up with the money to buy the land, I can prevent an Indian war."

"My father and yours will come up with the money," Annie said confidently. "And we won't have to get married for them to do it. And," she said with assurance, "you'll make sure there won't be any war."

Dan wished he shared Annie's optimism. They might

be able to come up with more money, but he knew that once Annie found out about the bet between Teddy Miller and Roylston Sinclair, she'd declare war herself.

After he ate, he gave a nod toward Red, picked up his dry bedroll and knapsack, and climbed the stairs. His search for quarters had been delayed. Tomorrow he'd figure out how he could find enough money to bribe Durant into exchanging sections of land.

Dan pulled off his hat, unrolled his bedding, and lay down on his side, pulling the blanket over him. Beneath his thigh, something hard poked into his leg.

Freeing one hand, he dug into the pocket and pulled out the offending object. It was the bead from Annie's masque, the bead and the feather.

Dan looked down at it for a long minute. Their first meeting seemed so long ago. He'd been such a fool, believing that all it took to succeed was knowledge and determination. So much of a man's success was out of his control. Either he pleased his father and the investors, or he saved a pitiful band of Sioux Indians who had saved his life. Annie had succeeded in making her future. She would be just the kind of woman he'd want to share his with once he found it. Until then, he'd have to put aside any personal needs, and focus on the spur.

So much for grand balls, mystery ladies, and marriage. It was time Dan Miller got on with his job, his future.

He had a railroad to build.

With grim determination Dan stood, pushed open the shutter, and tossed the bead through the window into the street. Moments later a man on a horse rode by, catching the bead beneath the horse's hoof, and burying it beneath the snow.

Annie watched Dan leave the room without saying anything to her. She'd thought that after this afternoon— what had she expected? Something had changed. She didn't know what. Of course they couldn't be together *that way*, not with Josie here and Ginny and Red. But he'd ignored her, speaking to Josie and the others, then eating alone.

He was worried; she knew that. Replaying her words, she realized that she may have sounded unconcerned, flippantly assuring him that their fathers would find the money. Suppose they couldn't?

Suppose Black Hawk had to be moved? If the Army tried to do that, the Indians would resist. New supplies were coming—she didn't how they'd managed that; maybe the committee had paid another bribe—but unless he worked out the new site, he couldn't build. There must be something she could do. Dan had been there at every step of the way for her. Now, it was her turn to take care of him.

Tomorrow, she'd telegraph her father and convince him to move the railroad. Dan needed the chance to do what he wanted without hurting the Sioux. Roylston Sinclair was a powerful man, and he had influential friends. Once he understood, he'd find an answer for Dan and she'd have repaid her debt to him.

But then what? What did she want from Dan?

She glanced around, taking in the signs of progress her little band had made on her behalf. When she'd started out, her goal had been to find Ginny's husband, and a place where she was needed. Though Red wasn't the husband they'd set out to find, he was a good man, and now that Caity was here, Ginny seemed happy. Laramie wasn't Fifth Avenue, but she had her office and they had a place to live. It was a beginning.

Still, as she lay in the darkness, her heart pounded inside her chest like a drum. Her mind recreated Dan's touch, his low groans of passion. Making love with a man was a powerful thing, and she was beginning to understand that what she'd thought she wanted might not be enough.

Long after the others had settled down for the night, Annalise continued to toss and turn. At one point she rose and stood at the window, looking out at the night. It had started to snow again.

Somewhere there was the sound of laughter. Then gunshots followed by more laughter. Annalise held her breath. Had someone been shot? Would there be a pounding on her door announcing a patient?

But there was only snow and silence.

Upstairs she heard the floor creak. Dan couldn't sleep either. She almost turned and climbed the ladder, then stopped. Life wasn't simple anymore. Twice he'd made love to her, and twice he'd walked away. Maybe he was smarter than she.

20

The next day, Dan left before Annie was up. He and his men helped with the repair of the bridge. Annie sent her telegram to her father explaining about the Indians and asking him to buy the new piece of land Dan needed. Then two days later, she got her father's answer.

LEAVING FOR LARAMIE NEXT TRAIN.
BRINGING SUPPLIES. FUNDS TO BUY NEW ROUTE
FOR SPUR OUT OF THE QUESTION.
ROYLSTON SINCLAIR

Annie read the telegram and her heart sank. Not only had her father refused to consider purchasing new land, but he was probably already on his way to Laramie. And he had ignored her concern about the Indians. And knowing him, he wouldn't take the cheap route. That meant that, without delays, he could be here in less than a week.

"What's wrong, Annie?" Ginny asked. "You look terrible, and it's me who ought to be having the jitters."

Annalise looked up at her old friend. As Ginny had said, she was marrying Red, and even though she'd given birth only ten days ago, she saw no reason to put it off. They'd come halfway across the country to find Ginny a husband, and they'd done it. She was wearing her best dress, freshly adorned by new green ribbon to cover the frayed seams resulting from her pregnancy.

"You look beautiful, Ginny. And I don't have the jitters. With my father coming, I just feel a little—queasy."

Ginny gave her old friend a long look. "Me, too. What's he going to think about what we've done?"

"What we've done?"

"Coming out here. You opening your office. Me and Red. I'm thinking your father will expect a match between you and Dan."

"There is no me and Dan. I've proved that I could succeed as a doctor. I don't intend to marry. You know that. Dan is my . . . friend."

"Uh-huh." Ginny heard Annie say *friend* but she was thinking that what she meant was *lover*. For days, there had been no mistaking the mounting tension between those two. Then suddenly everything changed. "I think you're probably right, Annie. Dan will expect a family, and you don't have time for that."

Annie frowned and paced back to the fireplace. "That's what I think. He came out here to build a railroad, and nothing is going to stop him. He's just feeling a little down right now, trying to find a way to do it without moving Black Hawk."

"Suppose he can't?" Ginny asked.

"Oh, he will. He's determined. But—I never thought about it before we came out here. Do you realize that we're taking land that doesn't belong to us to build railroads to bring more people who will do the same thing?"

"Annie, I'm going to say something you may not want to hear. You're fooling yourself, but you don't fool me. It's clear to everyone that you and Dan Miller belong together. I don't know if you're that blind or that stubborn. Don't you have any of your father in you?"

"I don't understand. How do you want me to be like my father?"

"He made sacrifices for you. He loved you enough to let you follow your dream. How many other men would let their daughters study medicine? He took a risk on you. He took a risk on the railroad, too. It messed up his finances but it will benefit ranchers in Wyoming, and people back east who need the food that farmers out here will grow. He knows that anything worth having is worth going after. Why can't you?"

"I don't know, Ginny. I guess I'm not so confident as I appear. Everything ought to be wonderful, but it isn't. It's all a muddle. You get what you want and it turns out that it isn't really what you wanted, only what you thought you wanted. There must be an answer."

Ginny nodded. "I suppose so. I could give up Red and we could all go back east and give the land back to the Indians. That would be the right thing to do, wouldn't it? 'Course we've killed their buffalo, so they'd starve."

"Don't be foolish, Ginny. You'd cheat Caity out of a father?"

Ginny turned to face Annalise. "Annie, there are times when no matter what we do, someone will be hurt. I'm going to marry Redfield, and our future has to come first. Laramie will be our home. Dan will build his railroad and if that means the Sioux have to go to a reservation, that's the way it is. As for you and Dan, I'm telling you, you're a fool if you don't marry him." Ginny shook her head. "I'm beginning to sound just like your father."

"Ginny, have I told you how proud I am of you?"

"No." Ginny grinned. "But I'll listen."

Later, in the railroad wash tent where the wedding was to take place, Annalise stood in the doorway thinking about

Ginny and what she'd said. Ginny had come a long way from the shy, downtrodden little country girl who ran off to the city to be a lady's maid. The future Mrs. Redfield O'Reilly had become a strong Western woman.

It was Annie who was standing here with knees like clabber in a jug. She'd never been a bridesmaid before. It had been years since she'd attended a wedding, and never one in a tent. Still, looking at Ginny's face, it didn't matter that they weren't in a church back home. All that mattered was that Ginny was happy.

Homemade candles turned the kitchen into a heavenly sight. Someone had cut greenery and fashioned an arbor, though where anyone had found anything green was a mystery. Annalise could see an altar, made from a stump and someone's white tablecloth. Behind it stood Dawson Harper, the banker who was also the mayor, assayer, and surveyor. In the absence of a proper minister he'd perform the ceremony, which would be repeated if and when a real man of God came to Laramie. Red, propped on his new crutch, was at the altar, with Dan beside him.

Dan. She hadn't wanted to see him, but she couldn't stop her eyes from seeking him out. He was wearing the same black suit he'd worn that night at the New Year's Eve ball. But now he had grown a beard. His face was weathered and he looked older. Had it only been three weeks since she'd stepped on that train in Brooklyn and her life had changed forever? It seemed a lifetime ago. At that moment, Dan turned his face to hers.

Before she could turn away, their gazes met and everything came rushing back; the connection, the arc of sizzling awareness, the physical asking.

The last few days had been easier—until yesterday, when Dan's men had returned from the bridge site for the wedding. The bridge wasn't finished yet—that was the excuse they gave to explain why Dan wasn't with them. Annie was hurt and relieved, then worried when he didn't come to "the Post," as her complex had become. When pressed, Red confessed that Dan was staying in the railcar camp with the workers.

Why?

She couldn't say her practice was bringing in a large cash income, but she'd patched up a few cuts and wounds from the ongoing celebrations of the workers who spent their spare time and money in the saloon, and pulled an abscessed tooth. So far, none of the families had needed her, or admitted that they did.

Except for this morning, she'd refused to allow Ginny to talk about Dan. He was avoiding them, and after she got over her initial feelings of hurt, she was grateful for the time away from him to come to grips with her confused feelings.

Annie no longer tried to conceal her identity, for one of the passengers, a would-be reporter, had contacted Andrew Greeley's paper by wire, and told the story of the doctor who'd saved the life of a savage Sioux chief. She did manage to convince him to give the Indian's side: The railroad was ruining their lives and their food supply. Now it looked as though Dan's spur would destroy the tribe's winter quarters.

"Annie? Annie!" Josie tugged impatiently on Annie's skirt. "I got on this dress Dan bought me so I can be a bridesmaid, but if you don't get on up there to the altar, Ginny's gonna have the wedding without us."

Josie was wearing the pink-and-white dress she'd worn the night of Rosco's dinner. She'd even combed her hair and tied it back with a ribbon. Annie smiled. So what if the dress needed another inch to cover the scuffed toes of Josie's boots?

"What's wrong with you?" Ginny demanded under her breath. "Are you feeling faint?"

"Of course not, Ginny! I'm going. I don't know why you're in such a hurry to tie yourself to a man. You're going to have to spend every day for the rest of your life with him. Are you sure that's what you want?"

"Oh, yes, every day and every night. Seems to me, Annie, that you'd be a lot less grouchy if you didn't try so hard to pretend you aren't yearning for the same thing with Dan. One minute you're giving orders, the next you're staring out the window. You say you're fine, but you aren't fooling me."

Annie whirled around. "How dare you, Ginny. I am no longer interested in Dan Miller—not in that way."

"Oh, yes, you are, and you have been since that New Year's Eve ball. He's the man who made your chest hurt, isn't he?"

"Yes."

"And it's hurt ever since, hasn't it?"

"Yes, but that doesn't mean I have to marry him."

"No. It doesn't," Ginny admitted. "It just means you want to. He's a fine man and he's trying his best to find a way to do his job without hurting Black Hawk's people. Why won't you admit it and admire his efforts?"

Because, if I do, I'll have to admit that I want to be with Dan for the rest of my life. Like a prisoner headed for the gallows, Annie took a deep breath and plodded toward the altar, making certain that she avoided any visual contact with Dan.

It didn't work. She didn't have to look at him to know he was there. She closed her eyes, trying to marshal her thoughts. He mustn't know how badly she missed him, how badly she wanted to be in his arms.

Just as she was about to plow into Red, Ginny grabbed her and shook her. "Annie!"

Her eyes opened with a start. She was standing directly in front of Dan. The man she'd danced with was back. Dan shook his head slightly, and turned away just as she realized that the pain and resignation she saw in his eyes was a reflection of her own.

The fill-in minister came close to conducting a real ceremony. At least he got the words right, down to the phrase that demanded Ginny obey her new husband.

Ginny gave a joyful yes. Red followed by promising to provide for her and protect her.

When he kissed Ginny, he transferred his weight from Dan to Ginny and proceeded to prove to all that a bad leg would in no way interfere with his being a proper husband.

After shouts of encouragement and congratulations, the tables were pulled out of the center of the hard-packed dirt floor that made up the dining area. A fiddler and a banjo player ripped into a rousing chorus of "Oh! Susannah," and the dancing began.

Annie gave Ginny permission to watch the dancers—as long as she felt all right. This time there was no fern arbor for Annalise to hide behind, and she knew that Ginny would be disappointed if she slipped away.

After several hesitant dancers started toward Annie, then backed off, Will finally got up the courage to ask, "Will you dance with a good ol' Southern boy, Doc?"

"I'm not much of a dancer, Will, but if you don't mind dancing with a Yankee, I'll try."

"Nice wedding," he said.

"Very nice," Annie agreed.

"Talk is that you and Dan will be next."

"Who's talking?"

"People who should know about those things are even betting on you two."

That statement caught her attention. She thought she'd left that kind of thing behind her. "Don't you know you shouldn't listen to gossip?"

"If you say so," he said, and let her go to the next partner.

There were three other townswomen, not nearly enough to satisfy the demand for partners. There was the wife of the storekeeper who'd set up the school, the wife of the railroad paymaster, and finally there was Agnes, who, after waiting in vain to be asked, jerked one of the workers onto the floor and proceeded to demonstrate a few steps none of them had ever seen.

At ten o'clock, the women brought out punch and a

wedding cake that looked like a large biscuit. It was obvious that neither Agnes's nor Ginny's culinary expertise extended to wedding cakes, but nobody minded. Toasts
were made, cake was eaten, and the musicians geared up
for one last tune.

Annalise heard the first few notes, turned, and made
her way through the crowd. The song was the same waltz
she and Daniel had danced to on New Year's Eve.

She made it back to the trading post and into the
"keeping room" where she pressed her head against the
door to her office and gasped for breath.

"I don't think that Red is going to appreciate an audience tonight," Dan said from the darkness behind her.

"What do you want?" Annalise said, trying not to reveal
her distress.

"Same thing I wanted a week ago. You—us."

He moved closer. He didn't touch her, but she could
feel the warmth of his breath on the back of her neck.

"Don't do this Dan. No matter what we want, there is
no us."

"I've stayed away from you and I've thought about that,
Annie. If you don't want to marry me, I can accept that. I
can't leave Laramie, and neither can you. I'm willing to try
to continue avoiding you if that's what you want, but I'm
not sure I can stay in the same town with you and not do
this."

He caught her shoulders and turned her, capturing her
protest with his mouth. In the background she could hear
the strains of the waltz as it came to an end. Her body, already on fire, burst into flames and melted against him.

No matter what she'd said to Ginny, no matter what
she'd told herself, this was what she'd been yearning for.
Her arms went around his neck and she parted her lips,
returning Dan's kiss with all the longing she felt.

She loved him. It was a simple truth that she'd fought
all along. But she'd lost the battle. Once she admitted that,

there was no turning back, and she resigned herself to him with her lips.

She was vaguely conscious of a sound behind them, identifying it only when the light from an oil lamp suddenly illuminated the room.

Dan gave a stilted groan and pulled back.

"Oops! Sorry, old man," Red said. "Didn't know the honeymoon suite was already occupied."

Annalise blushed, mortified at being caught kissing Dan. She glanced around, remembering his words about an audience. The two cots had been pushed together and covered with a lacy spread. Across the foot of the bed was the fur-trimmed dressing gown Josie had pilfered from the investors on the train, and Ginny's white nightgown.

Totally humiliated, Annalise raced past Ginny and Red and out into the clear, cold night. What had she been thinking? Dan was right. They couldn't be together and they couldn't be apart. For the first time since her brother's death, Annalise Sinclair totally lost control. She leaned against the post supporting the roof of the old trading post, and cried.

If she stayed in Laramie, she'd have to deal with wanting Dan. If she left, she'd have to start over again.

Maybe she ought to just go home. So far she'd focused her life on fulfilling her promise to herself. Now she was faced with dividing herself into two people—doctor and . . . lover. Could she do that? Or would one part of her suffer from the split?

And what about Dan? He was as dedicated as she. How long would he be content to stay in Laramie if his mission went unfulfilled? And if she truly loved him, what had she done to help him reach his goal? She'd taken from Dan, but what had she given? What could she give? Then it dawned on her. If all else failed, perhaps she could use herself as a bargaining chip. She'd return to New York if her father would find a way to buy the other section of land.

If the spur didn't get built, people would suffer. If it was built on Teddy's land, the Sioux would likely fight and many would die. Which choice offered the most good to the most people? And what was her part in all this?

A horse passed, digging into the snow and throwing it behind his hooves. Someone from the party crossed the street carrying a lantern, its glow casting a golden light on the snow.

"Lookee here," the man carrying the lamp said. "What's this?"

He bent down, digging in the rut, lifting something. He held it up so the other person could see. "It's some kind of bead, with a feather attached to it. Kinda pretty, ain't it."

"Ain't never seen nothing like that out here."

Annalise had. It was the bead from her masque, the one Dan carried in his pocket.

Had carried.

He'd thrown it away.

For nearly a week, Dan had grappled with the knowledge of the bet between Teddy and Roylston. There was no money for land, but there was money for a wager. He bet the truth was that neither man had the money. He'd also bet that neither man wanted Teddy to lose.

It was clear that *Miller and Sinclair* had been their goal from the beginning.

They had no idea that it was still Dan's.

It was the following day that Black Hawk and Bear Claw arrived at the Post. Black Hawk was all smiles when he stretched out on Annie's table and watched her remove the sutures from his wound. Bear Claw walked around the surgery, picking up items, examining them and being told, "Put that down, please."

"You're healed, Black Hawk," Annie finally said, leaning back with satisfaction on her face.

Black Hawk nodded. "Bring Medicine Woman present."

Bear Claw came forward, handing Annie a leather bag, polished and decorated with small turquoise stones and beads. She opened it. Inside was a bracelet, fashioned from large turquoise stones and held together with slender links of silver.

"Like mine," Bear Claw said, pointing to the elaborate decoration he wore on his bare chest. It, too, was made of stones, interspersed with hollow tubes, forming a lacy kind of breastplate. "Only chief wears the stone of the heavens."

Annie smiled and nodded. "Medicine Woman thanks you, Chief Black Hawk. I will wear this with honor. Will you and your son have refreshments before you leave?"

Ginny's customers stared wide-eyed at the two Indians who followed Annie into the kitchen. "Agnes, our guests are hungry. Do you have something for them?"

"Sure, Doc."

But Black Hawk took one look at Agnes and froze. "Strong woman," he said.

"That's right, Chief, come on over to the table." He allowed himself to be led to the table nearest the stove. Annie left them eating biscuits and chunks of meat from the stew with their fingers as she returned to the surgery to clean her scissors and put them away. There was a knock on the door. It swung open.

One of the railroad investors from the train was standing there. "Dr. Annie, my associate Walton, is very sick. Can you come?"

"Where is he?"

"In our railcar."

"What's wrong?" she asked as she began to check her bag.

"He can't breathe."

"Let me tell them I'm leaving." In the kitchen, Ginny was dipping more stew and handing out more biscuits. "They're bottomless pits, Annie." Then she caught sight of Annie's bag. "Where're you going?"

"To the railcar. One of the investors is sick."

"One of the men who donated the robe to Red?"

Annie nodded.

"Want me to come along?" Ginny reached for the strings of her apron.

"No. You can't leave Caity, and you don't need to be exposed to anything until I diagnose the problem."

"I don't like you going off by yourself," Red said.

"Bear Claw go with Medicine Woman," Black Hawk said. He grunted and signaled to his son. "Black Hawk wait here with big woman. Plenty good food."

Ginny shook her head. "Do hurry, Annie. I'm not sure I have enough food for a serious illness."

The man from the train was clearly uncomfortable with their escort, but he kept his concerns to himself.

"What's the patient's name?" Annie asked.

"Walton Flemming. I'm Gordon Ragsdale."

When they reached the car, Bear Claw took up residence in the parlor while Annie accompanied Mr. Ragsdale to the center of the car where the sleeping quarters were located.

"And how long has he been sick?"

"About a week," his companion said. "Wouldn't let me call you. I think he's dying."

Annie took one look at the sick man and agreed. The man was in desperate straits.

"Let me unbutton your shirt," Annie said, and started to examine him. He began to cough. Her fingers touched the swollen glands in his throat. *Dear God, how was he even swallowing?*

"Can you open your mouth?"

He tried. His tongue was coated white.

She reached for her stethoscope and listened. "His

lungs are congested. He's drowning in his own fluid." She considered the situation, then said to the sick man's companion, "I'll need hot water and a bowl."

"It'll take a few minutes," a familiar voice said.

"Dan." Her heart raced, then settled down. She was used to him, and confident when he was around. "What are you doing here? Where's this man's friend?"

"Halfway back to the Post and Agnes's cooking, I imagine. What's wrong?"

"I'm not sure. It may have started with influenza, but his throat is closing off and he can't breathe."

While the water boiled, Annie studied her medicines. She mixed mustard powder to make a poultice, then rubbed the paste generously on the sick man's chest and covered it with a cloth. Next, she mixed elixir with whiskey from the bar and spooned it into his mouth, hoping that some of it found its way down his throat.

The afternoon passed into the night. They kept changing the poultice and dosing Flemming. His breath grew steadily worse until each gasp was an agonizing effort for air.

"It's no use, Dan, his breathing passage is closing off. I have to find a way to open it." Desperately, she looked at the man who seemed to always be there when she needed him.

"How are you going to do that?"

"I don't know. He's going to die, and now you've been exposed to whatever he has and you could get sick, too."

"I'm not going to get sick, and if he dies, you will have done the best you could."

She listened to his chest again. "I think the fluid has stopped building up. If only he could breathe. If I could establish a passageway . . ."

"Too bad you can't jab something down his throat."

Annie began to pace. "I wish I could, but he'd just fight it. His reflexes would push it out. Unless . . ."

"What?"

"It might work. I need a hollow tube, something long and thin."

Dan frowned. "I can't think of anything hollow."

Then Annie remembered the breastplate worn by Bear Claw. It was made up of quills strung end-to-end across his chest. "That's it. Is Bear Claw still out there?"

"Was the last time I looked. He was wearing a dressing gown like the one Josie stole for Red, and smoking one of Flemming's cigars."

"Get him."

Moments later the suspicious Sioux stood before Annie. She gritted her teeth and peeled back the velvet robe. "Yes, it might work. Bear Claw, I need this," she said, jerking the necklace from around the startled man's neck. Instinctively, Bear Claw growled his displeasure.

Dan stepped between them.

Annie turned away, examining the breastplate in the light. She selected two of the hollow stems, and handed back the rest. Next she inserted them into the kettle of boiling water, then sent Dan outside to hold them in the cold air long enough to cool them. With Dan and the Indian watching, she dropped her scalpel into the pot, letting it boil while she assembled her needle, thread, and bandages.

"What you do with quill?" Bear Claw asked.

"I'm going to make the sick man breathe," she said, hoping that she wasn't halting her career by performing another bizarre procedure. She'd seen one of her instructors do something similar to what she was about to attempt. He'd made a hole in the throat and inserted a tube through the hole and down the trachea, establishing a passageway. His purpose had been to demonstrate the passage of air.

There was only one problem; the man on which he'd performed the procedure was dead. This man was still alive.

"You'll have to hold him down. He's too weak for any kind of anesthesia."

"I'll help," another familiar voice said. Annie turned

around in utter disbelief. "Father? I didn't hear the train. How'd you get here?"

"The train's on the other side of the bridge. There's still a bad post on the trestle. They're replacing it. But the crew found an abandoned handcar under a snowbank. We fired it up, and here I am. What do you want me to do?"

"Don't come in here. This man is contagious."

"Too late. I'm already here." Roylston Sinclair removed his hat and coat and took one of the patient's arms.

Dan nodded and moved to his head. "Bear Claw, you hold his other arm. But give Dr. Annie room to work."

Her father was right. She needed his help, and it was too late to worry about protecting anyone from exposure. She removed the scalpel from the water, located the indention between the ridges of the trachea, and said a small prayer before inserting the blade.

The knife entered, allowing the ragged inhalation of air. Annalise inserted the hollow tube, hoping beyond hope that it would work. The man breathed again, a deep, less labored breath.

Annie put a stitch in each side of the opening, sewing the skin to the cane, then sloshed the area with carbolic solution, careful to keep the liquid out of the tube. Moments later, the man was breathing easily. He soon fell into an exhausted sleep.

Annie leaned back and looked up at the men. Her father was studying her in awe. Dan was the steady rock of confidence he always was, and Bear Claw looked as if he'd been hit by lightning.

"Medicine Woman make magic," he said, backing slowly away.

"Not yet," she said. "And you can't leave here until you bathe yourself completely and boil your clothes. We can't take a chance on your spreading the germs to others."

He looked puzzled.

"Come on," Dan said, "I'll show you. I guess we all have to do the same thing."

Annie began to clean up. "Father, I'm truly sorry about leaving New York City the way I did. I didn't mean to hurt you, but I knew that you'd never—"

He cut her off. "Let you do what you do so well. I'm the one who is sorry, Annalise. I was wrong. What you just did was magnificent. If your mother had had you as her doctor, she might still be here."

"What I just did was attempt a desperate procedure."

His eyes twinkled. "You mean a desperate gamble. Seems to me that's a Sinclair trait, isn't it? I'd bet on you any time. In fact . . ."

Annie narrowed her eyes. "Why don't I like the sound of that? Have you and Teddy Miller been making wagers again?"

There was a twinkle in her father's eye. "Don't worry about that. Just tell me what you need me to do now."

"I want you to take off your clothes and wash yourself," she said, not believing his feigned innocence over his gambling for a moment.

"Really, daughter—" he began.

"Really, Father," she ordered and pointed toward the compartment beyond where Dan and Bear Claw were arguing. Annie didn't want to know what went on in the water closet but when the three men reappeared, their heads were wet and they were wrapped in clean bed linen.

"Is it safe for Bear Claw to leave now?"

"I don't know, but I don't think we can keep him here. He's probably all right, because he was already exposed to the illness when the members of his tribe brought it back to their winter camp."

"And I was exposed in New York. It's everywhere there," her father argued, "so I'm going to borrow some clothes from the owners of this railcar and leave, too. I promised my—associate I'd get right back." He gathered some clothes and slipped behind the changing screen.

Bear Claw tucked his cover tight around himself and left the car. Roylston Sinclair was right behind him.

Dan closed the door and leaned against it. Annie was watching him with great uncertainty. She didn't have a clue what he was about to do. God, there were times when she was too full of herself.

"I think," he said, "that what's good for the ganders, would be good for the goose."

"How's that?" she asked dubiously.

He put a solemn look on his face and handed her a sheet. "You just wait here until I tell you," he said.

"What are you doing?"

"Heating some water for your bath."

"You washed in cold water. I can do the same."

Dan dropped his sheet and tied it around his waist in the manner of the Roman togas. "I know you can, Annie. You can do anything you set your mind to. But this time, you're going to follow my orders."

She did, watching her patient while Dan heated kettles of water. When he finally finished, he stood by the door to the water closet and gestured for her to enter.

Her knees had been steadier when she was operating than they were as she moved past Dan. Inside, she came to a stop and let out a cry of disbelief. In the middle of the floor was a large metal tub, now full of steaming water.

"A tub? A real tub?"

"That it is, Dr. Annie. Compliments of Mr. Pullman. And this is a cake of sweet-smelling soap I'm holding. Take off your clothes. I'm going to scrub your back."

"You're going to do no such thing. It isn't—wouldn't be proper."

"Somehow I don't think that is relevant, do you? Nothing about you or me has been proper. Why should we change the rules now?"

"But . . ."

"You can't be a woman because you're a doctor. You can't marry me because you don't have time in your life for a husband. You're a woman who travels alone. Right?"

She nodded slowly.

"Wrong! If it hadn't been for me you would never have gotten out here. If it hadn't been for me, you wouldn't have living quarters. If it hadn't been for me, you wouldn't have saved Ginny. If it hadn't been for me, you wouldn't have pulled off this little miracle behind us. Right?"

"But I haven't, yet. He may die any minute. Don't you understand, Dan, it's all been me. I have done nothing for you."

"True, but you're going to. You're going to marry me. I've fought it as long as I can. I need you, Annie. I need your courage and your wisdom. You make me believe I can move mountains, and believe me, I have to move one to build this spur."

"Oh, Dan, if I thought marrying you would help, I'd do it. I owe you so much. I've been so lucky."

"It isn't luck. It's dedication and determination—talents that have served you well. I, on the other hand, haven't been so fortunate. At this point, I have no money to buy more land, and I can't build the railroad where I'm supposed to without causing grief to a lot of people. Does that make me a failure? Yes. Does that mean I'm giving up? No. It just means I need you. I have to marry a rich wife."

"I'm not rich."

"Not yet, but you will be. You're going to do great things, Dr. Annalise Sinclair. And I'm going to be there helping you—railroad or not. I do have a few other talents. And I plan to show you at least one or two of them now."

He did. She acknowledged this fact as a little spasm of heat ran down her spine and infused her other body parts, and she was a woman who believed in education.

"Dan, I'm beginning to think that washtubs are our fate," she said. "Do you suppose that tub is big enough for two?"

It was.

21

—❦—

Annie changed Flemming's dressing, then walked restlessly back to the windows. His lungs were clearer and his color better. To begin with, he'd fought the tube—until he realized that he could breathe. Now it was simply a matter of keeping the tube clear.

She looked out the window, but she didn't see anything. No answer came to solve the problem of more land for Dan's railroad. The only thing that came to Annie was a headache. She sighed.

"Tell me—what's—wrong," Walton Flemming rasped between breaths. "Maybe I—could help."

"Nobody can help. My father and his associates are five of the wealthiest men in New York. If they can't find an answer, there isn't one."

Flemming gasped, making a sucking sound as the air rattled past the quill. "Explain—might—help."

What difference did it make now? Annie told the man about the problem. "Everybody knows the Sioux winter in the valley where the spur is to be built. There's been bad blood between them and the army and the railroad workers. People have died. If anybody tries to move them, Will Spencer thinks they'll go on the warpath. That means a lot more people are going to be hurt."

Flemming grunted.

"Dan's father and my father assembled a group to buy the land between Cold Springs and Laramie from the government. They expected to sell it to the Union Pacific for the main line. Then the route got changed. To recoup their potential losses, Dan came out to build a spur line from Cold Springs to Laramie. Then he learned about the Sioux. He's found another site, but it belongs to the railroad. If he can come up with bribe money, he thinks that Durant will swap that land for Dan's."

"The—Sioux. The Indian here—was a Sioux?"

"You remember? I thought you were too sick to understand what was happening."

"Understand—because of you—the Indian—Dan Miller—I'm alive."

"That's true," she admitted.

"What happens—to Indians if Dan makes—swap?"

"He plans to talk to the officials in Washington about letting them continue to winter there. Dan was a diplomat during the war, and he knows how to deal with the government. But I don't think we can trust Washington not to try to move them to a reservation."

"I—have—idea. Want to—talk with Dan."

For Annie, sending for Dan Miller was hard. Facing him when he entered the car was harder. But when Flemming asked her to leave so that they could talk in private, she almost jerked that quill out of his throat.

Dan couldn't mistake Annie's frosty demeanor, nor the quiet fury she controlled when she left him with her patient.

For the next half an hour Dan explained the situation to the investor who'd accepted Dr. Durant's invitation to personally observe the future of the railroad he'd already invested in, a man now so grateful for his life that he was willing to intercede in a problem that meant no profit at all for himself.

In a quiet, unemotional manner, Dan laid out his plan, the same plan he'd already proposed to the representatives from the Bureau of Indian Affairs in Washington.

And, to his surprise, he found his answer.

Roylston Sinclair had been wrong. It was three days before the train finally arrived. Annie watched from the Casement car, where she'd been monitoring Walton Flemming's progress for the last few days. She'd have to remove his tube soon and go back to her office, but not yet.

"Who—who's come?" He managed to say, pacing his words with his breathing.

"The train. They've finally repaired the bridge."

As she watched, an escort of Army officers took their positions on either side of the train as if they were guarding the track. Roylston Sinclair, Will Spencer, Dan, and some of the railroad people leaned against the depot wall. Dawson Harper took a look at the cars, and stood by the steps of the shiny new one that looked the most official.

When the conductor stepped off the train and placed the stool beneath the steps, it was Teddy Miller who was first out the door, pausing on the platform as though he were campaigning for political office.

Dawson Harper stepped forward. "Welcome to Laramie. I'm the closest thing we have to an official mayor."

Teddy scanned the crowd until he caught sight of Dan. He nodded at Dawson, then came down the steps. "Hello, son. Understand there was a wedding. Was it yours?"

Dan shook his head. What else had he expected his father to say?

"Nope. Ginny got married."

Teddy frowned. "Who is Ginny?"

"Ginny is Annie's friend."

Teddy nodded. "And where is the famous lady doctor?"

"She's with a patient. You'll meet her later, Father."

"Good. I want to meet the woman who rejected my son." He started down the street, intent on showing the onlookers that he was a man of importance. He might have done it, if he hadn't been so intent on his target and if his boots hadn't been so new. Dan saw it coming but there wasn't a thing he could do about it.

In a matter of seconds, Teddy's feet flew out from under him and he landed on his rear with a jolt. Dawson and one of the soldiers raced toward him, apologizing profusely about the conditions of their street.

"You sure you're not Annie's pa?" Josie asked. "She likes the mud, too." She grinned at the man sitting on his rear in a melting puddle of muddy snow.

Teddy looked startled, then started to laugh as he pulled himself up. "Well, now, young lady, do you have a name?"

"Josie. Josie . . . Miller, sir."

"Miller, huh?" He cut a sharp eye toward Dan, who shook his head, motioning his father to silence.

"You got yourself pretty muddy," Josie said. "Ginny won't let you stay that way. She says cleanliness is next to godliness."

Teddy stood and looked down at his trousers. "Looks like I did. Guess I'd better get cleaned up before I go calling."

Dan made his way to his father's side. "Sorry, no hotel here. But you're welcome to come to Agnes's wash tent. When she's not cooking, she washes clothes."

A boy holding a piece of stick candy raced by, calling to Josie to join him. She looked at the candy, then at Teddy, who reached in his pocket and pulled out a penny. "Go on, little lady, get your own." She gave him a large smile and then raced off.

Teddy pulled out a cigar. "Don't need a washhouse. I brought my own." He started back toward the train, pausing beside the Casement Construction car, and making a sweeping gesture toward the new Pullman he'd come in on. "Isn't this a beauty, son?"

Dan shook his head again. He had already been studying the Pullman. He didn't have to go inside to know that it came equipped with every luxury.

"When did you get this?" Dan asked.

"Isn't mine yet. It might have been, if that wedding had been yours. You let me down, son."

"That's your bet. A railroad car? When you said you'd made a large wager, I thought it was money." Dan couldn't hold back his dismay. "What else don't I know?"

"The bet was money. The idea to use it as the down payment on the car came later."

"What exactly was the bet, Father? Spell it out for me. I don't want any more surprises."

"Why, Daniel, don't you trust me?"

"Not one bit."

Teddy grinned. "I bet Sinclair that you'd put a ring on the doctor's finger before the railroad is finished. He said it would never happen."

"You and Roylston Sinclair spent money you don't have to buy a Pullman car to come out here? Do you realize that with just a little of that, I could have bribed Durant to swap our strip for an alternate route?"

"Well, we both thought it would be a bet between families. I still have confidence in you, son. What kind of progress are you making?"

Dan swore. It would serve both fathers right if they lost the bet and the railroad. "Annie would never marry me to merge two businesses. I hope you realize what you two have done."

"Just think of it," Teddy went on, ignoring Dan's words, "*Miller and Sinclair.*"

Inside the Casement car, Annie was listening. She'd just opened the door to step out on the platform when she heard Dan's voice. Then she listened to Teddy Miller repeat the terms of his bet. The bet that Dan obviously had known about.

Her throat tightened up. Teddy Miller had bet her father that Dan would marry her. That meant her father had bet she wouldn't marry Dan. At least he'd supported her position. Either that, or he just couldn't turn down a bet.

But neither Teddy Miller nor her father's foolishness hurt as much as learning that Dan had known about the wager. When had he heard? Was that why he'd come to the car three nights ago?

Why he'd drawn her bath?

Why he'd . . .

"You're going to lose," Dan said.

"I don't think so, but what if I lose a little money?" Teddy said. "It won't be the first time I've lost. Besides, the issue isn't settled yet."

"Oh? How's that? What else don't I know?"

"The bet was that you'd marry her by the time the Union Pacific Line meets the Central Pacific Line. The way I figure, you still have some time to go. I expect you to get busy, Dan. I've taken a real liking to that car."

"I wouldn't get too attached, Father."

"Like I said, Dan, you've got several months to land the lady. You're a Miller. A lot can happen in a short period of time if you put your mind to it. At least consider courting her. You never know, she might agree."

There was a long silence. Annalise held her breath. What would Dan say? What did she want him to say?

At that moment, there was an uproar from the crowd, drowning out Dan's reply. By the time Annie looked out of the window, they'd moved away. Dawson Harper was making his speech again, this time to two gentlemen who were wearing black suits and top hats, the officials from the Bureau of Indian Affairs.

For Dan, it was just as well that the crowd interfered. He might have been tempted to physically put his father back on the train and lock the door. Instead he'd simply said, "We'll talk more about this later, Father."

"So we will, son, after dinner. I've arranged a little buffet in our car. We've brought more workers. You'd best get them started unloading our supplies. I see Sinclair's already down there."

"A dinner probably isn't a good idea for tonight," Dan said. "Give it a couple of days. There are a few things we need to talk about first."

"But I thought you'd like to speak to those representatives from Washington. They can explain their plans to clear those Indians off our land."

"Father, moving Black Hawk would be a mistake."

"Then how do you plan to build the cattle spur?"

"That's what I want to discuss with you. I've found another strip of land that I want to use instead."

"So we're going to give our land to the Sioux?"

"No, I don't expect you to do that. But they're going to stay right where they are."

"You're not going to tell me what you have in mind, are you?"

"You're right. I don't trust you not to do something to mess up my deal."

"All right. I'll wait," Teddy said, "What I want to do now is meet my future daughter-in-law."

Dan sighed. "She's with a patient, Father. I don't think she'll leave him yet. And, please, don't mention your bet if you want to be in the same state with Annie."

"You're right. Women are silly about things like that." He looked around. "Can't say Laramie is what I expected. It's pretty rough. But that's the way I was when I started. I had big plans then, too. Right now, I think I'll take a look at the bank."

Josie came out of the general store, licking reverently on her peppermint stick, and fell in beside Teddy. "Howdy, Gramps."

"Gramps?"

"Well, Annie's pa already decided I should call him Papa Sinclair. Where you headed?"

"Didn't know Annie had any children."

"She didn't—until me."

"I see. Well, I guess I could get used to being called Gramps. I'm checking out the town. Would you like to join me?"

She looked around. "Sure."

"Then, let's me and you take a little stroll." He offered Josie his arm as if she were a fine lady.

After a moment she looped hers around his and off they went.

"Your father is really something," Will said, joining Dan as he watched Teddy Miller strolling down the street as casually if he were taking a walk in the park. "Where'd he manage to come up with those supplies so fast?"

"I don't even want to know," Dan said. "But I guess I'd better go get them unloaded and check out the new workers he's hired. I've been bunking in with my men, but that space will have to go to the new crew and then some. Guess I'll need to find another place to stay while he's here. How about the jail? Think I could use Black Hawk's cot for a while?"

Will frowned. "Sure, but why would you want to sleep on a hard bunk when your father has offered you the luxury of the Pullman?"

"Spending the night with my father *and* Roylston Sinclair isn't what I had in mind when I came out west."

"Then why not stay at the Post?"

Dan shook his head. "I don't want my father getting any more ideas about me and Annie."

"You may be a little late," Will observed, as Josie and the old man seemed to be engaged in lively conversation. "Keeping secrets with Josie around is a lost cause."

Dan Miller groaned. Teddy had an uncanny ability to

find the one person who could give him inside information, even if it was a child.

Josie licked her candy in short little jabs. She wanted to
make it last as long as possible. Since Annie had put a stop
to her stealing, she was having a hard time satisfying her
sweet tooth. "Dan don't look much like you, Gramps."

"Well, looks can be deceiving."

Josie nodded. "You got any more cash on you?"

"A little," he said.

"Well, you should give it to Dan and Annie. They're
pretty broke."

"Tell me about how you got to be Annie's child."

"Well, I ain't—I'm not really. But I will be when they
get married. Never thought I'd want a ma and a pa, but
Dan and Annie, they're all right."

Teddy Miller made a choking sound, glanced behind
him at Dan and Will, then whispered, "You think they'll
marry?"

Josie hadn't missed his glance. She whispered, too. "I'd
put my money on it. Annie says not. But they're always
fighting and looking silly at each other. Ginny says they're
trying to convince themselves they don't love each other,
but they do. Ginny ought to know. She married Red.
'Course she calls him Redfield now."

Teddy flipped his cigar stub into the mushy snow and
stamped it out. "I knew it. Teddy Miller always knows a
good deal. Where's this Ginny?"

"She's at the trading post, that's Annie's office, with Red
and Caity."

"And Annie?"

Josie wrinkled her nose, then gave Teddy a stern look.
"Annie's not back yet from saving that stranger's life. And I
expect you'd better call her Dr. Sinclair. That's showing
professional respect."

"Of course. I will from now on." If this precocious child was right, he'd be calling her daughter soon. Dan's attitude still worried him. If they were interested in each other, what was holding them back? Maybe he'd have a little talk with Ginny. He picked up his pace.

But it was Agnes who greeted Teddy. "Howdy," the woman said, crushing Teddy's hand in her own and drawing him inside.

Teddy looked up at the mountain of a woman. "Eh, howdy, ma'am. I'm Dan's father. It's good to be here, Mrs. . . . ?"

"Agnes. Just Agnes. Buried three husbands but never felt cause to use none of their names. You hungry?"

"Agnes and Ginny's stew is pretty good," Josie said, following Teddy inside and claiming the bench nearest the fire.

"Well, sure, I'd love some stew, and some coffee, too, if you've got some."

"Josie, fetch the cream from the pantry and tell Ginny and Redfield we have company."

Moments later, Red limped in using his crutch, and Ginny followed behind nervously, holding Caity in her arms.

"New baby?" Teddy asked.

"Brand-new," Josie answered for Ginny. "Annie delivered her. She was turned the wrong way and Annie—"

"Josie!" Ginny said, "I don't think Mr. Miller is interested in the details. How was your trip, sir?"

"Well, it was easier than yours. None of the bridges gave way, though I wasn't too sure they weren't going to collapse."

By the time Teddy's bowl of stew had been placed before him the door had opened, admitting several workers looking for a midday meal. Ginny handed Caity over to Red and began serving their customers. Dealing with Caity took all of Red's attention, and he didn't notice the newcomer until he was standing beside him.

"Don't do nothing foolish, Irishman," the man said. "Or I might have to hurt the kid."

Red knew that voice. He didn't have to see the derby hat or the jacket with the fur collar. He'd been expecting him, just not in the middle of a crowded room. "What do you want?"

"Me and you and the baby are gonna take a little walk outside and talk about why you haven't lived up to our agreement."

"I would, but there's a small problem, meat packer. I can't walk nowhere without me crutch."

Across the table, Teddy Miller was carrying on a converstion with Josie, whose eyes were planted quizzically on the newcomer. "Red," Teddy said, rising, "I wonder if you'd allow me to hold the baby."

Josie looked at her newly adopted grandfather in surprise. "You want to hold Caity?"

"That I do. May I?" He leaned over and took the child before the man in the derby could object.

"Thank you, Mr. Miller," Red said gratefully, and reached for his crutch.

"Miller?" the stranger said. "You're Teddy Miller?"

Teddy backed away. "Yes, I am."

By that time Ginny and Agnes had realized that there was something going on. Ginny took Caity and retreated to a place behind the stove. "I know who you are, mister," Josie said. "You're the man I saw in the car, back in Boggy Gut. You were looking at Dan's things."

"Shut up, kid," the stranger said.

"Do I know you, sir?" Teddy asked, diverting attention from Josie by pulling a cigar from his coat pocket.

"No," the man answered, "but I know you."

At that moment the door opened, admitting another customer. Josie followed the new arrival and sat down beside him.

"You know me? And how would that be?" Teddy asked.

Agnes, coffeepot in hand, started toward the table where the new customer was sitting. "Coffee?" she asked, as though nothing was happening. "What else?"

He murmured something in answer.

"Let's go," Red said, and pulled the crutch beneath his arm. "You wanted to talk to me. I'm ready."

"So you're Teddy Miller," the stranger repeated. "I'm guessing that I know someone who would love to know why you're out here."

"You have the advantage over me," Teddy said. "You know my name, but I still don't know yours."

"You can just call me Jarvis. But I'm not important. Does the name William Russell mean anything to you, Miller?"

The name came at Teddy with such surprise that he couldn't conceal his reaction. "William Russell? I know the name. Hundreds of dead soldiers never knew it, but I did. What does he have to do with your being here, Jarvis?"

"I'm sorry, Mr. Miller," Red said. "I'm afraid I've involved all of you in something terrible."

"Red? What do you have to do with this man?" Ginny's voice was filled with fear.

"I told you in the beginning I'd done something wrong. I'm sorry to say that he works for William Russell, and I work for him. At least I agreed to work for him back in New York before I ever knew Dan or any of you."

"He did," Jarvis said. "Mr. Russell hired the Irishman to keep us informed on the progress of your little building project, but the Irishman got greedy, blew up the bridge, and threatened to blame it on my boss if we didn't pay him. That's how he got his leg broken."

"No!" Ginny cried out and started toward Red, only to have Agnes grab her. "My husband could never hurt anyone," Ginny sobbed. "I don't know what you're doing, but I don't believe you."

"Neither do I," Teddy said.

"Neither do I," the latest customer said, as he pulled off his hat and duster and stepped forward to reveal his badge. "Sheriff Spencer, Mr. Jarvis. Why don't you and me and Red take that walk you wanted, down to the jail. We'll see if we can figure it out down there."

Teddy watched as Jarvis looked from Red to Will Spencer and back. This was obviously not working out as the dandy had planned.

Suddenly Jarvis pulled a gun from beneath his shirt, gave Red a shove, and darted around the end of the table— straight into Agnes, who took a firm position between the gunman and the front door. "Whoa, Nelly!" she said. "Guess you don't know, we don't allow any guns in here."

"I'll betcha that's Dan's gun," Josie said, "the one that was missing after the train wreck."

Anges put her hands on her hips and stared down at Jarvis for a long moment. "I'll bet it is too, youngster," she said. Then, before Jarvis knew what had happened, she took the gun and lifted him off the floor in one motion. "I hate thieves."

"Let me go!" Jarvis demanded. "I haven't done anything except try to get my employer's money back. This man planted explosives under the bridge and blew it up. He ought to be in jail."

"Where you want him, Sheriff?" Agnes asked.

Will pulled out a pair of handcuffs and snapped them on Jarvis's wrists.

"Why you cuffing me instead of the Irishman?"

"Because, Mr. Jarvis, nobody knew for sure that explosives were planted under the track except three people: me, Dan Miller—and the man who planted them. That wasn't Red. That was you."

"And it was you who arranged the logjam back in Boggy Gut," Red said, making his way to Ginny's side. "I thought I saw you there."

"I want to send a telegram," Jarvis said.

Teddy relit his cigar and sat back down. "I'll just bet you do."

"Let's go," Will said.

"Tell me one thing first," Teddy said. "Why was William Russell interested in the Cold Springs Spur?"

"Forget it!" Jarvis growled. "You ain't getting nothing out of me."

"Guess it had something to do with shipping his beef to the Chicago meat-packing plant to be slaughtered," Red said. "He was a determined man."

Shipping his beef. It all came together for Teddy. Chicago meat-packing plant. William Russell. And finally, the sixth investor in the railroad, Mason Clanton.

"William Russell," Teddy said. "The sorriest excuse for a man I ever met. Sold tainted beef to the Army. Killed a lot of our boys. He thought Daniel turned him in so I could get his contract. Dan didn't. I did. And I never asked for his contract, either. The low-down slum rat lost everything he had, including a very fine woman, who married another man. William Russell. This was all a setup, to get even with me."

"Maybe," Will said, "but what does the spur have to do with getting even?"

"Not the spur, folks," Teddy explained. "I'm guessing that he's the mysterious money man who holds the mortgage on my house. His partner invested in the spur, except there's one little fact I didn't tell my associates. Mason Clanton demanded a guarantee of success. If the line failed, he got paid anyway. I gambled that we wouldn't fail. Russell intended to see to it that we did. He wanted to bankrupt me and ruin my reputation—all for revenge."

"Guess he didn't know who he was dealing with, did he?" Agnes asked.

"Guess he didn't. Thanks to you, Miss Agnes, ma'am," Teddy said, holding out his arm, "I may live to see what my son has arranged. I wonder if you'd care to join me for a piece of that pie I see on the shelf. I wouldn't want my associate, Mr. Sinclair to beat me to it. He's partial to pie and to . . ." he smiled, ". . . women who can cook."

"He is?" Agnes said, her face turning beet red. "I— well, I mean—"

"She will," Josie chimed in, "I'll guarantee it, if you'll throw in an extra piece for me. Come on, Agnes," she said, "Papa Sinclair is a rich man and I found out he ain't married."

For three days, Annalise managed to avoid meeting Teddy Miller. Avoiding Dan was less difficult since he was no-where to be found. Eventually, she realized that nobody was trying to get her out of the Pullman. Ginny kept assuring her that things were under control. She'd had no pa-tients. Laramie was entirely too quiet. Annie had the distinct feeling that she was on the outside looking in, un-til she received an invitation to the Sinclair-Miller Pull-man for dinner, along with the news that a substitute nurse had been arranged to take care of Flemming.

Meeting Teddy Miller was something she wasn't look-ing forward to. But that would be easier than facing Dan. He'd made no attempt to explain the bet or his knowledge of it. He'd visited her patient twice, but she'd not been al-lowed to be present. Now, she donned the gingham dress from the last dinner she'd attended at Boggy Gut, tried to arrange her unruly hair, then gave up. She wasn't sure that this was a good idea. She didn't even want to dine with her father.

The only thing she was certain of was that any possi-bility of marriage to Dan Miller had forever disappeared when she heard the conversation between him and his fa-ther. She'd been a fool.

So he'd kissed her. Men liked kissing women. So Dan had made love to her? It didn't mean that he loved her. It just meant he was a man with needs. At least he'd made her decision easy by keeping his distance.

Dan Miller might not be like his father, but then he

wasn't that old yet. And Annie had seen firsthand how the men of Wall Street always ran roughshod over the needs of the real world. She couldn't count on the relocation of the Indians being halted. She couldn't count on Dan finding a way to secure another route. It looked as if Wall Street would win out at the expense of the Indians, and Dan Miller would be the instrument of their financial success.

She'd proved she could practice medicine. But, in the end, her success wasn't as important as protecting the citizens of Laramie, and the Indians.

Delaying until the last minute, she finally left the Casement car and climbed the steps to the new Pullman that appeared to belong to her father. She stepped up into the light of the lamp and straightened her bodice, then reached for the door handle. Reached and stopped, caught by that familiar feeling.

She turned slowly. On the other car in front, a man leaned against the door.

"Hello, Annie. You look beautiful. I've missed you."

"Hello, Dan."

"I'm glad you came."

"I suppose congratulations are in order. Looks like your gamble paid off, even if your father's didn't."

"Too early to say."

"Why not? The Millers always get what they want, don't they? Including buying new Pullman cars when they're broke. You're definitely your father's son. Looks like you'll get Black Hawk's band moved, so you can build the spur and you'll all get richer."

He stepped over the rail.

Annie backed away.

Dan followed, pressing her against the door. "You still don't trust me, do you?"

He was angry, and at that moment, she felt the force of his anger.

"It's not you, Dan. It's just the way things are done. You

can't change it. I understand that now. The line isn't going to be moved, unless I find a way to do it."

"And you think you can?" Dan's voice was icy.

"I can."

"There is no way you can do anything this time, Annie."

"I can always go back to New York and pick a wealthy husband like my father wanted. All he'll have to do is agree to buy the alternate route for the spur and pay for a doctor to come to Laramie. That's the way it's done on Wall Street, isn't it? You should know."

Dan groaned. "Dr. Sinclair's grand gesture. She's the only one with the answer. She'll make a personal sacrifice." He caught her chin in his hand and lifted it. "I guess you were right. You could never be a frontier doctor *and* a wife, because you haven't any idea what it means to be a wife. It starts with trust. I told you that I love you. That means I care about what you care about. And you can care about everyone else but me. I have a heart that hurts, Annie. When are you going to treat my pain?"

He kissed her, feeling the tension, the longing she was trying to suppress. He hoped that this wouldn't be for the last time. The next hour would tell. Finally, he let her go.

"Dan, I'm sorry. I don't want to hurt you. It's just that we're only two people. Two people aren't important. We have to do what's best for everyone."

"Two people are important if they love each other. And you love me, whether you want to admit it or not. I also believe that two people joined together can move mountains. Listen, do you hear that?"

Annalise listened. It took her a minute to understand. It was the sound of the train engine starting up and purring—like a contented cat. "Why is the train building up steam?"

"It's getting ready for its passengers." Dan reached behind Annie and opened the door.

"What passengers?"

"That would be me and you." He pushed her inside. "Here's the bride, people."

They were all waiting; Josie, Agnes, Ginny, Red, both the fathers, Gordon Ragsdale, Will Spencer, Black Hawk, and Bear Claw.

"What do you mean, bride?"

Dan took her hand and pulled her forward. "Where's Dawson Harper?"

"Here," the mayor said. "I'm ready. Step forward, please."

Daniel slid his arm around her back and pulled her close. He leaned down and whispered in her ear. "You're going to marry me, Annie."

"No. I won't marry you with nothing resolved."

"Don't worry, everything's been resolved. I'm not moving Black Hawk."

"I hope you intend to explain how you plan to avoid that, son," Teddy said. "I'm not letting William Russell win."

"What do you mean you're not moving Black Hawk?" Annie asked.

"Just what I said. They can keep the land they're on for as long as they want."

"But your mother's house . . ." Annie began.

"It's too big, anyway. According to this telegram—" Dan reached into his pocket and pulled out a sheet of paper "—she's going to sell the house and pay off the mortgage. When she talked to that doctor you sent to see her, she decided that she would follow his orders and get well enough to visit her grandchildren. Why didn't you tell me Annie?"

"I sent my doctor friend a note. I wasn't even certain he would go to visit your mother," Annie said, "and I felt it was up to your mother to tell you about him or not."

Dan lifted Annie's wrist and kissed it. "Thank you, Annie, for sending someone who could help her." Then he kissed her nose and her cheek. Pulling her forward, he caught his hand between them, splaying his fingers across her stomach. "You love me, Annie. You know it. We belong together—no matter what. Admit it."

"You're willing to sacrifice your railroad and your father's reputation to keep peace?" Annie asked.

"I am. Tell me you love me, Annie."

He was sincere. He was magnificent.

"I love you, Dan, but I won't marry you if it means that you have to give up your future."

"I'm not. And you're not going back to New York to marry a man with enough money to buy another route for the cattle spur. You're going to marry me."

"Of course she's not going back to New York," Roylston Sinclair said.

Josie moved between the grandfathers, taking each of them by the arm. "Start the ceremony, Mayor Harper. We're getting married."

Teddy looked down at Josie and shook his head. "I don't understand why you're being so secretive, Dan, but I trust you. Start the ceremony. I have the ring right here."

Annie cut a sharp eye toward her future father-in-law and her father. "Are you sure you two don't want to wait until the railroad lines are joined? Or do you have another wager?"

Dan looked at her. "You knew about the bet?"

"We are gathered here—"

"I heard you and your father talking."

"And you believed that I was a party to that?"

"You did come to the Casement car and you—we . . . Are you certain your mother wants to come here to visit?"

"To see her grandchildren, yes. And we'll give her grandchildren, Annie."

"—to join this woman and this man as husband and wife and make it legal. Do you, Daniel, take this woman to be your wife?"

"I do," Dan said.

"And Dr. Annie, do you promise to love and obey this man?"

"I do not."

"Yes, she does." Roylston, Teddy, and Josie spoke at the same time.

"Give her the ring, Dan," Josie called out.

Dan smiled, ignoring his father as he slid a small gold band on Annie's finger.

"That's it, then," Dawson said. "You're married."

"Now we're really family," Josie said. "Dan and Dr. Annie Miller and their child, Josie, and Papa Sinclair and Gramps. Are we gonna have cake and punch, Ginny?"

"You are. Back at the trading post," Dan said. "But we're leaving. Everybody out."

"We can't leave here," Annie argued. "I just removed the reed from Mr. Flemming's throat. I'll have to monitor his progress."

Dan held on to Annie as she watched everyone filing out of the car.

"But I'm the first one you need to treat," Dan said, placing her hand on his chest. "Remember the pain in my heart?"

"Will Spencer, don't you dare leave. I want this man arrested for—for being a tyrant."

Will stopped at the door and grinned. "Don't worry, Annie. If we need you, we'll let you know. As for your patient, his car is attached to this train. Enjoy the honeymoon, Annie."

The door closed behind Will.

Annie jerked free. "I am not going on a honeymoon with you, Dan Miller. I'm not moving a step until you explain."

There was a shudder and the train started to move.

"You don't have to move, sweetheart." The train quickly picked up speed. "I've taken care of that. The wheels do it for you."

"Dan, you can't just give up on your railroad, and you can't force a woman to get married. That's wrong."

"Come and sit down, Annie. Tell me what you think is so wrong that we can't work it out."

Annalise let out a deep breath and followed Dan to the red serge sofa beside the window. She sat, and he sat beside her. He reached for her hand.

"No, don't touch me. My mind gets jumbled when you're touching me."

"All right. What do I have to do to make you happy?"

"You say we're a team, but you're still making all the decisions without consulting me."

"I can stop doing that."

"You have to consult with me first."

"I will do that."

"But you can't turn into a pussycat."

Dan chuckled. "A pussycat? How do you figure that?"

"I could never marry a man who could turn his back on his responsibility. You promised to build that spur and you have to build it."

"Even if it means war?"

"Well, no . . . I mean . . . Dan, I don't know what I mean. But I don't want you to give up. I couldn't love you if you did."

"So if I told you I'd found an answer, that I'd already bought the new route, you wouldn't say I should have discussed it with you?"

"Why would I say that? The railroad is your project, not mine." She wiggled closer. "Oh, Dan, have you?"

"I was able to convince Durant to sell that strip of land. That land is my wedding gift to you."

She shot him a skeptical look. "How? How'd you do it?" Then, all color drained from her face. "The bet. Your father won the bet. That's it. You gambled. If you marry me, you get the money. Oh, Dan, is that why you did this?"

Dan grinned and gave her a quick kiss. "Oh, I'd marry

you any way I could, but the money didn't come from gambling. It came from you, Annie."

"Me?"

"Yep, from your doctoring. You came out here determined to make your own life, to be useful and needed. You have. Now, because of your skill and my diplomacy, we've solved both our problems. We're a team, Annie."

"Stop this, Dan. I don't have any idea what you're talking about. How did my medical skill and your diplomacy do anything?"

Dan couldn't tease her anymore. She was liable to draw back and sock him in the nose again. "Annie, your patient, Walton Flemming, bought the land. He came out here to review his investment in the railroad. You told him about the spur and the Sioux. When you saved his life, he decided to buy the land outright as payment of your fee."

"You're serious, Dan?"

He nodded. "When I saw you set Red's leg I knew that you'd be a successful doctor, but I didn't realize your fees would be so high."

"Would you really have given up building the railroad because of me?" Annie asked.

"Would you really have picked a New York husband who would buy the new site?"

They both laughed.

"Annie, I do love you. I would have had a hard time walking away from the railroad, but I would have done it."

"I don't believe you. You're as big a faker as your father. Do we really own the alternate route, Dan?"

"We do, and we're going to build the finest cattle spur in Wyoming," he promised, drawing her close. "But, Annie, I'm not the man who's going to build it."

Annie looked stunned. "After everything you went through to get that land, you're turning down the job?"

"Yes, I'm giving that job to Redfield O'Reilly and Bear Claw. Red's going to supervise, and Bear Claw's braves are going to stick around to protect the workers."

"Why not you, Dan?"

"I came out here looking for a new life, Annie. I've found it. My mother was right I was trained to be a diplomat, and I'm a damned good one. As a start, I'm going to put those skills to the test by representing the Indians in the state of Wyoming. They don't have to go to a reservation. There's plenty of land for all of us. Tomorrow I'll tell you all about how we almost lost everything because of a meat packer who wanted to ruin my father. But tonight, Mrs. Miller, I'm devoting myself to you."

She put her hand on his chest. The connection arced between them just as it had the first time she'd seen him. "I guess you do have everything worked out. What do you want from me?"

The train picked up speed. Dan stood, blew out the lamps, and unbuttoned her dress. "You? I expect you to look after your patients, Josie, and me. Beyond that, I figure you'll probably be the first woman governor. You know there's talk about giving women the right to vote."

"Don't be foolish, Dan. A woman will never be a governor."

"Not just any woman, Annie. This is Wyoming Territory, and once the folks get to know Dr. Annie, you'll win by a landslide." He chuckled. "Make that mudslide," he said, and slid her dress from her body. "I love you, Annie."

"I love you, too, Daniel," she said and followed his plan, button for button. "I'm a doctor about to treat a very special patient with a recurring problem."

Dan's breeches fell to the floor. "How?"

She took him in her hand. "By doing just what my father was afraid I'd do—examine a naked man."

EPILOGUE

—❧—

Promontory Summit, Utah—May 10, 1869

Teddy Miller clicked open his gold watch and said, "Sinclair, I'll wager a five-dollar gold piece that the last stake will be driven in at exactly eleven o'clock."

"Go for it, Papa," Josie urged. "What you got to lose?"

"Five dollars," Sinclair said.

"You ain't gonna take the bet?" Josie asked in astonishment.

"No. Annie gave me a sermon on gambling. I'll pass."

"Well, I won't," Josie said, holding out her hand to her grandfather Miller. "I say it'll be before twelve o'clock. I'll take the bet."

Teddy Miller's eyes twinkled. "And where do you intend to get the money when you lose, young lady?"

"I ain't a lady, and I ain't gonna lose."

"And what are you gonna do with five dollars?"

"It's like this. I got a debt to pay off—to Annie. Thought I'd find a way to make me some money out here, but so far, nobody's got no real money. This ought to be just about enough."

At that point, the whistle on the Union Pacific screamed out a raucous cry. That sound was followed by a lower, equally urgent bellow from the Central.

"Let's get us a good place to watch," Teddy said. "I don't want to miss the ceremony."

"Yep, don't want you to miss the time. Gramps? Papa?" Josie offered an arm to each grandfather and rewarded them with a conspiratorial smile. "You think maybe some of them other gents would like to buy into the pot?"

Inside the Miller-Sinclair Pullman, Annie glanced at the clock. "We'd better hurry up! The ceremony is beginning, and we don't want to miss history being made."

She didn't know where the two old reprobates responsible for their attendance had gotten to, and she admitted that she was worried because Josie was with them.

Ginny stood by the exit holding Caity, and eyeing the Chinese Central Pacific workers with their yellow cone-shaped hats.

Annie gave a final pat to her hair and started toward the door. She hadn't known what to expect all those months ago when she stepped onto the train in Brooklyn, but everything had turned out to be just about perfect.

Just about. Her medical practice was thriving. Red's leg had healed, and he would soon be able to bring his family over from Ireland. The Cold Springs Spur was almost finished. And Dan, with his solid dependability and peacemaking skills, had convinced Washington to leave Black Hawk's people on the Miller Ranch, now being established on the site of the Sioux winter grounds. They weren't as free as they'd once been, but if Dan could prove that the

Indians and the white men could live together in peace, it would serve as an example to the other territories. Only time would tell.

For Dan, too, everything was just about perfect. He watched Annie tugging at the waistband of her dress, and wondered how long it would be before she confessed that he'd given her a child.

Just then she looked up, caught him studying her hand resting on her stomach, and gave him a guilty smile. As always, when they weren't touching, there was too much distance between them for Dan. Under the pretext of offering gentlemanly assistance, he came to stand behind her, sliding his arm around her and capturing her hand with his.

"Are you asking?" she whispered.

"Always," he answered. "Today I have a different question. When were you going to tell me about our child, Annie?"

She started. "Our child?"

"The one you're carrying."

This woman who was willing to take on the world's problems was still able to blush. "I don't know. What will people think? I'm a doctor."

"You're also my wife."

"Yes, but I'm worried. I mean," she gasped, "what if I'm needed, and I can't do my job because I have a baby to care for?"

"Well, there's always Agnes, and I'll help you. Haven't I always?"

"Yes, you have." She leaned against him, feeling the evidence of Dan's constant desire pressing against her. "You know, husband, I think you'd better find your hat."

"What do I need a hat for? The sun is shining. It's a warm day. There isn't even any snow."

"I didn't mean for your head. You're part of the government now, aren't you? And the government always covers up its problems."

He planted a kiss on her neck. "Problems?" He pulled her close. "You think this is a problem?"

"Only temporarily," she whispered, and pressed wickedly against him. "I'm a doctor, remember. And I've learned a few things they didn't teach me in medical school."

"Like what?"

"Like men don't always have to be naked."

The door opened. "Okay, you two," Red said. "Behave yourselves. If we're going to see them nail those spikes in, we'd better get going."

"Just think," Ginny said, "with just one spike, the East and the West will be connected."

Red laughed. "One spike? Never. You got two men representing two railroads. Leland Stanford brought a silver-headed maul all the way from California for the Central Pacific to use on its spike. Durant's not going to let the occasion get by without a spike from the Union Pacific."

Annie laughed. "And, knowing the owners of the new firm of Miller and Sinclair, they probably brought their own spike and are now betting on which one will get the last lick."

"At least it doesn't matter which one wins," Dan said.

"Are we going to have a ceremony like this when our spur ties in?" Red asked.

"We certainly are," Dan said. "Then we're going to buy out Mr. Clanton's share."

Annie glowered at Dan. "I suppose you convinced him that selling was to his advantage?"

"With Russell in jail, I didn't have to convince him. Besides, he's getting married."

"How's that?" Annie asked.

"My mother felt sorry for Mason, and invited him to tea. He met a young lady there who just loves steak."

Annie shook her head. "Your mama played matchmaker? I'm shocked."

"Why, Annie, matchmaking is a Miller family trait. Our fathers did a pretty good job, didn't they?"

"The jury is still out on that. Now that they're partners, we may need an attorney in the family, to deal with their shenanigans. Hadn't we better get out there before they make use of another family trait and put up our child as collateral for their next wager?"

"I suppose." Dan put his hand on Annie's back and directed her forward, then stopped. "Wait! You all go on, I'm going to get my hat."

Annie moved through the door and down the railcar step. Ginny turned and hugged her warmly. "Child?"

Annie nodded.

"I'm so happy for you. When will the baby come?"

Annie blushed. "Too soon," she whispered. "I'm going to be a mother, and I'm not used to being a wife yet."

"Do like me," Ginny advised. "Just keep practicing. I figure it ought not to take us more than forty years to get it right."

The band started playing, and the crowd noise began to die down.

"That's what worries me. I wondered how I'd ever be a doctor and a wife. With Dan around, I'm not sure I'll ever have time to be either."

Ginny looked puzzled.

"He seems to want to spend all our time . . . practicing."

"Let's go, Annie," Dan said from behind. "I hope this ceremony doesn't take too long, I'm thinking that I'm probably going to need some medical attention real soon."

Annie smiled. "Is your heart hurting?"

"Not anymore," he responded and twirled his hat.

Annie cut her eyes toward Ginny. "See what I mean?"

The Millers, the O'Reillys, Roylston Sinclair, several congressmen, the governors of Wyoming and Utah, three photographers, a brass band and members of the press were among the workers and railroad officials gathered around the two ends of track about to be officially joined. The two steam engines were nose-to-nose, as if in a stand-off.

"Who are those funny looking men in the blue jackets and straw hats?" Josie asked, tugging on Dan's arm to get his attention in all the noise.

"They're Chinese workmen. Some people call them Celestials," he answered. "Because they laid most of the Central Pacific's rails, they're going to lay the last two sections."

At that moment a photographer yelled out a command to those he was trying to capture on film, frightening the Chinese who scattered hysterically. After a few minutes, the workmen returned and railroad officials placed the last tie, a gift made of polished laurel wood with a silver plaque bearing the Central Pacific's leaders. It was almost noon when Stanford from the Central and Durant from the Union stepped forward to seat the final spikes.

"When are they going to get started?" Josie said, glancing secretly at Dan's pocket watch. She was certain he'd have given it to her, if she'd asked, but she didn't want to bother him. Picking his pocket was an emergency.

"Ceremony, my girl," Papa Sinclair said. "Be patient. This is a monumental occasion. You're watching history." Josie squirmed, trying to see through the crowd. History, yes. But she was about to lose a bet.

"Just watch," Teddy said, "I understand the Western States sent a Golden Spike with a large gold nugget on top. They're going to make souvenir watch fobs and rings for the bigwigs later. I intend to have one."

"Look at the maul they're using," Sinclair said, "pure silver."

"It's got a wire on it," Josie said, leaving her place between Dan and Annie to join her grandfathers who seemed to know "all the good stuff."

Teddy took her hand and leaned over. "It's connected to a telegraph key so when they tap in the last spike, the entire world will know. At last!"

Finally after several souvenir spikes were tapped into prepared holes, the speeches began. At 12:30, Stanford from the Central and Durant from the Union, stepped forward. Stanford swung the heavy mallet and missed the golden spike, hitting the rail instead. "It's done!" he announced triumphantly, as if he didn't know he'd missed and handed the maul to Durant who brought chuckles to the crowd by also missing.

"They both missed," Josie announced, her voice carrying across the crowd's silence. But the wire carried the message to the telegraph key that sent the premature message to the world.

"Of course they missed. They didn't want to destroy the nugget," Gramps Miller said as he stepped up, borrowed Stanford's maul and gave the golden spike a tap. As if they'd planned it, he handed the maul over to Papa Sinclair, who did the same thing. Officials of the railroad scurried forward, removed the ceremonial spikes and placed them in boxes. The polished laurel wood tie was taken away, replaced by one of hemlock and tapped into place.

But it was after twelve o'clock. Josie had lost her bet. She couldn't pay Annie or her grandfather. As the two trains inched forward, Josie jerked away and disappeared into the crowd, followed by the grandfathers.

"What's wrong with Josie?" Ginny asked.

"I don't know," Annie asked. "But I think it must have something to do with Dan's watch. She's been looking at it all morning. I can't believe he gave it to her."

"I didn't," he said as several officials came over to talk.

At that moment, Josie tore through the crowd and jumped the track, with the two grandfathers right behind her.

Dan reached out and grabbed her. "What's going on?"

"What's wrong, Father?" Annie asked, studying the child she and Daniel were raising as their own.

"Not a thing," Roylston Sinclair said, shaking his head at Josie.

"Josie?" Dan asked.

Josie, hands jammed in the pocket of her apron, rocked back and forth. "Ah—dragonflies and chopsticks! I swear I just found it. It was laying right there on the ground and I picked it up. I wuz gonna give it back. Honest!"

Dan held out his hand.

Josie removed her hand from her pocket and placed the object in Dan's open palm. It was one of the golden spikes.

"Josie!" Ginny gasped.

"It's worth a lot, isn't it?" she asked, beaming.

"It's worth a lot," Dan agreed.

"Good. Then I reckon there's a reward. I want Annie to have it to replace that money she lost. Guess I don't owe nobody nothing now, do I?" She looked from Dan to her grandfathers, beaming.

Dan looked at Josie and smiled. "Just your love."

Teddy Miller put his arm around the little girl who had already stolen all their hearts. "Thank you, Josie. Losing this piece of history would be a tragedy. I'm certain that Mr. Durant and Mr. Stanford and the Union Pacific Railroad thank you. Once you get some schooling, you'll start making a name for yourself."

Dan agreed, cautiously. "With a little schooling, I wouldn't be surprised if the name Josie Miller becomes famous one day."

Annie gave both her husband and her father a scolding look. She had no doubt that Josie would make a name for herself; she was already becoming a Wyoming woman.

"Josephine Miller," Annie said, "you march right back to our car. Your grandfathers—both of them—will accompany you, won't you?"

With great dignity, Teddy Miller and Roylston Sinclair each offered Josie an arm, and they all walked away. "Don't worry about all that schooling, Josie," Sinclair said.

Teddy agreed. "We'll teach you everything you need to know. I think we'll work on poker next."

Dan returned the spike and came to stand beside Annie.

She shook her head. "Some things never change," she said. "What are we going to do with them?"

"Just what you always say, Annie. We're going to do the most good for the most people."

Her husband was right. She knew that. And things did change. She'd run away from her home so she wouldn't have to choose a husband. But in the end the runaway bride had married the very man she'd run from, a man who shared her determination and her dream. Together they'd found a place to belong. And she wouldn't have it any other way.

The wind picked up, whispering across the wide open land. Its sound was half moan, half song. Pain and joy. Power and compassion. Strength and love. They went together.

Just like Daniel and Annie.

ABOUT THE AUTHOR

Bestselling and award-winning author Sandra Chastain has written thirty-nine novels since Bantam published her first romance in 1988. She lives just outside of Atlanta and considers herself blessed that her three daughters and her grandchildren live nearby.

Sandra enjoys receiving letters from her fans. You can write to her at P.O. Box 67, Smyrna, GA 30081.